Hurrah for

Peter J. Flores

Dedication

For my late wife Irene Cecilia Flores and our daughters, Iris Ann Peak and Carol Medina. And, the family in my life Andrea, Amanda, Greg, Javi, Rene, Star Layla, Callie, Isaac, Sandra, Dan, Tony and Jake. Last but not least, my nephew, Jack Trevino – many thanks, it couldn't have happened without you.

ACKNOWLEDGMENTS

I am a lover of the "Printed Word." I grew up reading Edgar Rice Burroughs and Zane Grey. Reading these great books instilled in me a great curiosity to read and learn more about the subject material that I read. I was somewhat like the character in 'Dirty Harry" who said, "I gots to know."

In my youth, I haunted the second hand bookstores and the San Antonio Public Library having a strong desire to read more and more books. Today, I have my own personal library.

There are so many individuals that have led me to this point and time in my life that the list would be longer than the actual book, so to them and you I say, "Thank you!"

PROLOGUE

"Gentlemen, I am the bearer of bad news." Hadley Fischer looked at the three men of the project, seated at the table. "As you may recall, the President hinted about it in his inaugural address. Late last Friday, the Secretary told me to wrap it up. There shall be no funds allocated for next year's budget."

"Has the Secretary, or even the President, been briefed on the project?" one of the men asked.

"After all, this is a new administration. Surely they are not acquainted with what we're doing."

"I briefed the Secretary when he was appointed," said Fischer. "I don't know if he told the President. It's immaterial. We're out."

"So, it's the end," one of the men mused. "We could have done so much. We were so close. For lack of a dollar, our penny-pinching President has blown years of research and the opportunity for this country to continue its dominance into the twenty-first century."

"Well, not exactly," Fischer surveyed his men, thoughtfully. "I've been thinking about this over the weekend, ever since the Secretary told me the bad news. We are funded for the remainder of the fiscal year, funds which the Secretary wants used to shut it down.

"So, since we're fading away into the sunset, they won't be paying too much attention to us."

"So?"

"Can we bring it in within this time frame?"

"What? You want to go on?"

"I'm waiting for my answer."

One man slammed his fist on the table. "Damn right!"

The other two nodded. "Why not. We can sure try," said one.

"Then it's a 'go,'" smiled Fischer.

THE PICKUP HALTED ON the shoulder of the road. The road was narrow. Two cars coming from opposite directions would have to edge onto the shoulder in order to get by. Heavy forested land pressed on the road from both sides. A few miles farther, the asphalt gave out and from that point on, it was gravel.

The driver slowly turned the pickup into the trees, winding through, searching for openings wide enough to let the truck through. The course they took twisted and turned, the only requisite being the spacing between trees was wide enough for the truck to squeeze by.

In spite of the contortions of the trail, they steered steadily eastward. A dozen miles must have gone by when a fusillade of gunfire brought them to a halt.

"What was that?" the other man was surprised.

The driver cursed. "I bet it's that damn Sam playing army again."

They resumed driving. About two miles farther they emerged to a cleared area at the base of a towering sandstone cliff.

The driver steered the truck into a clump of trees. There were three other cars there, camouflaged and hidden under the trees.

As they got out of the pickup, there was another burst of gunfire from the direction of the cliff. Still cursing, the driver slammed the door and hurried in the direction of the cliff.

Six men were lined up, facing the cliff. At the base were six targets, obviously the object of the fatigue-clad men standing by with rifles in their hands.

Fists clenched, the driver accosted a large heavy set man on the firing line. "Goddammit, Sam. We agreed there was to be no firing of weapons here. Do you want to attract the attention of everyone within ten miles of this place?"

"Who appointed you the boss?" Sam glowered at the intruder.

"Well, you're not the boss either. All of us have an investment in this venture. All we need is a jackass stunt like this to have it blow up in our faces."

"Harry's right, Sam," said the man who had driven in with Harry. "We're taking a chance being here without advertising it. Those shots could bring the law down on us."

Sam turned to him. "Well, Cal, we've been in and out of this place the last two years and nobody's bothered us. You and Harry are just scared of your shadow."

"Sure I'm scared," said Harry. "I know these rangers. We're lucky they're shorthanded in these times, otherwise they would have discovered us.

Nowadays they only respond to complaints. Which brings us back to this gun business. If anyone sees or hears us, they'll report us.

"You know Shel discussed this with all of us. We decided to do our target practice elsewhere so we wouldn't attract busybodies up here.

"We're all in this together. So help me, if you go off half-cocked, I'm pulling out, and so will some of the others. That will make Shel real unhappy."

Sam glowered and turned away.

"Where are the women?" Harry asked one of the other men.

"They're all in the cave."

Harry walked straight to the base of the cliff. He went around the narrow outcropping to reveal a low open cave. It was not high, the outcropping completely hiding it from the front. It was the discovery of this unique rock formation by Shelly Gorman that led to the formation of the group. Shel was involved in a survivalist group. Many of these had sprung up several decades ago. In the Seventies and Eighties, the country's economic problems had generated a resurgence of these organizations.

Shel had formed such a company that eventually numbered forty four people drawn from all over the state. It was only on rare occasions, however, that the whole group got together. From time to time, as on this weekend, a small group came in to stock the cave or just to spend time outdoors with friends.

The stronghold was in a wilderness area. It was forbidden to bring in vehicles or to establish any camp sites. However, in the last few years, the government had severely cut back personnel. It had meant the virtual destruction of the wilderness management teams. Which was why the group had been able to operate undetected.

Harry went up some steps carved out to get to the farther recesses of the cave. The group had enlarged the back part to allow the installation of bunks and shelves for supplies. Five women were opening boxes and stacking the contents.

As Harry came in, one of the women came running. "Harry!" she flung her arms around his neck and kissed him.

"Elaine," he returned her kiss.

"What took you so long? I thought you were coming in Friday."

"I had some last minute business to attend to, but Baby, we have nine days together."

"Harry, Have you, have you told..."

"My wife? No. Listen, she's all involved with this class reunion this coming week. We can go into Phoenix tomorrow or spend the rest of the week here. What do you say?"

"You're not going to tell her, are you? You've been making excuses for almost a year."

"Elaine, honey. I love you. I want you. Look, I'll tell her by the end of the month. School will be out by then and she'll expect us to make vacation plans. I'll tell her then. I promise you."

"This is it, Harry. If you don't make it this time, you and I are through."

"I mean it, honey. By this time next month, we'll be together for good."

She shook her head. "All right, Harry. I'll give you until then. But you've given me that story before. I mean what I say."

"And I mean it too. Now let's make plans for the next nine days."

CHAPTER ONE

May 7, 2020, The First Day

The rumbling roar built up and drowned the screams of the people in the basement. Jim's chair was violently jerked out from under him as if by a giant hand. He tumbled and slid on the floor along with chairs, tables and human bodies. The concrete wall was the brake that stopped the flow of objects and bodies.

Dazed, Jim felt and took the blows as everything movable seemed to target his body, creating a heap at the wall. He struggled to move, to sit up but a great force seemed to hold him down. It was not the other bodies because he had an arm and a shoulder free. He tried moving his hand, but it was like watching a movie in slow motion as it took will and effort before he could turn it.

A light was flashing on and off in his face. Who was up there? Straining against the pressure, he managed to turn his head enough to look.

No one was there. It was a light on the wall, jingling back and forth. He remembered now. It was a battery operated lamp mounted on the wall. It came on automatically when the main power supply was cut off. He could see the dust particles swirling in and out of the light beam like falling snowflakes.

The rumbling had not stopped. It continued loud, over-powering, drowning out everything else. He could see a couple of the women, their mouths open in soundless screams.

His ears, his senses could no longer abide the appalling clamor. His eyes followed a crack on the wall as it zigzagged down to the floor, then another, any moment now, that ceiling would come crashing down.

Fear gripped him as it had never done before. He felt helpless, out of control. He closed his eyes, not wishing to see the impending collapse of the ceiling, but could not shut out the horrible and shattering din.

How insignificant and powerless we really are, the thought came, inanely, to mind. Dorothy, the tablets, Linda. Is this what they mean by your life flashing through your mind as you await that final moment? What regrets we've accumulated?

The roar did not abate. The walls shook; the lights jiggled; the floor rolled; the pressure pinned down everything. Time seemed endless. But the end, his end, did not come.

Damn you, Martin! Is this it?

He heard screaming and slowly turned his head in that direction. What now? What could be worse...then he realized the implication of the screams. He could hear them! He could distinguish them from the roaring demon in the closed basement.

The rolling stopped; the din subsided. He could raise his arm, aching, but without having to exert force. In contrast to the hideous roar of a few moments ago, it was suddenly quiet.

Then came the groans and cries. Others had survived.

He pushed off a body that produced a moan in reply. He found reliable footing and slowly stood up, feeling like an old man on shaky legs. He cast a wary eye on the ceiling. He shook his head. It had to be a miracle.

"Are you hurt?" he bent down to help the woman he had pushed off. He recognized her as Stella Mundick, one of the nurses.

She put a hand to her rib cage. "A painful bruise, I think. I hope I didn't break a rib."

"We're lucky to be alive. Can you move about? We're going to need your help. See if you can find Walter Heerlson and your buddy Ellen. Think you can manage?"

She nodded and stumbled off.

The basement was a mixture of lights and shadows, forms standing up or on hands and knees. A huge figure materialize on his left. It was Oscar.

"My God! Jim, what was that?"

"Don't know. Maybe an earthquake. We'll have to wait for the evening news anchor to give us his analysis.

"It's not important now. We have to help the injured and then get the hell out of here." In the dim light from the lamps, he and Oscar began checking the others. First checking they had no injuries that could be further aggravated by moving them. Coughing and whimpering, the survivors were slowly coming out of their trance. Stella returned with Walter and Ellen Service.

"Let's clear a space where we can get the most benefit from those lamps," said Walter. The dust was settling providing more light.

"Jim! Walter!" a disheveled Dorothy, a bruise on her forehead clutched Jim's arm. "In the back of the hall, the storeroom under the staircase. We have first aid kits, medicine and blankets, and flashlights."

"Great! Get some help from those that are able. Anything you have that will help the injured and to get us out of here."

He saw John and David and beckoned to them. "Let's find the door and start getting out of here."

They picked their way through the debris, chairs, tables, pieces of masonry. Jim marveled that anyone could have survived, but even more amazing was the survival of the basement, a sub-basement really. True, it was a Civil Defense Shelter, but then, whatever it had been, had been definitely out of the ordinary. Judging by the sound, it could have been the end of the world.

He stumbled, missing a step. Martin's prediction. Why couldn't he get it out of his mind?

"There it is, Jim," John broke into his thoughts. They were confronted by bulging double doors standing askew. Rock and dirt blocked the doorway and partially spilling into the basement.

"It looks solid," said David, picking at a piece of masonry sticking out. The other two joined him. After a few minutes and the creation of a dust cloud, they backed off, coughing.

"It's going to take a while and more effort to get through that," Jim remarked. Turning around, he saw they had acquired an audience.

"I suggest everyone sit down and try to relax. The doorway is blocked. We have to wait for them to dig us out or we have to do it ourselves."

The statement elicited cries of anguish and concern. "Oh My God! We're trapped!"

"I've got to get out! Don't you understand! My babies are up there!"

"Yes! Yes! Our children! What's happened to them?"

They surged towards the door.

"Stop! Stop!" Jim held out his hands to hold them back.

"Where are you going? You can't get out, so don't panic. Slowly now. We'll take turns digging at the doorway."

Oscar and Dorothy pushed their way to the front of the group. Oscar had two shovels in his big fist. "This should help. Dorothy had them in her storeroom."

Dorothy was handing out flashlights. "We have more things in the storeroom." Jim pointed to the shovels. "Take turns, two men at a time. Get a handkerchief over your nose, you'll last longer." He stepped back as the first couple attacked the rubble at the door.

"What now?" Dorothy asked.

He saw the bruise on her forehead. "Did you get Walter to look at that?"

Without thinking he reached out to her head, but she drew back, stumbling over a chair.

He caught her, drawing her to him. "I'm sorry. That was a stupid thing to do. Are you all right?"

"Yes," she said breathlessly, her face almost on his dusty shoulder.

All of a sudden, he felt like holding her very close. A feeling of protectiveness came over him. Quickly, but gently, he stepped back, holding her by the shoulders. Hastily, to cover any embarrassment, he returned to business.

"Dorothy, are there any more exits? Surely the fire department must..."

"Yes, yes. There are two more. One on the east side and another inside leading to the library on the ground floor."

"Then let's check them. Oscar, get a flashlight and do the east side. Dorothy and I shall check the library stairs."

She led the way, his hand on her arm as they carefully stepped around the debris. "Here we are," she pointed in the gloom and he flashed his light to guide their way. The beam of light traveled upward to reveal a landing and a door at the top of the stairs.

"C'mon," he took her arm and started to scramble up the stairs.

"Wait!" she cried. "These high heels weren't meant to bound over steep stairs, even on a mission of mercy."

"You never know if you're dressed correctly for the occasion," he remarked.

"Even if you're forewarned?" she looked at him.

He sighed. "For the last hour, I've been trying to reject such thoughts."

"I think it's important that we consider it," she replied. "For instance, if true, there may not be anyone up there to dig us out."

He nodded. "Right. And we're about to find out the answer to question one, part one."

They had reached the top and as he surveyed the door, he had a sinking feeling. It looked solid. And since it led into a Civil Defense Shelter, it was built to withstand punishment. It would take a direct hit to blast it open.

"Stand back," he warned. "We don't know what's behind it." He placed his hand on the handle and pulled. The door did not budge. He placed one foot on the wall and pulled with both hands. Again, nothing. "Stuck! I guess that eliminates this exit."

"Maybe we can pry it open," she ventured.

"With what? Even if you had a crowbar in that stockroom of yours, it wouldn't do the trick. Nothing short of a stick of dynamite will open that door."

"Oh God!" she thumped her temple with the flat of her hand. "Somebody goofed. I'm sure we had that item on my list of things to store."

He smiled. "We're going to need some humor to get us through the next few..."

"Yes?" she inquired when he stopped.

He shook his head. "No more of that."

He helped her down the stairs and at the bottom they met Oscar. "I checked the other door, Jim. It's blocked like the west entrance."

"So is the one up here. Well, since we started on the west entrance, we might as well continue our efforts there. But let's not broadcast it to the others."

"Sooner or later, someone familiar with the building, namely Sylvia, Esther and Linda, will ask questions," said Dorothy.

"By then, we'll be out of here."

"I can't see in the dark, Jim," Oscar commented, "but are your fingers crossed?"

"Now there's question two," Jim held up his hands, fingers spread so Oscar could see. "Are there air vents in this hall? How many and where?"

"We have six. Three on the north wall and three on the south wall," Dorothy supplied the information.

"We've got to check them and see if they're operating. But quietly. With all exits blocked, it leaves us with the vents as out only source of air. Luckily this is a big basement and there are so few of us. If they're blocked too, then what's in the basement is our only source. And speaking of air, we don't know the quality of it up there.

"Dorothy, since this is a Civil Defense Shelter, did you stock a radiation counter?"

"Yes we did, and a radio too. I just forgot with all this excitement. Do you think it was a nuclear attack?"

"I doubt it. Why would anyone pick Stonecliff as a target? And we're not anywhere near a primary target. No. Most likely it was an earthquake. No matter. Oscar, get the counter and radio and meet us at the north wall vents. But first I'll check with Walter on the casualties."

They found Walter administering to one of the women. "Give us the bad news, Walter, injury list and fatalities."

"Well, as far as the latter is concerned, just one. Shirley Adkins. And as far as I can figure, she died of fright. I couldn't find any reason for her demise."

"Poor Shirley, she was a quiet one," said Dorothy. "She didn't deserve this."

Jim took her hand and Walter continued. "As for the injuries, we had four people knocked unconscious and now back with us with nothing worse than headaches and some dizziness. There were also three broken arms, various sprains, cuts and bruises. That's the extent of it. Damn lucky, since we don't have medical facilities, and extra-ordinary, considering the circumstances. I thought this was going to be my tomb."

"We're lucky you and the nurses were here," said Jim.

"Well, I can think of better places to be," grunted Walter. "Do you know what happened?"

"An earthquake would be my guess. Beyond that I don't know. Better have anyone not working to lie down. That should lessen any discomfort from the dust."

"What about the air supply in here?"

"That's what we aim to find out. So no undue movement. Try to keep them together under the pretext you have to check them periodically. We don't need panic now." The two went to the north wall where she pointed to the louvered openings. "It doesn't seem damaged," he said. "Is there a fan in each unit?"

"Yes."

He pulled a chair against the wall and under the vent. Standing on the chair, he was about even with the lower part of the vent. Reaching with his hands he could just reach the two upper screws. He pressed the side of his face against the louvers. Nothing. No sound or flow of air.

"Feel anything, Jim?" Oscar asked as he arrived with the equipment.

"No, nothing.

"Oscar, would a Forest Service type be carrying a pocketknife? You know, one of those with a bottle opener, nail cutter, eyebrow tweezer and a screwdriver?"

"Never leave home without it. You figuring to take off that vent cover?"

"This might provide another avenue of escape. But let's finish checking the others. If we find one with a draft, it might be easier to clean out.

"Give me the counter and I'll check out the vent. Dorothy, you try the radio."

He turned the knob on the Geiger counter and held the box to the vent.

"Any reaction?" Oscar inquired.

"No, But, I don't know what that means. It would seem that whatever is behind this vent is not contaminated. It doesn't necessarily tell me how it is topside. Then again, what's the depth or range of this thing? Can it detect through some forty feet of dirt and rock?"

"I don't know, Jim. You need some scientific types for that answer. In my business, I'd look for the thickest tree to hide behind."

"Any luck, Dorothy?"

"Nothing here either. Just static."

"Isn't there supposed to be an Emergency Broadcast System?"

"Yes. It's supposed to cut in the regular programming when an emergency arises and give instructions on what to do and where to go. But there's nothing."

"We might have missed it. Keep the radio on, but low," nodding towards their unseen classmates in the dark.

A tired and obviously frustrated David Granhill joined them.

"How is it coming at the door, Dave?"

"We're not making much progress. You can't stick there too long with the dust. We've been constantly changing teams.

"We're about two floors down. If that stairwell is solidly blocked, we may never make it out of here. There is nothing to suggest anyone up there is making any effort to reach us."

Jim nodded. "We're practically helpless, but we've got to try. We can't give up. If nothing else, for appearance sake. These people are ready to panic."

"Everyone has family up there," said David. "It's the not-knowing that's gnawing away at us."

Jim glanced at Dorothy who had tears in her eyes. He squeezed her shoulder. "I know. I wish there was some way to make it easier for you and those other mothers over there. You're all going through hell just thinking about all the possibilities up there. Harsh as it may sound, we can't do anything until we get out of here, through outside intervention or on our own. We just have to hope someone up there has taken care of our loved ones."

"I don't hear an encouraging word," said Oscar. "Is this the Big One?"

"I don't know, Oscar. God! I don't know how many times I've had to say that. I feel helpless. There's no answer except to keep on doing what we've been doing. We're alive. For how long?" he shrugged.

"We have, or we had, a two-story building above us," he continued. "Judging by the sound alone, it seemed like we were in the epicenter of an earthquake. The only time I was in one, I only felt a slight tremor. The epicenter was miles away though I observed selective damage around us. This one felt like the granddaddy of all quakes. Yet aside from a few cracks, this basement survived. It is against all logic. I felt a rolling sensation as if the whole building was on rollers. That might have been our salvation. The whole basement, heavily encased in concrete must have been carried along rather than twisting vertically. The motion seemed to be in one direction."

"You think that was it?" said Oscar.

Jim shook his head. "It's a guess. I'm no expert."

"This place was built to withstand all but a direct hit," said Dorothy. "My grandfather was on the school board back in the Fifties when they built the school. It was him and several others, at the height of the 'bomb' scare, who insisted this be built."

"I don't think it was a nuclear explosion," said Jim. "It's strange, but, well, I'll take my turn at the door. Oscar, you and Dave try the other vents, and don't forget to test for radiation. Dorothy, keep checking that radio."

A half hour later, Jim took a rest from the door detail. He sat down with a group that included Dorothy, Sylvia Remner, Esther Bonococci, Jean Ansuelmo, John and David.

Everyone was quiet, conserving their energy, and unknowingly for some of them, the remaining air. For those who knew, that problem was uppermost in their minds. The scraping at the door and an occasional sob or moan was just a reminder of their basic problem, getting out.

"To think I was responsible for bringing everyone here, to this," Dorothy broke the silence.

"Speaking from hindsight, of course," Jim replied. "If we take any incident, then trace back the lives of those people involved, we might find out what brought them to that place in time. But it was a conscious decision, whether it was for fun, for greed, for nostalgia or a social obligation. We cannot live our lives holding back making decisions for fear that dire consequences might result. Yes, this is an extraordinary event, but there was no way to measure that ahead of time. So here we are, accountable to no one but ourselves. Our free will made that decision for us."

He saw them, grieving and full of guilt. How can you blame them? It's only human nature. Now me, why did I come? He grunted. Yeah, why? He looked at Dorothy.

CHAPTER TWO

June 3, 2019, The previous year

The man stood at the top of the hill and watched the two young men as they approached. He could have been anywhere from his late fifties to the late sixties, straight black hair speckled with gray, chunky, of medium height, his skin darkened by heredity and environment. He was dressed in the universal uniform of the outdoors, flannel shirt, denim jacket and jeans and the inevitable boots. The only break from traditional garb was a cap with the name, University of Arizona on the bill.

The two men were both tall, although the tanned white man was a couple of inches taller. They too were dressed for the outdoors although bareheaded. The white man wore bomber jacket while the darker one had only a flannel shirt.

As they were almost upon him, the older man sucked in his breath. His eyes wide, he drew back a step. "Another one?" he muttered in amazement.

"Jim, this is Martin, Martin Hill, although he rarely uses his last name. Martin is our medicine man, my mentor, my second father. He is that and more to me," the darker young man made the introductions.

"And Martin, this is Jim Fenzer."

"So, you are the archaeologist John was talking about. How interesting that he would pick you."

"Not so strange," replied Jim, "seeing as how we went to high school together."

"You were with John in high school? At Stonecliff?"

"Yes. Is that significant?"

Martin shook hands with Jim. His left hand covering the handclasp. He held it longer than usual, looking straight at Jim's eyes. Finally, he stepped back and nodded to John. "Yes, he will do."

Jim noted the exchange. "Did I just pass some test?"

"With flying colors," said Martin.

John stared at Martin. "I'm glad you approve. As I recall, you were not happy at bringing in an outsider."

"He is another one of the 'chosen' ones," replied Martin, looking at Jim.

John sighed, smiling at Jim. "Martin claims I am a 'chosen' one, destined to survive some cataclysmic event. Are you saying he is one too?" addressing Martin.

"John, you still do not take me seriously. I thought I had taught you better."

"Martin, you must admit that a long time has elapsed since you told me that story and nothing has happened. You've given me no clue as to what my role is. Shouldn't I be skeptical under the circumstances?"

"Speaking for myself," said Jim, "I'm interested. While I'm not up-to-date on your people, I know that many stories and legends abound about your culture and heritage and those of other tribes in the area. On the other hand, I too, become skeptical when you include me, a white man, as part of some tribal legend. I know you are a people proud of your land and culture and it would be heresy for whites to be involved."

"Yes, of course. You barely get here and right away you get words thrown at you that sound like something out of science fiction. Oh yes, I saw the arch of the eyebrow. This is another Indian medicine man shaking and rattling the bones and mouthing weird incantations. Shades of Sitting Bull!"

"The eyebrow went up when you included me in your legend. However, unless you read minds, you would know I do not scoff or belittle other cultures. I wouldn't be in this field if I wasn't interested and eager to learn of the past."

"I apologize. I guess I was overly sensitive. If we're going to work together, I should establish my credentials. After serving in 'Nam, I went to good old Arizona U. After the requisite number of years, I now have the right to a string of alphas after my name. That is my modern, USA side of me."

"As the resident shaman descended from a long line of medicine men, many secrets have been passed on to me. Among them is the one of the First Children. When the last world ended, a small group survived to repopulate the new world. They are our ancestors. But it was also foretold that even this new world would die. Thus, there would be a new group of survivors to start the new world. They are referred to as the 'Chosen Ones' or the 'First Children.' One day, it was said, the chosen ones would be revealed to the shaman. Then he would know the time is near when another world would end."

"It is said the children must first come together. So, when I saw you with John, it hit me. In fact, several things are now of great concern to me with your appearance."

"If I might ask," Jim squinted as the clouds parted and the sun shone straight into his face. Martin's eyes widened. "How do you know I am, what you say I am?"

Martin sighed. "How can I explain that without sounding weird as the young people say? It is an aura around your body. It is a feeling or a force when I touch you. I cannot explain. I just know. Having been educated in the white man's schools, I can understand your disbelief. Indeed, there is often a clash of cultures that raises doubts within me sometimes.

"As John said earlier, nothing has happened since I first discovered him, and I told him of his destiny. That was many years ago and it certainly caused me to question those beliefs. Then today, you appeared. Worse, you were a white man. It was a shock. It told me I had fallen into the mortal trap of racism and intolerance because I looked no further than my own people. It was an Indian thing; therefore, the survivors would come from our own people. Right? Well, I didn't find any more after John. You've proven the fallacy of my thinking, my narrowmindedness. How much time have I lost? How much time do I have left?"

"You pique my interest with your story, as an archaeologist," said Jim, as he absently plucked a blade of grass. They had sat down on the southern slope of the hill but still had the cooling breeze from the northwest. "But I must tell you I've heard that tale, or some variation of it, many times in as many cultures. Moreover, so-called modern society has its own variation of the Doomsday story. There is 2000. A year that some have predicted would spell the end of the planet. The year 1999 was also another favorite. Maybe it was those repetitious digits that captured the public's fancy. The same predictions were around a millennium ago when the year 1000 approached. Nothing happened, of course. We're still here. There is no significance in the numbers of a calendar year, especially to Christians. The birth of Christ is at variance with our present calendar. Calendars and the Bible have been tinkered and tampered by emperors and empresses, kings and queens, popes and bishops, all for ideological, religious or self-interest. Words that can have several meanings have been misinterpreted. An untold number of translations have been made. God only knows what has been lost in the translation. The Bible contains Jewish, Christian and pagan events, thoughts and dogma. There is just so much that can go wrong over that length of time. Stories have been handed down through the ages and much has been dropped or added that makes the whole unreliable."

"Indeed, we see much of it in today's society. The cover-ups, the protection of someone's ass. There are still many mysteries within our own lifetime that we cannot solve. So how can we be sure what happened 20, 200 or 2000 years ago? How reliable is the historian or story teller? What self-interest did he have? Who was he beholden to? I could go on and on. Every year produces some dire predictions of extinction and the usual groups of people trudging to the mountain top after having disposed of all their worldly goods. That is the reason for my disbelief."

"All right. I'll accept that for the time being," said Martin. "Perhaps later I can convince you as we proceed with the task that brought you here."

"Yes, that part seems to have been lost with all this attention to, other matters. John said you would explain."

"Better than telling you, I'll show you. John, get some horses while I get food and water."

They walked down the slope towards a cabin and corral with several horses. John had brought him out on a pickup. Apparently, this trip would be over terrain inaccessible to a truck.

John saddled three horses and Martin brought canteens and a bulging knapsack from the cabin. As they mounted, Jim noticed a blanket roll on each horse.

"Looks like a long trip." he remarked.

"Overnight, at least," replied Martin. "It's about twenty miles, but I'm sure you'll want to spend some time there after you see it."

"See what?"

He smiled and shook his head.

It seemed farther than twenty miles, but it was the terrain that made it so. There was no well-defined trail. The way was heavily forested, at times dark with thick foliage blocking out the sun. Then they would burst out to open grassland or sunbaked rock.

In mid-afternoon they entered a small canyon, the entrance slightly smaller than the length of a football field. Most of it was shadowed by the escarpment now almost overhead. Farther on, Jim could see the walls on both sides curve as if to form a giant dome. Perhaps in times past, an immense cavern might have formed here, but now it was open to the sky.

Martin stopped and indicated to the others to dismount. He took out a couple of flashlights from a saddlebag.

"Better bring your rifle, John. Never know what kind of wildlife might be cooped up in there."

For the first time, Jim became aware of a Winchester stuck in John's saddle. He mentally shrugged. At the very least there must be rattlesnakes to avoid.

Jim saw nothing but canyon wall with brush and some foliage seemingly growing out of bare rock. He couldn't imagine what it was that he was supposed to see. Martin disappeared into the thick brush and John motioned Jim to follow. Jim plunged through expecting to come abruptly against canyon wall. But no, there was about two feet of cleared space in front of the wall. He followed the others laterally along the wall. And then, there was a gaping hole on the wall. A cave!

"This is the last thing I expected," he exclaimed to the others waiting at the entrance. "I thought you had some ancient pictorials on a wall."

"There might be some of those on the inside," said John. "We haven't explored all of it."

"How did you find this? This area is so inaccessible,"

"Actually, I brought John here," said Martin. "That was a few months ago. You are the fourth person to know of its existence. Before that, only the chief of the tribe and the medicine man knew it was here. The knowledge has been passed on for generations of medicine men and tribal chiefs."

"And now you're revealing it to me, an outsider and a white man. I know enough of your culture to realize this is sacred ground if so few know its whereabouts."

Martin nodded. "Just bear with us for just a bit longer."

Jim followed Martin into the cave, John brought up the rear. The passageway was about ten or twelve feet high and just about as wide. The sides were rough, but as Jim could see, it looked almost smooth. It had been worked to its present dimensions. But how long ago?

They continued for some two hundred feet when they came to a fork. "We take the left," said Martin.

They went on. Jim estimated they had gone a good quarter mile before they came to a huge room. As Martin flashed his light farther on, he saw a ledge overlooking an even larger chamber. Jim saw a large pool of water below, the light reflecting from the water as it swept over the pool. Off to one side, in the shadows, he saw what appeared to be a long bench or table, no, not a table. It had no visible legs.

"And there you are," said Martin.

"Beautiful," said Jim. "I didn't know a cave this size existed in Arizona."

"Oh, there's many people that don't know about them, and then there's some that do. But we know them all. After all, we were here first."

"Is this what you wanted to show me?"

"Yes. You've seen it."

"I don't understand. I haven't seen anything that could require my services, archaeologically speaking."

"Yes, you did. But let's get a closer look."

Martin led the way down from the ledge. Jim saw that some crude steps had been fashioned to go down into the chamber. They were narrow as if made for people with small feet. He had to step sideways. A mental picture of the pyramids in Mexico came to mind, also with narrow steps. He shook his head, a coincidence. They descended to the floor of the chamber, indeed they had been steadily descending since they entered the cave. This room must be over a hundred feet below the outside entrance.

"As an archaeologist, I know you will appreciate this," said Martin as he flashed his light on the bench Jim had seen from above.

For a moment nothing registered in his brain. Then as the light revealed, the bench was not a bench, He gasped. He reached to touch the top of the object. He saw and felt the indentations and the edges separating one from the other, tablets! Tablets, heretofore seen only in museums.

He knelt and ran his fingers over the stack. Only it wasn't just a stack. There were four more, each about four feet high. They had to number in the hundreds.

"I, I can't believe this," Jim's heart was pounding. "Do you know what this means? Nothing like this has ever been discovered in North America, possibly in all the Americas." He turned his attention to the tablets and blew away the dust on the top layer. There were inscriptions!

"This is a written record! Not a bone or a piece of pottery that you theorize as to its origin. Do you realize this find may be on the level as the Dead Sea Scrolls or the Middle Eastern tablets? And here, of all places."

The others could not see Jim's face in the darkness, but they heard the excitement in his voice.

Then Jim had a thought. "Is this a hoax? These things are out of place here. They don't belong in this environment."

"This is not a hoax, Jim," Martin looked at him sadly.

"I would never play tricks with you. What would I have to gain? They've been here all my life and for several generations of medicine men before me."

"Can you vouch for them? They're dead."

"No, I can't vouch for them. But I sincerely believe they had no intention of playing tricks on their descendants."

"They might have used them as a means of controlling their people. Medicine men have been known to do that."

"Our people have no knowledge of these tablets. As I said, only I and the chief of the tribe know about them. No one comes to this cave on their own."

"All right, that's no matter. I can authenticate them by radiocarbon dating."

"No, I can't let you publicize this."

Jim's suspicions went up again. "Why, Martin? Why have you brought me here, shown me these things, supposedly as genuine, then refuse to follow procedures to authenticate them? You need a team of experts to do this job. I can't do it alone."

"There are several reasons. We don't want to be overrun with reporters and tourists. Secondly, this is our land, set aside for a special purpose, as I suspect you will find out from those tablets."

"You let in a stranger like me."

"You are a stranger no longer. You are a part of this. Can it be mere coincidence that you, an archaeologist, are also one of the 'children'?"

"John told me you consented to have an archaeologist to come here, presumably to show him the tablets. What would you have done if I hadn't passed your test?"

"I would have brought out a few for your inspection. Never would I have taken you or anyone else to the cave."

Jim sighed. "All right. So, I can't tell the world. Exactly what were your plans after you had shown me the tablets?"

"Exactly what you would want. Work on them. Translate what they say. I think they will verify everything I've told you and more. The question is: How much time do we have left. What are the particulars?"

"How can I do this without it becoming public knowledge?"

"Then do it here. Not in the cave. We can build a cabin in the canyon for your workplace and living quarters."

"My God! Martin, if this is what you say, then this is a project. You need a team of experts. And talking about time, this will probably take several years."

"I don't think we have years, Jim."

Jim shook his head. "Then I can't promise you anything. Even if you build a cabin, this place will be snowed in by late fall at least. You could have trespassers that could become curious of a lonely cabin in the wilderness.

"No, Martin. You're setting obstacles that negates everything you want to know."

"Please, Jim," said John. "Won't you reconsider?"

"You're handcuffing me, Martin. If you're looking for a quick translation, this is not the way to go."

"John will help. I will help. I'll get the best and most trusted men from the tribe to help."

"Isn't that letting in more people on the secret? It wouldn't be sacred ground anymore and sooner or later someone will talk, and it would get to the outside. And what training do any of you have? This is not a 'dig' where manual labor is required. The artifacts have already been dug up, so to speak. We need to know the age of the tablets and the cave. Were there previous occupants and how long ago. And who were they? Did they leave any clues on the walls or buried on the ground? Are there other entrances? How did they get in here? Who brought them and how? And what..."

"I'm interested in the tablets only and what they say," broke in Martin.

Jim threw up his hands. He was silent for a few minutes as he flashed his light on the tablets, then on to the wall and into the darkness beyond.

"Only the uniqueness and the implications of this find forces me to accept your terms," he finally replied to Martin. "But I can't guarantee results without expert help and within any time limits."

"I'll agree to that," Martin nodded and put out his hand to seal the agreement.

"Which brings up another problem. I'm going to need equipment, reference material and other supplies. I'll go to Stonecliff to get some of it. The rest I might have to go to Phoenix or Flagstaff."

"John and I will go to Stonecliff with you. I'm curious about your background and others in that town. Could there be more of you? Your schoolmates are they still there?"

"I imagine there are some that left. I haven't been there in years. Probably John has a better idea."

"When I picked you up, it was the first time in eight years I've been there. Funny thing, it's only seventy miles away, the largest town in the vicinity, yet I avoid it like the plague."

The others made no comment.

John laughed. "Just some unpleasant memories, I guess. Thelma Rattling is probably still there. George Perez is in Tucson. Maybe, Jean is there."

The two noted the pause but said nothing.

"Anyway, we can check," John continued, "if you think it's important, Martin."

"Yes," Martin replied, "I've got a feeling that I've delayed too long. It is my duty to pass on this inheritance to the rightful heirs."

Jim glanced at John who shrugged.

THE NEXT DAY.

The three men met in the lobby of the small motel where they had registered. The motel was on the outskirts of Stonecliff, on Highway 87, where it hoped to lure some of the passing tourists. Not that Stonecliff couldn't attract visitors. Its main attraction was the cliff dwellings north of the town. In addition, there was a wide variety of game during the season and many lakes nearby for fishing. It was a scenic area and there were national forests wherever one turned. Indian reservations were a few hours away to the northeast and around to the southeast. In the last census, it had counted twelve thousand people. Now almost ten years later, at least two or three thousand had been added. On a straight-line basis, it was about equidistant from Phoenix and Flagstaff. But as Jim well knew, in Arizona nothing was ever on a straight-line basis. Mountains, forests and deserts made detours inevitable.

"Well, are we agreed on the agenda?" Jim asked.

"Yes," answered Martin. "We'll drop you at the Western Post. It's next to the supermarket owned by Hart Perkins. He owns the Post too. You get what you want, I'll take care of it, or rather the tribe shall."

Martin scribbled a note and handed it to Jim. "We do a lot of business with Hart."

"And what will you and John be doing?"

"Martin is still interested in our high school relationships," said John. "I've called Thelma and we're going to see her. She's the only one I know here."

Jim looked at him. "All right. How about if we meet for lunch at...at....," he looked at Martin

"The old Cattleman's Diner," he said. "It's only three blocks from the Post and they only care about the color of your money."

Jim hesitated. "Right. Let's make it for twelve thirty."

Later at the Western Post

"Yes sir," the clerk looked at the list, "we have all these items. You say the chief wants them charged to his account?"

"Yes," Jim handed the clerk Martin's note. "Here is his authorization."

"Ah, Yes, Ah, no offense, sir, but I don't know you. Perhaps I'd better check this with my boss. I hope you understand..."

"Of course. If it will make you feel better, I can bring him around this afternoon and we can pick up the equipment then."

"Yes sir, I'm sorry, sir. Obviously, you're not Indian, uh, that is..."

"Tony? Is something wrong?"

The new voice came from behind Jim, definitely feminine. He turned around. The new voice belonged to a vision of loveliness. She was of medium height with dark shoulder length hair, green eyes, slim and wearing a dress. a few inches above the knee. That, from what he could see, suggested gorgeous legs, a great body overall.

"Oh no, Mrs. Walters, I believe we have resolved the problem."

"Are you the manager, Mrs. Walters?" Jim asked.

"No, I have no official capacity. It's just that my father owns the store, and as all my friends would tell you, I have a tendency to butt in on other people's business."

"If I were to choose someone to butt into my business, I could never pick anyone as lovely as you."

She blushed. "Thank you, your very kind. But, don't I know you?"

"That's supposed to be my line," he saw her blush again. "I was born here, went to school, fourteen years ago. I haven't been here in ten years and then only briefly. And, oh yes, name's Jim Fenzer."

"Jim Fenzer! Of course. I'm Dorothy Perkins or was. As you heard Tony, it's Walters now."

"Dorothy Perkins, our cheerleader, class valedictorian, vice president of the senior class, how could I forget."

"Yes, how could you forget, Mr. President and captain of the football team when we were class officers and I was on the sidelines leading the cheers for the team?"

Now it was his turn to be embarrassed. He laughed. "I have no excuses. I deserve a whack from your baton."

"Well, as you said, it's been a long time. And since we were in the same class, I don't even have the female prerogative of lying about my age."

"I can't think of anyone looking at you and caring about your age."

"Well," she was disconcerted by the compliments, yet strangely elated at this meeting. She was glad she had made an extra effort in her appearance in what would ordinarily have been a routine errand to her father's store. "Let's forget about past history and get back to the present. What brings you back after these many years?"

"A job, sort of. You remember John Edleman, don't you?

"He had some, artifacts on the reservation that he wanted me to study. I'm getting some equipment and supplies for the job."

"Does that mean you're going to be around for a while?"

"Depends. I'll be out in the reservation most of the time. I might be able to make some weekends here to break the monotony."

She laughed. "First time I ever heard anyone coming to Stonecliff for diversionary purposes. It's usually the other way around."

"I guess any town short of Phoenix is going to come off short. I've never been much of a city boy. Not much beauty to be found in a city, present company excluded."

"Thank you again. If I were younger and unattached, I'd be having a giggling fit."

He smiled, nodding. "Actually, meeting you today might be a help to us. Are you free for lunch by any chance?"

"Is that an invitation?"

"Definitely! That is, if it doesn't compromise your standing as a respected lady of the community by dining with a stranger. I know how small towns are."

"Oh, think nothing of it. Anyone who knows me will tell you I do as I please, if I think it's right. Besides, you're an old friend, a classmate."

"Good. Before I met you, we had made plans to lunch at the Cattleman's Diner. It's not the most elegant place to impress a lady, but it's too late to change."

"Who is 'we'?"

"John and Martin, the medicine man at the reservation.

"He does quite a bit of business with your father. I want you to meet him."

"Yes, I've heard my father mention him, but I've never met him. Any special reason why I should?"

"Well, it could be. Martin has expressed a desire to meet our ex-schoolmates. In fact, they were meeting this morning with Thelma Rattling whom John knows."

"Thelma? Oh yes, we meet now and then. Poor girl. She has a weight problem and she doesn't seem to know or care how she looks.

"But why this interest in old schoolmates?"

"Well, I, I'm not exactly free to tell you. Let's wait until we see Martin and see how much he wants to tell you. And since you've never met, you qualify for his inspection."

"Inspection? Now I am intrigued. You've aroused the Dorothy Walters curiosity."

"Then let's go. It's only three blocks away. We can talk and do some catching up."

JIM AND DOROTHY WERE sitting in a booth at the diner when John and Martin came in. Jim was facing the door, so he saw them first. He waved them over.

Martin was excited. "Jim, you wouldn't believe this, but we found another..."

He stopped as he saw Dorothy. Jim heard a sharp intake of breath as he stared at her.

"Martin, John, this is Dorothy Walters, formerly Perkins. John, you should remember. She was the cheer leader and our class valedictorian."

John nodded and shook her hand. "Yes, you don't forget someone like her."

Dorothy laughed nodding towards Jim. "He did. Of course, he showed his appreciation in other ways."

Jim joined in the laughter.

"May I shake your hand?" Martin addressed her, still staring at her.

Dorothy was plainly flustered, but she extended her hand. Martin covered it with both hands.

"Two of them in one day!" he exclaimed with glee. "All the time they were right here. I've been such a fool."

"Martin met Thelma," John explained. "He says she is one of us."

"And Dorothy too?" Jim looked at Martin.

He nodded. "No question about it."

"Will someone please explain what's going on here?" she asked.

"Martin?" Jim glanced at him. "You started this. Are you going to tell her or is it forbidden?"

"No, of course not. She's one of the 'chosen.' She figures into everything."

Martin told Dorothy essentially the same story he had told Jim. Which wasn't much, Jim thought he was still skeptical of the 'chosen' story. Even today there were the religious sects which claimed they would be saved at the end of time. That Jesus would return to signal the arrival of a new age.

Still there were the tablets. That was real, if they were genuine. What could they have to say about the 'chosen'? Martin could believe what he wanted so long as the tablets were available for study.

"I see..." Dorothy said as Martin finished his explanation. But Jim could see she was being polite.

"You say Thelma is one of the , group?" somehow Jim couldn't bring himself to say the word 'chosen.'

"Well, you have to know Thelma," said John. "She's never been one to get much attention. Naturally she was thrilled, but just as confused as Dorothy as to what it all means."

"Well, I am confused," said Dorothy. "What you're telling me is that I, a, excuse the expression, white woman, is involved in an Indian legend. I know that sounds racist, but what else..."

"Exactly what I once thought, Mrs. Walters," Martin interrupted. "I've known about John since he was twelve years old. When I first saw him, all doubt was erased from my mind. Then the years went by and I saw no more of the 'children,' even though I searched the entire reservation. Doubt crept into my mind, challenging my beliefs. My white man's training screamed to reject such nonsense.

"I finally resolved to tell John everything. I took him to the cave and revealed the existence of the tablets which I had sworn to protect from outsiders. Of course, we didn't know what they said. John said we should have them translated. At first, I resisted. It would mean strangers in our sacred land and danger of being overwhelmed by all sorts of people. John said he knew an archaeologist who could be trusted, and I finally agreed. Not with misgivings and with reservations as to how much I could tell him. So, I met Jim. It was then that all my theories, and prejudices, crumbled. A white man was one of the 'children.' I had searched in vain among my own people, now here he was, and so you see Mrs. Walters, I too, was guilty of racism. God does not dis-criminate, whatever your color, race, nationality or religion. That is the message we should all learn in this world but never do. We seem unable to overcome this animosity.

"The common denominator among all of you is that you come from Stonecliff and went to school together. Mrs. Walters and Miss Rattling have confirmed that today, at least to me. How many more of you are there?"

No one replied. Jim could see the lack of credibility in Dorothy although John was noncommittal. Martin couldn't fail to see it too. The older man was very likable and very obviously believed this legend. It was not some con game to him. Certainly, he hadn't asked for anything that was out of line, so far. If anything, he was the one putting out for expenses and was loaning his pickup for Jim to travel to Phoenix. No, it was definitely not a con game.

And this ability to see or sense some difference in them from all others, well, Jim had both seen and heard of people so gifted. Psychics, clairvoyants, ESP, all these were supposed to have special powers. Not all, fortunately, or unfortunately, were 100% in their predictions. Perhaps it was the human animal that couldn't always control its emotions that played a part to flaw their psychic abilities. Who really knows what powers we have and don't know how to use them? Perhaps the world is better off that we don't. Martin has never made any claims for psychic abilities except for his obsession with the 'children' and his supposed ability to discover them by sight and touch.

So, Jim's involvement came down to the tablets. He still wasn't sure of their authenticity but was willing to find out. And for that he was willing to put up with Martin's eccentricities.

"Assuming for the sake of argument, this is all as you say it is," he addressed Martin. "What is supposed to be our role in this scenario?"

"If you are to survive this coming event, you must all come together and seek shelter in the cave. I am firmly convinced that it is a safe haven."

"A bomb shelter," said Dorothy.

"What?"

"A bomb shelter. That's what you're saying the cave will serve. We have one at the school, under the library. And curiously enough, my grandfather help push it through during the 'bomb' scare of the Fifties. You can carry that oddity a bit further if you consider that I have been the one that has kept the shelter updated and stocked through all the years I have been a teacher at the school."

"Bomb shelter or cave," said Jim, "it still depends on the cataclysmic event you're predicting. There are some events from which no shelter will save you."

John grinned. "Does that mean that your belief factor has gone up a notch?"

Jim snorted. "Enough of this. I'll leave for Phoenix tomorrow and should be back the day after. Then I can start work on the tablets."

"We'll wait for you here," Martin nodded.

"Can I see the cave and the tablets?" Dorothy asked.

"Why not," said Martin. "But let's wait until we get set to accommodate visitors. Say by July?" He looked at Jim.

"It's all right with me. You're the one, as I recall, who was talking about keeping out the tourists."

Martin shook his head. "She is not a tourist. A child is coming home."

September 2019

So, she came in July. Then again in August. Now it was September and she had returned for a third time.

"Your accommodations are much better than what I saw last time," she said.

"We finally finished the cabin. A small corner to eat and sleep, the rest is work area. I doubt I'll get much use of it this year. The weather will change soon, and I'll have to leave or get snowed in."

"Where shall you go?"

"Move in with John and Martin. We'll find a winter place to continue some of the work. John has been taking photographs of the tablets. That should enable us to work through the winter on the translation."

"Any progress on the translation?"

"We can't even identify the language. It's like nothing I've ever seen before."

"How ancient could it be?"

"I need to test the tablets, but I doubt Martin would agree. If I knew how old they were I would be inside the ballpark."

"What happens if you're not successful?"

"That may be a problem. Martin is worried about time but doesn't help me in that respect with his refusal to bring in additional help."

"He's very obsessive about keeping all this a secret, including this 'chosen' business. Why do you put up with it?" said Dorothy.

"That's easy, the tablets. Why do you put up with it? For instance, this is your third trip here. The first I could understand, curiosity. But the others?"

She hesitated before answering, apparently thinking her reply. "It's true, I don't believe. But as a history teacher, this intrigues me. And I like the old man and his enthusiasm. He's been so happy since he found 'us.' I guess part of me wants it to be true for his sake."

"Including this world-ending catastrophe he's predicting?

"Of course not! It's just that, Oh, maybe it's the excitement of something new. I've been stuck in this mountain town where nothing ever happens."

"Regrets?" said Jim.

"What's 'regrets'?" she moved to look out the door. "Regrets are useless, because you can't do anything about them. All they do is serve as an experience you can learn from. Even then, I'm not sure that time or wisdom would cause one to change one's decisions. Or maybe to mope around and feel sorry for yourself. Until you asked, before this happened, I hadn't given it much thought. I have my family, my friends, my duties. Yes, it's probably dull, if you think about it. There must be millions out there with the same problem, Did I say problem? That suggests I have one."

He smiled. "No problem for you. I remember in high school you were always involved in some cause raising money, circulating petitions. Is it still that way?"

She laughed. "Just ask Sylvia, Esther or, Linda."

"Ah, yes, Linda," he smiled. "Should my ears have been burning all these years?"

"I imagine you both came in for your share of talk and gossip," she shrugged. "Is anyone really immune from that? I presume I've also been a target."

"Well, that was long ago. Everyone has moved on to a new and presumably better life."

"I guess you're right. We're all old married women with kids making life noisy and demanding. Is there a Mrs. in your life?"

"Are you kidding? With my lifestyle?"

"But is that the way you want it?"

"It's my work. Look around, this is very typical, no, take that back. This is luxurious. A tent in the wilds is typical. Why would any woman want to put up with this?"

"She would if she was in love with you."

"I wouldn't ask her to. It wouldn't be fair to her."

"How many women have you asked?"

"Why would you like to know?"

"Listen to us," she laughed. "We don't have answers, only questions."

"That seems to be the sum total of this venture, one big question mark."

"And I have to leave. No question. Just a statement."

"Will you come back?"

"I thought we were through with questions."

"Haven't you heard? Generalizations are always invalid."

"I don't think I should. You were right in saying three trips were two too many. And I could give you a couple of more clichés, but they're better left unsaid."

He put his hand on her arm. "I'm sorry. I'm taking my frustrations out on you. It looks like both my personal and business life are going nowhere. Maybe this next world will be different," he smiled.

She nodded. "I understand. Nevertheless, I think it best I don't return. As you said, the weather will turn bad in another month or so. My school schedule is set too, so that will limit my activities. If you make any progress, give me a call."

"I feel I've put a strain in our friendship," he replied. "It was never my intention to do so. Time and circumstances have changed many things for all of us."

"Yes, right now, in some ways, it's fourteen years ago. Good-bye, Jim."

He didn't say anything, following her out the door and watching her mount her horse and ride away. Damn, he didn't want her to leave. Already he felt an emptiness. He felt like she was riding out of his life. But what could he do? He was right in cutting it off. There was no future in getting close to her. No entanglements was the best solution. His work with the tablets was getting him nowhere. Now this. He didn't need it.

December 15, 2019

"John, this photo," he paused, shaking his head. "This is so different from the others. What does this number mean, 'four dash eleven'?

"There were twenty stacks of tablets in rows of four, eighteen tablets to a stack. That is the fourth stack, eleven tablets down. Here, I'll draw you a diagram."

John drew a series of rectangles representing the tablets, writing numbers in the blocks. "That photo would have come from this stack."

Jim spread out the four pictures on the table. "Look at this. These are numbered in succession, 4-9, 4-10, 4-11 and 4-12. Compare the inscriptions on the first two with the last two."

For a few minutes John studied the four pictures with a magnifying glass. "They are different. Like two separate writers or languages."

"Exactly! That's got to be why we haven't made progress. We've been looking at these in the order that they were in the stacks. We presumed that the intelligence that produced these tablets would leave them in sequence like you would in writing a book. What we've been looking at has made no sense of any known language.

"Here," he picked up a book from the table. "Turn to any page and you'll see a repetition of words, letters, vowels and consonants. It's only natural in any language. The first two have hardly any that repeat themselves but look at the others. See that inscription that looks like a little tree. It's repeated several times, or some variation of it. So is this one that looks like a funnel."

"My God! My God!" Jim stared off into space.

"What is it?"

Jim looked at him. "We could be looking at five or six thousand years of the history of mankind!"

He got up and went to peer out the window, deep in thought. It was snowing outside. It was December. They had left the cabin early in November, bringing only the photos John had made of the tablets.

"What are you saying?"

"John, these two tablets are definitely Middle Eastern, possibly Babylonian, or even Sumerian."

"What would they be doing here, of all places, halfway around the world?"

"Why do they have pyramids in Mexico resembling those in Egypt? Why is there a universal Flood story in several cultures, thousands of miles apart? Why? Why? That's why people like me go all over the world turning up dirt hoping to hit the Mother Lode.

"Your culture and that of many other tribes in the Southwest has been handed down orally, perhaps some pictographs here and there, but not in tablet form like these. They cannot be indigenous to this area unless they predate our present knowledge of this land. Why are they here? I don't know. I can speculate that they might have been placed here as a safe haven. Isn't that Martin's theory? Sort of like we place our valuables in a safe deposit box at our bank. Destructive wars exact their toll on many of the earth's treasures,

37

historical documents, not gold or diamonds. For instance, the great library at Alexandria was wantonly destroyed. One source claims there is a Hall of Records buried beneath the sand between the Sphinx and the Pyramid of Cheops. Who knows where others may be. It would make sense to bury a copy out here in the boondocks where it would be safe from warring factions in the Middle East. And all that is a guess, mind you, based on the history of those ancient people who had a tendency to bury their treasures for safe keeping."

"All right. That sounds as logical as anything I've heard," John still looked puzzled. "But how do you transport several hundred tablets some eight thousand miles, without breakage?"

Jim laughed. "I'm glad you included that last phrase. I don't know. A spaceship, maybe? There's plenty of people out there who swear they've seen them flying around for centuries."

"How do you explain these different tablets?"

"I can't. All they accomplish is to slow us down. Almost made me throw up the whole project, and come to think of it, maybe that was their purpose."

"How is that?"

"Did you ever hear that story of the opening of that Egyptian tomb? I think it was in the 1920s. There were warnings and curses to anyone defiling the tomb of the Pharaoh. Several people of that original party who opened the tomb later died."

"Yes. I remember reading something to that effect. What does that have to do with these tablets? Are we to be cursed for messing around with them?"

"Maybe these false tablets were placed here to throw us off from the real ones."

"That means separating the good from the bad."

"So, we'll do it. Then I'll have to go to Tucson or Phoenix to research the new data. What I wouldn't give to have a team here. We're trying to do too much by ourselves. Martin claims he's running out of time, but he won't give me expert help thereby extending the time it will take to translate the tablets."

"Are you stopping by Stonecliff to tell Dorothy?"

"No. I told her I would give her a call when there were new developments, but I don't intend to say anything until I have something more definite."

"She seemed very interested in the project. Then all of a sudden, she stopped coming. Is there something wrong?"

"My big mouth is what's wrong. I said some things I shouldn't. She turned cool after that. I can't blame her."

"She's a beautiful woman."

"And also married, and a mother. It's best not to start something that leads nowhere. That's the story of my life when it comes to women."

"Yet, she is supposed to be one of us. Destined to survive along with an undetermined number of others."

Jim grimaced. "The tablets are the only thing that have held me here, not saving civilization. Stonecliff holds nothing for me anymore. It was that way fourteen years ago. It's that way now. "Hell! Maybe even the tablets aren't enough to keep me here."

John put his hand on Jim's shoulder. "I know how it is. I've been through it myself. Why do you think I avoid Stonecliff?"

Jim laughed. "We're two of a kind. That's one thing Martin didn't figure on. How much baggage his 'children' will be carrying into the new world."

"Still want to leave?"

"In the worse way. But I'll stick it out a while longer."

CHAPTER THREE

M ay 7, 2020
Aaron Sherland came to, a monstrous headache tearing away inside his skull. His mouth was dry and gritty. It had the taste of dirt. What had happened? He had been shoved, no, he remembered the person next to him falling forward. And, yes, that rumbling roar. Then he remembered nothing.

He groaned as he tried to turn his head and was hit by a stabbing pain.

"Aaron, are you all right?"

He opened his eyes and slowly turned in the direction of the voice. In the dim light of the basement, he made out Linda, sitting on the floor next to him, her back against the wall.

"My head," he gingerly touched the back of it. "Must have taken a nasty crack. Still feel a little dizzy."

"Walter said you should be all right. Just take it easy. You were knocked out."

"Were you hurt?"

"I slid against a table leg, broke it and the table fell on me. Nothing broke, thank God, but my leg is uncomfortable and achy."

"Tell me what happened, or do you know?"

"I heard Jim say something about an earthquake. Seems like we're trapped in here. The door is blocked. They're trying to dig us out."

Someone came by, flashed a light and inquired if they were all right. It was one of the nurses, Ellen Service. It gave him a chance to see Linda's face. Her hair was in disarray, her mascara running. She was, or had been, crying.

"You're crying. Is your leg causing you pain?"

"I wish that was my only problem," she sniffled. "My children are up there, and I don't know what's happened to them. It's an effort not to break down and scream and cry like the others."

For the first time Aaron became conscious of his surroundings. The pain in his head and the surprise to find Linda next to him had rendered him oblivious to other disturbances in the hall. Now he became aware of the crying and sniffling, the occasional cough and the scraping at the entrance. A scream to his left evinced a stab of pain as he turned to look.

"My babies! My babies!"

"That's Edna Hobbes. She has five children. I wish they would shut her up. It's hard to keep your mind off the subject with her screaming. Does she think she is the only mother here?"

How strange events turn out, he thought. Only yesterday in Charlie Durian's garden, he had been pumping Charlie about Linda, her breakup with Jim, her marriage to a lawyer named Storey. He remembered Charlie's snide remark about teen-age infatuations. But what was unusual in having an interest in Linda? Many others did, no doubt including Charlie. Of course, Charlie was smart enough to know he would never be in the running in the Linda sweepstakes. No, sweepstakes was the wrong word. Not when there was only one entrant and one winner, Jim Fenzer. That didn't keep others like himself from yearning for the unattainable. He recalled Tom Wadley's remark that only his friendship with Jim kept him from going after Linda. Oh yeah! As if that would have made a difference. In those days she had eyes only for Jim.

She had been an ornament to be hung on one's arm, Jim's in her case. It was the blonde mystic that made her the sought-after beauty of the class although that wasn't a fair designation. The class had been blessed with a bevy of beauties like Dorothy, Nancy Grother, Jane Sestos, Susan Gilbert and Jean Garcia. Someone had said, unkindly, that all she did was stand there to be admired. She was not as active as Dorothy or that Mexican girl, Jean. It was just that Linda always dressed for the part of beauty queen, while the others dressed in sloppy, oversized clothes, in ponytails and sandals. She was always dressed to fit in anyone's drawing room at tea time. Looking at her now, she didn't look as formidable as the teen-aged princess of high school days. She was sad-faced, struggling to hold her composure. Aaron wanted to reach out and comfort her, but the wrenching pain in his head stopped him. Then again, it might provoke her to move away and he didn't want that. He lay back and closed his eyes. There was nothing he could do or say at a time like this.

DAVID, DUSTY AND TIRED, came away from the door for a quick rest.

"David, are we making any progress?"

He peered into the shadows, recognizing Jean's voice. She was sitting on the floor, her back against the speaker's platform. Thelma was next to her. He hesitated as he saw Nancy and Margaret Stanton sitting nearby. He wanted to move on but could not ignore Jean.

"We're still trying, but no luck yet."

"Will we, will we be able to get out?" Margaret spoke to him.

"Oh sure. We'll get out. I don't know why I'm so certain, but I'm sure we will," looking at Nancy as if to assure her, not Margaret.

"You look worn out, sit down and rest," Jean invited.

"Spending my time behind a desk hasn't prepared me for this type of work," he grinned.

"You look all right to me, Dave," observed Thelma. "I'll bet you haven't gained a pound since high school."

"Ah, Thel, but I have, all of thirty pounds. I weighed only one thirty-five in high school. Not big enough for the football team," he glanced at Nancy, but she seemed focused elsewhere.

"But good enough for the track team," Thelma persisted.

"Right now, I wish I could run, and I would, even if I had to carry you."

Thelma giggled. She was used to her friends joshing her about her weight problem.

"Oh, for God's sake!" interrupted Margaret. "What are you two prattling about? Can't you see that we're trapped here? I know I never should have come. If only Arthur..."

"Margaret, please be quiet," Nancy admonished her. "I'm sorry..." she looked directly at him for the first time. "She's just upset."

David's skin tingled at her look. After so many years, it hasn't changed. I shouldn't have come, but oh no, I'm a masochist. What can I say? Nothing. Be a gentleman. He shrugged. "No offense taken. Are you, are you both all right? You didn't get hurt?"

"Oh no, we're no worse than the others. Jean has kept up our spirits."

Jean smiled. "That's too much credit. We should give thanks to Walter, Stella and Ellen. They've done a tremendous job with only first aid kits available."

"I saw them with a radio," said Nancy. "Is there, have you heard..."

"No, only static. Your family, up there. I know how hard it is..."

"Of course, you idiot," Margaret cut in. "Why are you sitting there. You should be getting us out. My husband, Arthur will gladly pay you for..."

"Enough, Margaret!" Nancy burst out. "My God! How insensitive and self-centered can you be? Your offer of pay is in such bad taste and embarrassing to all of us. Everyone here is doing their best to get us out, but they are not our lackeys and don't deserve to be treated as such. God only knows what's up there. Yet all you've done is complain about your personal problems. And where is your concern for Arthur? I know I haven't contributed very much, but I've sat next to you and listened to your complaints..."

She got up and went to sit at the other side of Jean, leaving Margaret with her mouth wide open in amazement.

"Hey, Nancy, you're all right," chuckled Thelma. "That's telling Miss High and Mighty where she stands."

"That's enough, Thelma," interjected Jean. "We have enough problems without creating more. The best way to help is to sit quietly while they figure a way to get us out."

David stood up. "I guess that's my cue. Tote that dirt! Lift that shovel." He looked at Nancy, caught her looking at him. But with swirling dust and dim lighting, it was hard to read the expression on her face. It was starting all over. He must control his emotions. It was past history. You couldn't go back. Every time he thought about it, the hurt and embarrassment made it worse....

It started when they had classes together. Since he was a GRA and she was a GRO, the teachers assigned them desks in line, he in front of her. From this vantage point, he picked or passed on papers from her. Sometimes their fingers touched. Thrilled, David would blush and was rewarded by the most beautiful smile in the world.

One day he finally got the courage to ask her for a date. To this day he could remember his shy, unsophisticated question. "You, you wouldn't care to go out with me, would you?" Happily, for his ego, she had accepted.

He went about preparing for the Big Date. He borrowed a car and pulled money saved from his after-school job.

Saturday night arrived, and so did the fates that would spoil his big day. Arriving at Nancy's home, he was awed by her mansion, or so it seemed at the time. That was understandable to a boy who came from the River Road area which was the closest thing to a slum in Stonecliff. He sat in his car, his stomach in knots, wanting to run to the bathroom. She must have been watching for him because she came out and waved at him. Having no choice, he went in. He was introduced to her father and he, making conversation, asked him what his father did. Mr. Grother of course was one of the richest men in town while David's father could not compare, nor did he mix in the same company as her father.

Mercifully, Nancy pulled him away from the inquisitive parent. They had gone to the Palace Room, one of the two ritziest clubs in town. To this day David didn't know what had caused him to go there. Showing off, perhaps?

At the door he was confronted by a haughty headwaiter who demanded his name.

"I'm sorry, Mr. Granhill, but I don't see your name here. You did make a reservation, didn't you?"

"Uh...I, ah...I don't..." he was overcome with shame.

"Well, 'sir,'" the man emphasized the last word, "under the circumstances I don't see..."

"David, are you sure it was the Palace Room not the Executive Club, my father recommended?" Nancy interrupted. Turning to the waiter. "My father, Walter Grother recommended us to the best club in town, but perhaps we came to the wrong place."

"Walter Grother...Yes, yes, I know Mr. Grother. There is no mistake. I'm sure this is the place he recommended, Miss Grother. I'll have to get after that boy, Mr. Granhill.

"He must have forgotten to put your name down. Please come this way." Damn hypocrite! There was plenty of space. Nancy apologized for pulling rank. No, no, he didn't mind. But he did.

Then he had seen the menu. He had mentally calculated how much the dinner, the tip, movie and snacks would cost. He had only a thin margin of safety. He had pulled out fifty dollars from his savings, more than he needed but with some feeling of acting the big shot. She must have read his face for she only ordered salad, apologizing for having snacked earlier.

So, he had escaped his stupidity. His stomach was churning. He imagined the waiters sneering behind his back. What a jerk!

There were no more problems. The Big Date went on to a successful conclusion, but not to him. On Monday the tribulations of his date were still on his mind, and the embarrassment he had suffered. He spied Nancy in the school hall in the company of Gwen Sweet. Nancy waved as he approached. Then she turned to Gwen and started talking and giggling and glancing in his direction.

Damn! She's telling Gwen what an ass I made of myself. How could she do that? Indignantly, he strode on by without acknowledging their presence. How could that sweet beautiful face be so deceitful?

That question had haunted him for fifteen years and he was no closer in finding the right answer.

Nancy watched David walk away. It hadn't been that hard, had it? Ever since she had received notice of the reunion and had decided to come, she had dreaded the meeting. But look what it took to bring it about. It makes your personal problems look small in comparison. After all, one can hardly maintain a grudge in such close quarters. It didn't matter. It was like being trapped in an elevator. After a few hours everyone would go their separate ways, never to cross paths again.

She suddenly felt ashamed for thinking of her own problems. After all they were in the past. What was up there? Everyone has family. And she had a mother, all that was left. Poor Mom. She lowered her face and covered it with her hands and wept. Jean put her arm around her and drew her close.

Nancy looked at her. "You have more up there than I do. And you're comforting me?"

"How do you measure love or concern whether it's for one or ten?"

"But you have your whole family, your parents. I have only my mother. And I'm not sure she doesn't think she would be better off dead since Dad died."

"Perhaps you have more than you think," Jean glanced towards the door.

Nancy followed her gaze. "No, that was over a long time ago. It's a strange situation. I'm supposed to be the rich girl who had everything. Yet I've suffered more loss than most. I lost a son, a father and a husband. In retrospect, the husband was not much of a loss, but it shows money can't buy happiness. You're lucky, you've led a happy home life."

46

Jean sighed. "Don't be too sure that my life was so wonderful. As you've found out, the private lives are not as wonderful as the public ones seem to portray. Maybe there's someone in this world who has lived a life without problems, but it wasn't me. The fact you lost so much doesn't mean it won't change in the future. I think God allows each of us a little while when we can find happiness for ourselves. And what happened long ago isn't over. If we make it out of here, you should find out for sure. I've seen it in his face since he came back, He was so in love with you. I don't know what happened between you two or how serious, well, don't give up too soon."

So, It's not just me. She has seen it too. Still, it doesn't explain....

THERE WAS A SUDDEN scraping, a thump and a cry that echoed across the hall. All eyes turned to one corner of the building. In an open-air vent, two men were pulling at the legs of a third one whose upper body was stuck in the vent.

Jim left the door and ran towards the commotion, dodging debris and sprawled bodies on the floor.

"What happened? Who's in there?"

"It's Larry Wilk! He was trying to pull out the fan. It must have collapsed," Tom Wadley replied.

A coughing sputtering Larry was pulled out by the legs.

"That damn fan...' spitting dirt. "I was suffocating. Fan and dirt just came down on me."

"How bad is it, Tom?" Jim asked him.

"Don't know, but it doesn't look good. Must have been a lot of pressure on that fan. Once you loosened it, everything came down."

"If it came down like this, it might have left an empty void. It might not take too much to clear."

"I don't know. There's still more dirt or some form of obstruction in there. We don't have thirty feet of dirt that has come out of that vent," pointing to the meager pile on the floor. "Moreover, in order to dislodge anything in that vent, one person is going to have to pick at it from the bottom and then let it fall on him like Larry."

"I'm not going back in there," huffed Larry.

"I don't see how you ever got the guts to go in there in the first place," snorted Tom.

"I don't see any of you football heroes' volunteering. Maybe you ain't got the guts," sneered Larry.

"You hear that, Oscar?" Tom turned to him. "There's some jocks around here minus their guts. You come across any lately?"

"All right, you guys, lay off Larry," Jim broke in. "Doc, you want to take a look at him?"

"Hey! The self-elected boss has spoken," Larry jeered.

"All you jocks stick together. First thing you know, I'll get gang-tackled."

"I feel like gang-tackling you all by myself," Tom growled.

"Let's stop it here and now," Jim ordered.

"O.K., but that sniveling little twit needs to get his ass kicked. Maybe that will straightened out his brain."

"It's beginning to strain people's nerves," David said in an aside to Jim. "And we're still not showing any progress at the door. We must have removed a ton of dirt. Just look at that pile."

Jim shook his head. "Dave, maybe Larry's right. I've been pushing my decisions on everyone else. The door is still blocked. Our air will give out soon. Maybe you or Oscar or Tom, anyone should take over."

"I heard that," said Dorothy, coming up behind him. "You can't be faulted for what you've done. What else could anyone have done that we haven't? Who has voluntarily stepped out to offer a solution or an alternative? You've always been the class leader. It's only fitting you should take over."

He smiled. "That's very flattering, but it's quite a difference in some high school project to this situation. Time is running out. The air, the next tremor. We're walking a..."

He stopped as one of the battery-operated lights went out. Immediately, there were cries of surprise from those left in the dark.

"And that's another problem, although a minor one by comparison," Jim frowned. "It's not surprising though. How long has it been, five, six hours? We can expect the rest to give out in the next couple of hours."

"I've got candles and more flashlights." said Dorothy.

Jim nodded. "We can use the extra flashlights, but candles use up oxygen and we need that for ourselves."

Then the basement started tilting again. Jim seized Dorothy, stumbled and they both went down together.

"Oh Jim, hold me, I'm afraid for us..."

He held her tight, his body over hers, protectively, his face buried in her hair. Even in the dust and dirt, he could smell her perfume.

"Aftershock, I hope..." he gasped hoarsely in her ear. "It may not last too long."

Once more there were the cries of terror as the rumbling underneath mounted in intensity. Then the screams were once more overcome by the roar emanating from below.

Then it was over, as suddenly as it began. It had lasted only a few seconds. Once more the basement had survived though having gained a few more cracks.

There was a period of silence. No one moved, not trusting it was over. Mentally, if not physically, the terror, the pain, the uncertainty, had now built up to the boiling point.

Jim rolled off Dorothy. He sat up and pulled her to a sitting position. "Are you all right?"

"Yes, yes," she gasped, brushing herself off and modestly pulling at the hem of her dress that exposed dusty but shapely thighs. "Look at my clothes. They're a mess. I bought a new dress for the occasion. Now look at it."

He laughed at her priorities, then she joined in. "Yes, look at me, look at the situation we're in and I'm fussing about my clothes."

He got up and then bent down to help her up. Once more he had that disturbing sensation as he held her close. They looked at each other for a moment, then let go and started dusting off their clothes.

There was a rising murmur from the others. Jim saw a group gathering with heated words and gesticulations. They turned in his direction. "Oh, oh, here comes the lynch mob."

"And we haven't got cake to feed them," said Dorothy. "History hasn't changed much. When in trouble, blame the leader, whether or not he's responsible."

A choleric Charlie Durian led the pack. "Fenzer, you've had enough time to do something. You're no longer on a football field making like a hero. It's time somebody else did something."

"Yeah," piped up Larry, "you take these jocks off a football field and they couldn't find their way out of a wet paper sack."

Inwardly Jim was fuming, ready to explode. The stupidity and ignorance of his classmates was not to be imagined. But he knew he couldn't lash out. He could understand their anxiety.

"Well, Charles," ignoring Larry, "I don't think shoveling dirt is heroic or related to football. I thought we were doing the obvious, digging ourselves out of here. However, now that the councilman is ready to take over, I'm listening. Give us your orders, your plans. How do you propose to get us out of here?"

Before a sputtering Charlie could reply, a furious Dorothy sprang into the fray. "You just back off, Charlie! You make me sick, you, you pompous ass! Who are you to point fingers? You've never done anything on your own without Daddy clearing the way for you. But Daddy's not here now. You've been lying there like a sick puppy whining while the others worked. Let's face it. You don't have anything to contribute to this group, and certainly no idea on how to get out of here. So why don't you just crawl into Larry's paper sack."

"Why you, you, you interfering..." Charlie fumed.

"Just hold it, Charlie. Don't say anything more," warned Jim.

"You're being too hard on Charlie," interrupted Aaron Sherland, shouldering his six three, two hundred thirty pounds to the forefront of the group. "He's only voicing the same doubt and concern that the rest of us have. It seems only a matter of time until..."

"Well, now," Dorothy turned her guns on the new target. "So, you're well enough to get up. As an ex-jock yourself, you should have been doing some heroics with a shovel. Or is that beneath a self-made millionaire? Then again, why are you taking up for a person like Charlie unless he's got you involved in one of his nefarious schemes?"

Aaron flushed, his mouth open in astonishment. Dorothy, as if suddenly aware of her outburst, drew back as Jim held on to her arm.

"I don't care who gives orders or is in charge," he told them. "We all want to get out of here and we're losing valuable time arguing here. The only way out is through that door. If someone has a better idea, let him or her speak up. In the meantime, I'm going back to digging while the rest of you can hold an election, if that's what you want."

"You've got my vote, Jim," Oscar boomed. Several others nodded and followed the two.

AARON SURVEYED THE small group left, which even then was dissolving. He, Charlie, Larry and Don Burins ended up as the lone dissenters. "The people have spoken and you're not their choice, Charlie," Aaron remarked. "I think they know you too well."

"That damn Walters hussy! I'll get her, just wait. I know a lot of things that are going on," Charlie fumed.

"It would seem she also knows some things that are going on," Aaron glanced at Don. "But even so, you've got to admire her. She has a lot of spirit and backbone. Yeah, she's, interesting."

Charlie just glowered at him.

"That's a strange comment," observed Don. "Seeing as how she savaged you as bad as Charlie."

"No, she didn't gore me quite as bad as Charlie. Verbal attacks made in the heat of emotion don't bother me. She was defending Jim. I can understand that. And those two make an interesting couple, I wonder."

"She just needs to be slapped around a few times," Larry made his contribution.

"Yeah, Larry," Aaron looked at him. "Then when you wake up, you'll be on the ground looking up, because if Jim doesn't get you, I will."

"Hey! What's the matter with you guys? You ain't got too many friends left. You can't afford to insult me."

"I can afford anything." Aaron stared him down then, he returned to his seat next to Linda. She hadn't moved except to lie down and cover her head during the last tremor.

"I see you haven't moved since that last quake," he said.

"What for? It's not going to get me out of here any sooner. We could conserve more air if everyone sat down and shut up."

"I guess that's meant for me. You heard?"

"How could I not hear you? No one held down their voices, or their temper." She looked at him for the first time since he had returned. "You got yourself told, didn't you?"

He scowled, then laughed. "I sure did, but good. She's quick to defend her friends."

"I thought I knew Dorothy," she mused. "But I've learned more about her today then in eighteen years. She reminds me of a heroine in the movies. All through the movie, she has her hair up in a bun, wears glasses and frumpy clothes. Then at the end, down comes the hair, off go the glasses, she puts on sexy clothes, Walla!, Lynda Carter."

"Lynda Carter?"

"She was a beauty queen in the Seventies. Later she played Wonder Woman on TV. That's why Dorothy was called Wonder Woman by the rest of us. Always looking for a cause to right. Esther and Sylvia are the movie buffs. They played a game of pinning movie star names on classmates or people we knew."

"I'm afraid I'm not a movie or TV fan. Didn't have time for such things. Who were you compared to?"

"Grace Kelly."

"Now her I heard about. And it fits you. You were regarded as a princess in high school. And you still are, by my judgment."

She glanced at him. "Thank you."

Slow down, he thought. He was getting too personal. And certainly, this wasn't the place or time for such things.

"Weren't those movie stars getting along in years when you were in high school?"

"Not all of them. Lynda was always high on the list of beauties in the Eighties. But then, through the magic of TV and the late movies, they were very much alive and young looking. No matter. It was a silly game."

"I wouldn't call it silly. What name was I tagged with, or was I?"

"None that I know."

"What a crushing blow to my ego. It means that I went unnoticed. If I had known this in my youth, I would never have recovered from the trauma."

"You'll have to take that up with Sylvia and Esther. It was their game; they assigned the names. Dorothy and I just played along with them. Oh, why are we even discussing such an inane subject?"

"Sorry. I thought it would help keep your mind off more serious and immediate problems."

"No. I'm the one to apologize. I shouldn't let..."

From the direction of the door came a dull roar that kept mounting until it burst inside the hall with an ear-splitting howl. There was a great rush of air and everything and everyone was being sucked towards the door.

At the door, David, Oscar and Carl Umbral dived away from the door as a hole appeared in the doorway, sucking away the debris.

"Get out of the way!" screamed Carl. Oscar grabbed him and pulled him away from the doorway.

David grasped the edge of the door frame and watched in horror as the door hinges started to come loose. He felt his breath being sucked from his lungs. With every ounce of strength remaining, he dug his feet into the dirt and pulled his body out of the path of the howling terror. Then he let go and rolled over the side, away from the opening.

The huge pile of dirt and masonry removed from the doorway during the past few hours began to be sucked out the door.

Jim pulled Dorothy down and together they crawled behind the staircase leading to the library. There were others there, holding on to the steel steps. He placed her behind the steps and then started to crawl towards the door.

Dorothy pulled at his arm. "Don't go!" she screamed in his ear. "Please...it's dangerous..."

"I have to help them, at the door, keep others from being sucked out!" With eyes almost shut, he crawled towards David, but avoiding a direct line with the doorway. A chair went flying by, just missing him. His eyes stinging, he made it to David's side.

"What happened?" he shouted in David's ear.

"I don't know exactly...noise started to build up...that gave some warning. Suddenly the doorway cleared, and we were being pulled out. We were lucky to get out of the way. God! I thought my arms would be pulled out of my sockets as I hung there."

"Did anyone get sucked out?"

"I don't think so. I see Oscar and Carl on the other side. Out reliefs were resting. So, we're the only ones at the door."

"O.K., keep an eye out and be ready to grab if you see anyone heading this way."

They crouched by the door, their backs to the wall. Across the doorway he could make out Oscar and Carl. He tried to convey with hand signals what they were to do. Oscar nodded and made a thumbs up sign.

The rush of air slackened although the roar could still be heard through the open doorway. Jim estimated only a few minutes had elapsed. Cautiously he stuck out his hand and felt only a slight tug. Encouraged, he slowly crawled to the opening, David holding one of his ankles.

"It's all right," he called out and stood up.

The other three men joined him. "Wow!" exclaimed Oscar. "What was that? I can still hear it up there."

"Had to be a big difference in pressure," said Carl, who was the science teacher at the school.

"But what could have caused that big a change?"

"Sounds like a tornado up there," said Jim. "But it did accomplish our rescue."

"There's some weather instruments in Dorothy's storeroom," said David. "I'll get them."

"There's also some rope there," added Jim. "Bring that along. I'm going up there." He turned to the others, now beginning to assemble by the door, "Is everyone accounted for? Anyone missing?"

No one was missing and they started surging towards the door.

"Wait! We can't leave now. Listen! There's a storm raging up there. I'm going to take a look. The rest of you stay here until I find if it's safe."

"Must you do everything?" Dorothy questioned, a look of disapproval on her face. She turned to face her classmates. "Now's the time for Charlie and Larry to do some leading, like finding out what's up there. What? No takers...? I'm waiting."

No one took up her challenge. There were a few nervous giggles.

David returned with a weather kit and a coil of rope. Jim took the weather kit which was really only a thermometer and barometer and stood by the doorway. His eyes almost popped as he saw the barometer plunge down. Twenty-seven! No, it was just barely under twenty-seven. It couldn't be!

"Carl, look at this. Tell me what you think."

Carl looked at him, then peered at the barometer, turning it to get the proper angle to read it. He gasped. "My God! Jim, I've never heard of a reading this low, except perhaps in a hurricane."

"How about a tornado?"

"I don't see how anything, man or machine, could survive inside one to take a reading."

Jim nodded. "Neither have I. There is, or there was, a tornado-like storm up there. That's the only thing I know that could produce a reading like this."

Carl looked up the opening. "I heard of a twenty-eight three in reference to a hurricane, but never this low. I guess you would have to go to a trivia book to find the lowest ever recorded, but this is it as far as I'm concerned. Certainly, the change in pressure accounts for the sucking effect, like an airplane losing pressure. Happily, the change wasn't as it would be at thirty thousand feet."

"Yes, "Jim said. "Who would think a tornado would be our savior." He tied the rope around his waist and motioned to Oscar and Tom. "I'm going up there, so I'm depending on you guys to hold me or bring me down if I start to take off like a kite."

Dorothy, standing by, hands on hips, shook her head. "I guess it's useless trying to talk you out of this."

He shrugged. "I could act like the boss and order some-one up there or even ask for volunteers. An archaeologist has a need to know, a curiosity. Yeah, maybe I still want to be a football hero."

She shook her head in resignation. "I've felt the need to climb a few mountains myself. But I have to remember that cheerleaders have to cheer the football hero no matter how dumb he acts sometimes."

He laughed. "Too bad I won't be able to see you in that skimpy skirt, but I'll keep my ears open for the cheers."

He started up the stairs, feeling the upward draft. Like a chimney, he thought. The roaring increased as he climbed higher as did the tugging sensation. It had to be a tornado. What else could sound like that? But he had never heard of one that lingered over the same location.

A folding chair was wedged between the bottom of the railing and the steps. It was jiggling up and down. He pulled it out. He held the chair over his head for protection as the dust swirled making it hard to see.

Suddenly the chair was torn from his grasp and he was slammed against the side of the staircase. His body was now exposed to the fury of the storm. He felt himself being dragged out by the cyclonic wind. Frantically he tugged at the rope, hoping those below would understand the signal.

He closed his eyes tightly and covered his face with one hand, reaching out for the railing with the other. The rope tightened against his waist, but apparently to no avail. He felt the sting on his face, probably loose dirt or gravel. The howling of the wind deadened his hearing. His fingers holding on to the railing bleeding exposed to flying debris. His breath shortened, from the exertion and from the wind sucking it away.

Then slowly, those below began to win the battle for his body. He was down below ground level as the outside forces battled to regain their prey. He was spent. A lassitude spread over him causing him to loosen his hold on the railing and he tumbled backward as those below pulled him. A blow struck his head and he lost consciousness.

HE CAME TO, FEELING sore all over and a king-size headache on the back of his head. Walter was peering at him.

"Welcome back to the world, such as it is," he said soberly. "How do you feel?"

"Who ran over me? I hope someone got his number."

"Some monster up there. You look like you should survive. Nothing broken, except maybe your reasoning in going up there in the first place."

"If I hadn't, some other fool would have tried it with worse results. However, if you tell me all my body parts are still in their regular place, I'll take your word for it."

"You looked a bloody mess when we pulled you in. A fish at the end of a pole would have looked better. Luckily all cuts were superficial. You were lucky you weren't hit by anything larger than a few pebbles. Most of the damage was by that knock on the head. That wind must have been terrific."

"Yes, I've never experienced anything like that," he croaked. He had to clear his throat several times. How much dirt had he swallowed? "There's no way to measure that force. No tornado or hurricane was ever that powerful. But then, who knows. I was never in the middle of one before."

For the first time he became aware there was someone next to him. It was then he noticed Dorothy leaning over him. As he turned his head, he found it was resting on her lap.

"Dottie, what are you..."

"She's been your nurse," said Walter, before she could reply. "Wouldn't let Stella or Ellen near you. She was climbing those stairs to drag you back. Dave had to hold her back."

Dorothy's face was red. "Walter! I...I wasn't that...I mean I wasn't aware I was doing that. I...we couldn't afford to lose a good piece of rope. Could we now?" she laughed.

He laughed too, then winced as he felt a stab of pain in his head.

"I didn't say that to make you laugh," she adjusted the bandage on his head, gently. "Sorry."

"I'm not. It's not often I get this much attention from a pretty girl. Now that you got your rope back, I'm glad you think me worthy to look after."

She blushed again. "I'm going to drop your head on the ground if you don't stop that."

"All right, but I don't know how it looks like to some people. You know Charlie and the other folks in this town. Tongues will wag, as they say."

"I have never cared what people thought or said as long as I think I'm doing right. Jim, to get serious. Do you think there's anyone up there? The quake, the wind. Look what it did to you, and you were only partly exposed. We were protected by this shelter. But those up there, what protection did they have?"

He saw the tears in her eyes and knew she was thinking of her child, her parents and, her husband?

At that moment Oscar came up hesitantly. "Jim, can you talk?"

"Oh boy, can he talk," Dorothy smiled through her tears.

Oscar saw the tears, then glanced at Jim. "You all right? Walter led me to believe you were."

"He's all right. Don't mind me." she sniffled.

"What's the situation up there? Can we get out of here?" he asked.

"The best thing to do is to stay here until that storm blows itself out. Right now, as you see, it's too dangerous to go up there."

"Oh, don't worry. They all got a good look at you and that quickly killed any ideas of breaking up this reunion.

"Uh, Jim, there's something else," Oscar hesitated, glancing at Dorothy.

Jim caught his glance. "Are there some hens indulging in a little gossip about Dorothy's actions?"

"What?" Oscar looked confused. "I don't understand. I wanted to talk to you about the situation upstairs. I didn't want to alarm Dorothy."

She giggled. "I think Jim was thinking in terms of saving my reputation because I was, somewhat anxious about his health."

"Oh that!" Oscar guffawed. "I'm sure Esther and Sylvia have made that their main topic of conversation for the last hour."

"Oh well," she said, "I expect that from Sylvia. She will rake me over the coals, but if someone else does it, she'll tear into them."

"What is this business you wanted to talk about?" asked Jim.

"Did you, did you see any signs of life up there?"

"No. There wasn't much time. I never got to the top and I had my eyes practically shut. We'll find out soon enough."

He smiled at Dorothy. "I think I'd better lie down somewhere other than your lap. We don't want to wear out Sylvia's tongue. It's a wonder she hasn't already come over and given us hell."

"Oh yes," she agreed. "Sylvia was in her element at the reunion brunch. If she were writing her life story, that would have to be one of the high points. I think she stabbed everyone with that sharp tongue of hers. One moment it was all fun, then this."

CHAPTER FOUR

E arlier, January 7, 2020
"A reunion!" Sylvia exclaimed. "Dorothy, your tight shoes are affecting your brains."

"How quaint?" said Linda. "Is that the latest, fifteen-year reunions?"

Esther sighed. "First you get us all involved in that Civil Defense Shelter. God! How many hours did we spend in that gloomy basement? Then you got us all hot about having a new college built in Stonecliff. I don't know what became of that. Now..."

"It's still on," Dorothy interrupted. "I've been trying to interest Aaron Sherland into endowing a college for our town. Aaron is a millionaire who could afford to do that and he's our classmate."

"Ergo, a reunion? Is that it?" Linda frowned.

How could she answer that? It was true as far as it went. She had corresponded with Aaron about the college, but the whole thing was on hold. Aaron had not said yes or no.

No, the reunion was really for the old medicine man, Martin. He had called her during the holiday break. How could he arrange to meet with more of her classmates? The fact that all four of his 'chosen' were from the same town, had attended the same school and were in the same class had to be significant. From his viewpoint, she had to admit it was a logical assumption. She had different ideas, however, and could not bring herself into believing an old Indian legend. She had finally agreed to help him, not seeing any harm and the possibility of a joyous get-together.

Inwardly though, she knew it was not the old man that had decided her course of action. Why was she, a married woman so concerned about another man...? Maybe because she couldn't say she was a happily married woman and hadn't been for a long time. The quarreling, those long trips he made. Going hunting or fishing, he said, but he never brought back anything except lipstick she found on his clothes.

But it went farther back than her husband. A crush on the captain of the football team while she led the cheers from the sideline. Working next to him as a class officer, he the president, she the vice president, later valedictorian of the graduating class. Yet seemingly, she went unnoticed and it was Linda who went everywhere with him.

So, they went their separate ways after graduation. Whatever her feelings, she had brushed them aside. It would never be. It was just another high school crush for the most popular boy in class. Who knows how many other girls had the same idea. No one could compete with Linda. Eventually, even Linda lost him. No one knew why, because Linda didn't talk about it. Jim never came back except briefly on the death of his parents in an automobile accident.

Her meeting with him at her father's store had been an unexpected surprise. She had gushed like a schoolgirl this past summer until he brought her up short that last meeting in September. She felt embarrassed at her actions and had vowed not to return.

Then Martin had called and pleaded with her to set up some occasion where he could meet others in her class. She wanted to refuse. Indeed, she did, but she liked him, and she did not want him to think it was a racist thing. That was not what her father had taught her. It was further involvement with Jim that made her hesitate.

In the end she relented. She would help as best she could, but it was not in her nature to do things half way. She was like a bulldog once she got some project in her teeth. Then the idea of a reunion took shape. It was the perfect way to get an unsuspecting group together where they could be observed without inciting questions.

However, there were other questions which she could not dodge. The three women here, classmates, friends and fellow teachers at the high school, had already initiated some of them. They were her cohorts in all her projects and under-takings, however reluctant they might sound. She couldn't keep very much from them and she pondered whether or not to tell them her real motive. Doubtless they...

"Dorothy!" she jumped as Sylvia's voice cut in her thoughts. "Earth calling Dorothy. Beam her down, Scotty. What's the matter, girl? What devilish schemes are making the rounds in that head of yours?"

"Why does there have to be anything up there?" she smiled at her little joke. "Really, what's wrong with getting together with old classmates and having fun?"

"There's very few of them I'd care to see again," said Sylvia. "And even less of them that know what fun is."

"I've known you too long to know you never go into a new cause without a purpose," said Esther.

"Yes," added Linda. "And I'm not too sure I want to renew acquaintances with some people."

"Oh? Anyone we know?" Sylvia looked at her innocently. Linda scowled but didn't reply.

"Well, Esther wouldn't mind seeing Oscar again," Sylvia leered at her friend. "You're still in love with him."

"Trust you to keep a friend's secret, Sylvia," Esther scowled. "How can you embarrass your friends in public?"

"We're not in public. We're friends among friends. We know your situation and we're rooting for you and Oscar to get together. After all, it's not uncommon for ex's to get back together. At least you've got an ex-husband. Linda and Dorothy have ex-boyfriends. But what have I got? Nothing!" she wailed.

She didn't get much sympathy. Linda looked at her sourly. "Dorothy and I are both married. I'll thank you not to lump me in with those women who want to re-live their teen-age romances."

"So, I suppose the reason for this meeting is to get us involved in this scheme of yours," Esther grumped. "Some-times you stretch friendship too far. Don't you think we have other things to do?"

"What's so important about watching those old movies on TV as you and Sylvia do?" Dorothy smiled at the two women knowing they were ardent movie buffs.

"That's our form of relaxation," said Sylvia. "Yours seems to be digging up new causes and involving us in them."

"Oh shut up, Syl," Dorothy gave her a playful jab. "You always end up liking them. Think of all the fun you'll have with your old classmates. I can see you flitting from group to group, that sharp tongue of yours just clacking away." The others smiled at that image. Sylvia's caustic wit was known to all.

"All right, so you have us hooked. Tell us the who, what, where and other details we need to know." Esther said.

"I'm planning it during the Frontier Days celebration. Our first meeting will be a brunch on the seventh of May. I've tentatively set up a picnic for the ninth and a Saturday night dance on the twelfth."

"You actually want to drag it out that long?" Linda stared at her.

"Well, Frontier Days is a week-long and, oh, I ran into an old Indian medicine man at Dad's store the other day. He's an old friend of Dad's. I thought I would invite him to the picnic and he could do some dances or tricks for us."

"Oh great," said Sylvia. "As if our old class didn't have enough characters."

"That's an unkind cut at a very nice man," replied Dorothy. "I didn't finish telling you that he was in company of two other men we know. It seems there are some old Indian artifacts being dug up at the reservation. The two men working on that project are John Edleman and Jim Fenzer."

"Oh ho!" exclaimed Sylvia. "So much for ulterior motives."

"What do you mean by that?" Dorothy asked, glancing at Linda.

"Suddenly, a reunion out of the clear blue sky, an unusual fifteen year one at that. Come to think about it," Sylvia peered at Dorothy. "I recall talking to your son at school and he mentioned you had brought him a gift from the reservation. Why this sudden interest in Indian affairs?"

"There is no sudden interest. I have a history class which also includes our Indian brothers as well as our so-called American ones. Come to think about it, don't we have that turned about? It's American history and our Indians are just as American and more so than the white ones."

Sylvia clapped her hands. "And away we go on yet another noble cause starring our beloved leader, Dorothy Walters."

"Oh, shut up and listen. I needed some firsthand experience with Indian life for my classes and the old medicine man provided that. It was then I learned that Jim and John were on the reservation. It was very natural with no sinister motives involved."

"Does Jim, do they know about this reunion?" Linda asked.

Sylvia looked at Linda. "Are you getting all itchy-koo at the thought of seeing Jim again?"

"Of course not!" Linda snapped. "I've already said I was a married woman. I don't choose to dwell on nostalgia like some people I know. And where does an English teacher pick up such an expression as 'itchy-koo'?"

"The late, late show, where else," supplied Esther.

"You said we're opening this glorious occasion with a brunch. Is it catered, or do you expect the alumni, namely us, to sweat in a hot kitchen?" Sylvia glared at Dorothy.

Dorothy gave her a sweet smile. "Your looks say you dare me to say the latter. But no, it shall be catered except for cakes, cookies and the like."

"Where will it be?" Linda asked. "The Palace Room or the Executive Club?"

"Uh, no, at the school."

"School?" said Esther. "Tinner Hall, the library, the faculty dining room?"

"No, none of those."

"Well, what else is left?"

"Oh no!" exclaimed Sylvia. "Not, not the Dungeon. Please tell me it's not the Dungeon."

"If I told you that I would be lying."

"I knew it! I knew it!" cried Sylvia. "I always said the Russians would nuke Stonecliff just to get me back into the Dungeon. But I'll take my chances on the outside no matter how many bombs they drop."

"All right, I give up," Dorothy looked at Esther. "Is this her Bette Davis or Bergman or somebody I don't recognize?"

"Actually, aside from you," Esther replied, "I don't think you'll find too many people that love that place."

"It was the only place available. Mr. Humphreys wouldn't let me have any of the regular meeting halls," Dorothy giggled. "You might say I tricked him into using the shelter. I pouted, managed a few tears and reminded him of how much I had helped him evenings and weekends on his pet projects. I stammered out how people might talk about us spending that much time together. You know, 'man-woman,' that kind of talk. That got him flustered. Then he said he owed me a few favors and if I could come up with a place, he would agree to let me use it. Well, I did, and you know what place it is."

Sylvia shook her head. "Dorothy, you'd do anything to get your way, but look out. One of these days it's going to get you in trouble."

"As far as I'm concerned," said Linda, "any trick you play on Humphreys has my approval. The old goat has taken advantage of his position to try to romance every female teacher in school, including Esther and me."

"Not me," said Sylvia.

"He wouldn't dare," said Esther. "He figures you might take him seriously."

"So much for our beloved principal," Dorothy got up.

"One last item, since we were on the subject of the shelter. Last year I promised the kids in my class they could bring items for the shelter. Word got around the school and other classes wanted in too. So, among other things, I got Mr. Humphreys to approve a Civil Defense Shelter Day when the kids will bring in their version of what is needed to survive.

"Can you girls help out in the Dungeon?"

"Oh no!" Sylvia pressed her hand to her temple.

May 7, 2020

"Well, John, what do you think of the old alma mater?" said Jim.

"School was never that important to me in those days. It was a chore, a duty, something I had to do. If anything, this should be a triumphant return for you, most popular man in school, class president, captain of the football team. Did I miss anything?"

Jim winced. "I must have been an insufferable bastard."

"No, I disagree. You carried it off well. I should know. You always treated me as an equal when others didn't. I can't forget that."

"Time has a habit of reducing such achievements and putting them in their proper niche.

"As for the treatment you got, I'm sorry I couldn't do more to make life easier with the others. So, it goes to show you that my popularity didn't run very deep or was transferable."

It was a cloudy day as the two strolled through the high school campus. With the change of seasons, the weather could change from day to day.

"Are you going to tell Dorothy about the tablets?"

"Don't have very much to tell her. She and I have agreed to act like strangers, admitting to only one meeting. This is to allay suspicion that it was set up for Martin."

"Have you come around to his way of thinking?"

"No. I'll just play what comes along. Who knows what the tablets will say. You have to remember that the ancients spoke and recorded symbolically.

Gods were not gods as we think today. Natural phenomena were looked on as warnings or retribution for one's evil ways."

"Well," said John, as they stopped before the school library, the Lander Building, the name was inscribed on the cornerstone. "Martin sure believes his legend. If there's any more of the 'Chosen' to be found here, it will mean they have come together as he claims. That is the prelude to, what? Disaster?

"Anyway, he's putting off coming here to the last minute, so he can finish stocking the cave. According to him, it's anytime now."

A hand-made sign read "Class Reunion" and an arrow pointed down a flight of stairs. They went down two landings before coming to a set of heavy double doors.

"I don't remember this," said John. "Is this a bank vault?"

"I believe the Drama Club had this place, but I didn't go in for that," Jim opened the door. Just inside was a card table lined with several rows of name tags.

"Class of '05?" asked the woman sitting behind the table.

"Yes, Jim Fenzer and John Edleman."

"Oh yes, I saw them here. But then, I should know our class president by sight."

She came around the table to pin the tags. Jim saw the name on her tag was Laura Ostender.

"I'm sorry to confess I only vaguely remember your name."

"You and three dozen others," she laughed. "Everyone is so excited," she chatted on. "Nobody expected a reunion so soon. There's a rumor of some announcement. I know there were efforts to have Aaron Sherland endow a college in Stonecliff. Do you think that could be it? Wouldn't the class president know what's going on?"

Jim smiled at her. "All I got was an invitation to a reunion, same as everyone else, I presume. John and I were in the vicinity, so here we are."

They moved into the hall, sub-basement was what it was. It was large, extending the length of the building, but only the end they had entered was fully lighted. There were two rows of tables set for a meal. Against the wall more tables were loaded with food tended by caterers. At this end of the building was a stage which must have been the one used by the Drama Club.

"Jim, here we part. I see some of my people from my side of the tracks. You belong on the other side."

"None of that! At least not with me. Go and have a good time with your friends but forget about the past."

"The past is what I've been trying to forget."

Jim remained by the door, undecided where to go. The loud boisterous voices of two men behind him did not get his attention until he heard Laura repeat their names.

He turned to see two men, one huge and heavy set, the other about his size. "Oscar, Tom! Are you guys for real?"

The two rushed him, embraced and pounded him, shouting insulting imprecations usually heard in a locker room.

And indeed, it was fitting for three of Stonecliff's better contributions to the world of football. Oscar Bonococci, six foot six, two hundred sixty pounds of defensive lineman with big fists was still the friendly bear Jim had known as teammate and roommate. Tom Wadley was Jim's size, six two possibly two hundred pounds which would make him about ten over Jim's weight.

"Hey Oscar!" cried Tom. "Look at this skinny fellow."

"What's the matter? Digging old bones not paying you enough to eat?"

"Digging old bones has kept me in shape. There's nothing like walking, bending, stooping and general hard work to keep down the weight. From the looks of you two, I can't say the same."

"I didn't think you would make it, Jim," boomed Oscar. "Thought you would be deep in some South American jungle."

"Nope. I was close to home, you might say. Of course, I know what Tom is doing in the NFL, but I heard you were in the Forest Service. Is that right?"

"Yeah, why not. I love the outdoors. Football just wasn't my cup of tea and it caused me other problems, well, you'll know soon enough. I divorced Esther."

"No secret," said Tom. "I told Jim when he stopped by after a game."

"Yeah," Oscar was staring behind Jim's back, "and I see the moment of truth fast approaching. Esther is over there with Sylvia and..."

"...and Linda," Tom finished for him. "Still a beauty, that girl. Isn't she?" looking at Jim.

"Be my guest." Jim shrugged.

"I intend to," staring in the direction of the women.

"Well, what are we waiting for?" said Oscar. "Let's get over the rough part."

Jim sized up the women. Dorothy had told him how close she was to the three and their silly game of calling each other by movie star names. Sylvia was Eve Arden and Esther was Brenda Vaccaro. And the description was not too far off the mark. Sylvia was taller and thinner than Esther, somewhat dour. While Esther was more genial. They made perfect opposites which was probably why they got along so well together. And Linda was, well, Linda. Aptly named after Grace Kelly.

The three men marched solemnly up to the women. Well, at least two were solemn, thought Jim. Tom seemed enthusiastic at the prospect of seeing Linda again. Had he sought his permission with his remarks or was he just daring Jim to differ with him?

"Well, the three bears cometh," cracked Sylvia.

"Are we welcome?" asked Oscar.

"Why not," replied Esther. "You're members of the class and you got your invitations."

"Hello Jim," Linda's tone was not unfriendly, but she was unsmiling.

"The world hasn't changed where you're concerned," replied Jim. "Still beautiful. It's nice to know you haven't changed."

Linda laughed nervously. "Thank you for the compliment, but the world has changed and we're not what we used to be."

"Looks like working outdoors has done wonders for you," Esther told Oscar.

"I love it. Best decision I ever made."

She raised an eyebrow. "Best decision...? So, is it lonely out there?"

"Yes," Oscar couldn't relax. "But you work long hours and sleep soundly. How about you? Is everything going well with you?"

"I have a career as a teacher. No complaints. I'm happy."

"Okay, if you two are at ease," said Sylvia. "Let's get on with this."

She turned to Jim and Linda. "How about you two? Have you anything to get off your respective chest and bosom?"

"Sylvia!" gasped Linda.

"I'm glad you took up teaching, although I wonder about those young minds under your control," Jim smiled. "You would have starved in the diplomatic service."

"I don't appreciate your comments," added a furious Linda. "Some things in the past should remain in the past, and private."

Tom was the first to break the silence that followed. "Hey! Doesn't anyone believe in saying hello or welcome?"

"Well, well, here's another of these worldly men," cut in Sylvia. "Are you still throwing that ball around? Or perhaps 'bull' is the better word."

"Ah, Sylvia, there is no way you can cut me up," said Tom, but he was looking at Linda. "How's my favorite blonde?"

"Oh? I didn't know I was your favorite blonde. As usual, no one tells me such things until too late."

"Too late for what?" piped up Sylvia.

"Sylvia, don't you have something else to do?" Linda snapped.

Tom chuckled. "You and Jim were such a couple that the rest of us had to worship you from afar."

"It's been quite a while since I've been worshipped by anyone," she glanced at Jim. "Suppose you escort me to the brunch, Tom. Will that make up for my neglect?"

"It's a start. But I would need more of your time before I would consider your debt paid," Tom grinned slyly at Linda.

"Well, I'm a married woman. But for the rest of the reunion activities, you're welcome to worship at my side."

Jim could feel several eyes on him. The others expected a reaction from him, but he kept a smile frozen on his face.

They all knew Linda's flirtation and subsequent date with Tom were made to spite Jim. How silly. Did Linda think he had come back just to take up with her or make preposterous demands like Tom's? Sure, it hurt because the little charade was directed at him and he didn't deserve it. More than anything, it had been Sylvia's remarks that had triggered Linda's wrath. Why couldn't she have laughed it off as everyone else had when Sylvia had targeted them?

Esther broke in with obvious relief. "Here comes our leader and guiding spirit."

Jim turned, his eyes lowered, still inwardly brooding. The first thing he saw, and recognized, was her legs. And there was only one person who owned them. When he stopped his survey, he was looking into her green eyes. She had a half smile as their eyes met.

"Jim, you remember Dorothy, don't you?"

"Yes, I remember a girl in blue jeans and pony tail, always in a hurry to get somewhere. This lovely lady can't be her."

A flustered and red-faced Dorothy stammered. "Ah, thank you for the compliment, I guess."

They had agreed not to acknowledge their recent meetings and limit it to one meeting at the Western Post. A wise decision, given Sylvia's slash and burn tactics. It was now eight months since they had seen each other. Even so, he had pondered how to initiate their meeting at the reunion.

"The ladies are looking very lovely today," he observed, smiling at her. "Why didn't you dress like this in the old days?"

Dorothy was still taken aback, but before she could answer, Sylvia was back at it. "Why, you big oaf," she snapped. "She was just as lovely fifteen years ago if you had bothered to notice."

"I'm trying to make up for it now."

"Ha! Now you say that," Sylvia sniffed. "Unlike spinsters, bachelors feel safe in flirting with married women. Their words can't come back to compromise them."

"Oscar," Jim raised an eyebrow, "do you feel a distinct chill in this hall?"

"Ah yes," Oscar sighed. "Perhaps we'd best go seek the company of less hostile classmates."

"Come on," laughed Dorothy. "We may be frustrated, but we're not hostile. After all, we had to stay in this old, unexciting town while you men of the world were out doing your thing."

"Yeah," observed Sylvia, "like digging holes in the ground, hugging trees and carrying a football in their arms."

"Sylvia," Oscar chuckled, "with your sense of humor, I can understand why you're still a spinster."

"By the way," said Jim, "since making luncheon dates is acceptable at this reunion, I would like to ask Dorothy if I can be her escort to the brunch."

"Ah, yes, but what is this 'escort to lunch' business?"

"Oh, Tom is escorting Linda to lunch," volunteered Sylvia. "That's Linda's way of repaying Tom for her neglect of fifteen years ago. That will let him worship at her side."

"Serves me right for coming in on the middle of the movie," said Dorothy, "and asking you to explain what has gone before."

"Believe me, you wouldn't want to know," Esther grimaced.

"Come on," Jim took Dorothy by the arm. "I want to say hello to some of the others."

"You go along, Dottie," said Esther. "Enjoy yourself. Sylvia and I will take care of things. We'll draft Oscar if we need any muscle."

"Come on, Tom," Linda took his arm. "Guess we should mingle too."

"Well," said Sylvia as the two couples left. "What's coming off here?"

"I hope I'm wrong," Esther shook her head, "but it looks like Jim and Linda are squaring off. What's bad is they're using Dorothy and Tom as pawns."

"Maybe so. But I saw Jim looking over Dorothy. He even winked at her. I think his invitation was sincere. Now Linda, I don't know. For someone who's always bringing up her marital status, she was quick to commit herself to Tom for all the functions this week."

"Or else she was trying to forestall Jim from getting too close and bring up old memories."

"Excuse me, ladies," interrupted Oscar, "but I'm still here."

"So you are," said Esther. "I suppose we could talk or go and mingle too. That is, if you don't mind being seen with your ex-wife."

"Hey!" exclaimed Sylvia. "Everyone is partnered off except me. Are you going to leave me alone?"

"Ah," replied Oscar. "She wonders why she's left alone. Is it bad breath? Is it her deodorant? No! It's the acid dripping from her tongue. There! I've said it. But it had to be told. Unfortunately, there is no cure. Our only recourse is, amputation!"

"Ha! Very funny," Sylvia stuck her tongue at him.

"Come along, little aunt," Oscar continued. "Maybe you can chaperon us. Or better still, maybe we can find a fella for you. Poor guy."

"Look, Buster, don't do me no favors!"

"Yecch!" Esther threw up her hands. "Double negatives! An English teacher she is?"

"GEORGE LOOK! IT'S JOHN," cried Jean. "I'm so glad he could make it. Now all we need is David."

"That's one guy you won't have to worry about recognizing." The tall, handsome Indian joined the two, hand upraised in the universal sign of peace. "How, Brown Brother and Sister. What you do'um on red man's land?"

"Oh no, John, you're not still doing that old act?" George shook his head.

"Couldn't help it, George. I knew it would get to you."

He came to Jean. "And this is what I've been looking forward to seeing," he took both her hands and kissed them. She blushed.

"I've been here all the time, John. Why haven't you come to visit?"

"Because," George cackled, "your father's shotgun scared him away. Just as it did every boy that liked you."

"As you see, John, George hasn't changed much. He's still recycling the same old jokes."

John smiled, still holding on to her hand. "I would have come, but you are a married woman. Your husband might have objected. Then too, I'm an Indian. There are people to whom it still makes a difference."

"Never mind what anyone else says or thinks. You are my friend," she said softly.

"Thank you. That means a lot to me. Where is David and Thelma?"

"Thelma's around somewhere. Probably over by the snack table," chuckled George. "As for Dave, he hasn't arrived."

"Are you still living in the River Road area?" John asked.

"Yes, but we've improved the neighborhood. Otherwise, I'm just a housewife and mother, nothing very exciting about that."

"Just a housewife!" burst out George. "Don't let her kid you. She's very active in civic work. The River Road area improvement is mostly due to her efforts. You ought to see the town council shiver and shake when she shows up for a meeting."

"George Perez! How would you know?"

"Thelma told me, between snacks."

"Look!" said John. "There's Thelma with David."

"David!" Jean embraced the tall, slim young man. He kissed her on the cheek.

"He kissed me on the lips," said Thelma.

"That's because we're not spoken for," he told her.

"Your mother said you were married to some girl back East." Jean peered at him. "Are you and her..."

"Jean, it's been over for two years. Listen, this is supposed to be a happy occasion. Let's just talk about the good old days."

"In the next few days," observed John, "we're going to tell each other what great times we had. But in truth, there were many days of sadness, frustration and disappointments."

David nodded. Jean gave John a sharp glance. There was a moment of strained silence.

"Hey," George broke in. "Like David said, let's have fun. Besides, with all this kissing, I want my share."

NANCY GROTHER HEAUME had walked in the door along with Margaret Stanton and Gwen Sweet. They had been pinned by the effusive Laura. Now they were milling in the crowd, shaking hands and laughing at some remembered incident of the past.

As usual, the warmth of Margaret's greeting ran up and down the scale according to the social level of the recipient. Nancy smiled. Margaret was a snob. The local banker's wife and social leader had everything an ambitious woman could want. However, Nancy remembered a young girl in high school coming up to her and asking if she was THE Nancy Grother. From then on, Margaret had stuck to her like gum on a shoe. So even then, she had her ambitious goals working overtime. It had stung Nancy when she found out Margaret's character and how she had been singled out to open doors for Margaret's entrance into her circle of friends. However, she had relented, mostly because, at that time, Margaret had other good qualities that Nancy hoped to nurture. The girl had been so intense and single-minded, she couldn't help admiring her. She became an interested spectator, or perhaps like a scientist observing an experiment coming to fruition.

And fruition it did, but not to Nancy's expectations. With attainment of power, Margaret became more obnoxious and power hungry, especially after marrying the town banker. Now at the reunion, it was the perfect place to flaunt it. Nancy had avoided her as much as possible lately, but like the old days she had attached herself to her for the reunion. Nancy mentally shrugged. Margaret was at the top of the social heap, but with few friends and with hordes of others who detested her imperious and lordly manners.

Nancy, on the other hand was going through the motions mechanically. Her eyes kept darting around the large hall, searching for a face or familiar figure. Why am I so concerned? After all, more important things have happened in my life. I've lost a son, a father and divorced a husband.

How does that compare to public humiliation?

Her eyes sought out the hall entrance. She could go over and talk to Laura and sneak a peek at those name tags. She mentally kicked herself for not having done so when she came in.

Her heart skipped a beat as a tall, slim young man stood at the door, greeting Laura. Although she had a clear view of the door, there were several people between her and the entrance. The man at the door would have to search a sea of faces before he could possibly focus on her. She had a few seconds to observe.

Yes, that was him. She recognized that nervous gesture, the momentary fingering of his ear lobe. How many times had she seen that from behind his chair? He had filled out from the skinny kid she had known. Face a little long, but he was quite attractive. She remembered his eyes. On that log-ago Saturday night, she had read his anguish and despair as his date degenerated under the onslaught of arrogant waiters and overpriced menus and, yes, his naiveté.

The thought came to her head. If she could look into his eyes again, she would know. They were like an open book to her. How often had she sat behind him and waited for an opening to talk to him? But in the endless shuffle of paper, the best she could get was a shy smile. But his eyes spoke volumes. There was an adoration in them that both embarrassed and delighted her.

So it came as a pleasant surprise when he blurted his negative invitation. She could have destroyed him, but she didn't. It was something that didn't enter her mind then. When she saw him hesitating in front of her house, she had gone and got him. She had quickly steered him away from her father and his questions. She had been surprised when they pulled up at the Palace Room. Inwardly she ached for him as the Fates conspired to make a shamble, at least from his viewpoint, out of their evening. She did her best to reassure him. When the evening ended, she thought she had succeeded.

The following Monday, Nancy felt like a freshman girl on her first date. Gwen Sweet had met her and bombarded her with questions. So it was that Nancy and Gwen were chattering and giggling when he came into view. Nancy waved as he approached. Ooh, he's so handsome, but so grave, said Gwen. He's sweet, she had replied. He just needs tender loving care. Said Gwen: So, it's like that? Nancy had walked out to intercept him. But eyes looking straight ahead, he strode past her.

She was thunderstruck, the color rising on her face.

She saw Gwen's look. Then she was running... Nancy covered her face with her hands as the memories came flooding back.

"Nancy? Is something wrong?" Margaret asked.

"No, It's nothing. It's passed. It's all over," she said as she watched Thelma rush over and kiss David.

Dorothy and Jim were among the last to get to their table. Mostly because Dorothy couldn't resist some last-minute supervising at the buffet table. Jim stood by, admiringly, watching her instruct and argue with the caterers. He caught a flash of shapely limbs as she whirled from table to table conversing or laughing with other classmates.

He recalled in high school she was like a Jekyll and Hyde. One moment at rallies and football games, she was the beautiful cheerleader with flouncing dark hair, sparkling green eyes and gorgeous figure. Then every day in the school halls or classrooms, it was blue jeans, ponytail and sandals. Next to Linda she registered zero.

Had he been fair to her in those visits to the reservation? There she had been in his environment. He regretted his treatment of her. Yes, life was full of regrets that could never be called back. The water had flowed and the debris was far downstream. Regrets were the residue.

Now at the table, with semi-privacy assured because of the hum of conversation, he attempted to reverse the flow of that stream.

"I want you to forgive me for that caddish attitude last September. I shouldn't have taken out my frustrations on you."

"I forgave you long ago because I think I know why you acted as you did.

"Your job was frustrating you. You didn't know what you had in those tablets and Martin wasn't much in the way of offering you help.

"And from what you told me, your personal life wasn't any better. That's a double whammy in any person's life.

"You want happiness. What's wrong with that? It's a universal goal and need. You think everyone has it and you don't? Behind that white picket fence and model home are not always blissfully married couples. It seems so ironic that men and women pursue each other so ardently only to find they're so incompatible living together.

"I too owe you an apology for probing into your private life. Call it the eternal curiosity of the female. I had no need to know. Certainly, on such short acquaintance, I was getting too personal."

"Don't think about it," he said. "Perhaps I was too sensitive on the subject. Coming home I was confronted by unpleasant memories. My parents were gone. My father and I had a great relationship. We tramped over all these hills, traveled over the state and the surrounding ones. We camped at night and I listened to those stories that hooked me to go into archaeology.

"After college I set out to discover the next lost civilization. And I wanted Linda at my side. I don't know what her idea of an archaeologist's wife was. My first job was in Africa. Maybe things would have turned out better if it had been a more civilized country. For her, Africa was the end of the universe. She wanted a life among her family and friends, and a husband who came home nights. I chose my job over her, angrily, perhaps. I don't know if I did right. I thought so at the time. It was what I had trained and studied for and what my father encouraged. Linda could have waited, but she didn't want that. All those years we were together, we never discussed the future. Real dumb, right? I guess we took it for granted there would be a happy ending.

"So there it is. I've been moderately successful in my profession. The personal side is blank. You didn't make me feel so good asking those questions. Whom did I fail? Linda or myself? Was it that I didn't love her enough?"

"Who is to say what love is in your teen years. Maybe her idea of love wasn't love. The type of love that makes for commitment. Perhaps both of you failed each other. She should have known more about your future profession, not only on her own but also from you. Did she read up on it?

Did you tell her what life was like in your line of work?"

He shrugged. "Perhaps not clearly. I, we, both probably had an exaggerated and romantic view of it."

"I've known Linda for a long time. I know she was broken up by your leaving, but that's all anyone knew. Then she got married about a year later to a lawyer named Storey. They have two boys. I do know one thing. She has a habit of telling everyone she's a married woman whenever any discussion arises that involves relationships. Maybe a psychologist could find that significant.

"But we were young and naive. We made mistakes. Go around and ask the others if they've made any. If they're honest, they'll say yes."

"Did you?"

She laughed. "Questions again?"

He raised his hand. "Peace. Let us be friends. If there's something we don't want to discuss, we just say so and that's the end of the discussion."

"It's a deal. But, you didn't let me finish. I can answer yes to your question. Also, let it drop there."

HE NODDED. "OKAY, LET me bring you up-to-date, which isn't much. There seems to be two sets of tablets. I believe one set, very conveniently on top, to be gibberish, because we couldn't identify the language. However, there is still an outside chance that it is a new language completely unknown at this time. The other set is Middle Eastern, Sumerian or Babylonian. I'm not an expert in that area so I've gotten some materials on the subject plus I've set an appointment next week with someone who is."

"Sumerian or Babylonian? What could they be doing here?"

"That is the big mystery."

"As a history teacher I know that's going back a long way, although I'm into American history and not too familiar with history in that area."

"Sumerian is the oldest language we know of. Some call it the primeval language. No other language has been discovered that predates it. Indeed, the Sumerians recorded events and discoveries that were lost and only now in this century have been rediscovered."

She shook her head. "It's unbelievable."

"Yes. Now the mystery is what they say, why are they here on an obscure Indian reservation and how were they transported here."

"You left out 'when.'"

He nodded, "The questions do mount up."

"How about the other thing. You know, Martin's legend."

He shook his head. "I don't even want to get into that. There's still a lot to be done. I can't even set a timetable, maybe fall at the earliest."

"You know Martin is coming Wednesday. This is his opportunity to find out if there are more of his 'children' in the Class of '05. And don't forget he said when the children get together..."

"Yes, I'm aware of all that. He's very impatient with our progress, but then I have to remind him it's his fault for not allowing me to get outside help."

"God! I hope this is just a legend and no more."

"I'm still not sure he ever really found us as he says. I like the old man, but to believe him is to stretch reality to the limit."

"So what," she shrugged. "You'll have the tablets and the legend will be just that, a legend. Someday you'll get the credit and acclaim for their discovery."

"If he'll let me go public, and if they don't turn out to be fakes."

"Hmmm, you do need cheering up. Martin has kept you in that cave too long."

"You're right! So to make it up, can I have the pleasure of your company for Wednesday and Saturday?"

"Why sir! I'll have you know I'm a married woman. Whose husband will be gone all week," she blushed. "There I go, doing a Linda. Pushy Dorothy."

"Hey stop! I would never judge you that way. Besides, I'm beginning to know you better. And I like it. If you were a man, I would never dare you to do anything."

"Is that supposed to be a compliment?"

"It is. So let's enjoy today's events."

JOHN LISTENED AND TOOK in the view as Jean's animated chatter occupied the attention of their friends at the table. Like all the women in the class, she had dressed and made up to look her prettiest. In her case it hadn't taken long. Jean was among the top beauties in the class. She was easy going, gregarious and caring with other people. He wasn't surprised she was active in civic affairs. Even in school she had been called the "Mexican Dorothy Perkins."

Her social life had been limited because of her father's strict upbringing. She and her mother had finally persuaded the father to let her work after school. So she had taken a job at the drugstore where the group frequently met.

It was there one Saturday night that John offered to escort her home when she had worked late. How could he forget . . .

For a few blocks they said nothing although he had always made his contributions in the group. It was left to her to break the silence.

"You don't talk much, do you, John?"

"With George around, who gets a chance."

"Ah," she smiled. "You have a sense of humor. You're not the fabled stoic Indian."

"It depends. Sometimes it's my Indian part that takes over. Other times it's my paleface side. I'm half Indian, you know."

"Yes I know. And most of the time it seems your Indian side has taken over."

"That's what they expect when they see me. Another Indian. What's he doing here? Everyone looks down on you and kicks you around. I don't want to give them the satisfaction of knuckling under to them."

"So, you retreat inside yourself and confirm what they think of you. That's no way to fight ignorance and prejudice. So you're Indian, so what? You should make yourself the smartest Indian there ever was. That's the way to kick those people in the teeth. By showing them you're just as capable of living and competing in their world."

"That's easier said than done. In the white man's world a half breed is automatically labeled as undesirable, a villain."

"I can't argue with that, John. But you can't lie down and let them run over you. You and I, we both have to rise above these roadblocks put in our paths because of our heritage. We are first and foremost, human beings. We were brought into this world without our say so. Did you choose to be born? Did you choose your parents? Your sex? Your race? Your country of birth? We came screaming into this world frightened and helpless. There is your equality. From then on, everything becomes less equal. Some get lucky, most don't. It's up to the individual from then on to rise or fall on his own. Oh, you'll get help, if you're willing to accept it. And if you can distinguish between what's good or bad for you."

"Jean, you're the first person who has talked to me like that. To make me understand that I'm a person too. Would it be out of line for me to ask, to ask for a date?"

"No, you can ask, but you know how my father feels."

"I would settle for this, taking you home. Surely they can't object to that?"

"Yes they can, but, what they don't know they can't object to. So ask."

So it began. He escorted her home, well, almost home. He left her two blocks from her house, then followed her at a discreet distance. They had drinks at the drugstore after she finished her stint. On the way home they found a deserted spot by the river. It became their place. They would sit and talk and toss stones into the water. Most of the time John listened and she talked. She encouraged him to set goals and to ignore the hatred against his race.

It was inevitable. He fell in love. He didn't tell her, afraid she might stop seeing him. She gave no indication she returned the feeling.

It was the graduation that forced the issue. He would be making his annual return to the reservation, but unlike previous years, he would not be returning to Stonecliff. The tribal council would decide whether to finance a higher education for him. A foregone conclusion since John had the grades and his mentor, Martin, the medicine man carried a lot of weight in the council.

He would never forget the last meeting with Jean. He explained why he was leaving and what was expected of him. He also told her he didn't want to leave.

"You must, John. This is your chance to do something for your people.

"What about something for myself? Don't I have a right to happiness?"

"Why do you want to stay here? What happiness can you find in a place where you encounter hate and intolerance?"

"I don't care about them. I only care, about you. There, I've wanted to say that for a long time."

She was obviously distressed. "I know. I sensed as much a long time ago. I should have stopped it then, but I was weak. I'm to blame for misleading you."

"You didn't lead me on. I wanted to be with you. I couldn't wait..."

She held up her hand. "John, stop. You're making it hard for me to say what has to be said. Yes, my parents are strict, but loving with all of us. They have been poor all their lives mostly because of a lack of education. So, they want the best for me. They believe at this point of my life I must dedicate myself to my education and not be sidetracked by a love life."

"But Jean, are you going to spend the rest of your life doing as your parents tell you? Aren't you entitled to your own happiness?"

"I don't know if happiness now, is happiness forever, or if I'll ever have it. I'm only seventeen. I hope I have a long way to go yet. I need to know more about life and myself. What about you? You want to stay here, doing what? What would they offer you with only a high school education? The kind of jobs you would get are those that will subject you to more of what you hate. On the other hand, you have an opportunity to advance your education and do something for your people. Doesn't that count for something? Isn't that what we spent many hours discussing?"

"Jean, can't I make you understand?"

"Yes, I know how you feel. But can't you understand how I feel? We're still in our teens. Our future is still ahead of us. This is only the beginning. We have our wants and needs, but we also have our obligations. Maturity and obligation go together. It's confusing and it tears one apart. All I know is that I can't commit myself right now. And if you stop and think, neither can you."

"All right, but later. Is there a chance?"

"Please, John. We'll have to wait and see. So, go to your tribe and be the smartest Indian there ever was. Use that knowledge to better their life so the next generation of children won't know the hatred and prejudice." She flung her arms around his neck and kissed him hard and long. He felt her trembling, felt the tears on her cheeks. Then his tears mingled with hers. She released him, looking in his eyes. "Good-bye, John." She turned and ran. He never saw her again until today.

The tribal council impressed with his record sent him off to college. During his second year, Thelma wrote and told him Jean had married. John was crushed. He quit school and returned to the reservation. The tribe assigned him to work on one of the ranches they owned. This suited him fine as it provided the solitude he craved.

A year later he went to Stonecliff. He called on Thelma. After exchanging greetings, Thelma brought up Jean in the conversation.

"She told me about you before she got married. It was very hard on her. There was this nice Mexican-American boy, Pete Ansuelmo, who was doing very well in the construction business. Her family was pushing, and she was resisting. She finally gave in. She said her family never would have accepted you. It would have torn her apart to have a husband and children that would be disowned by her family."

"I can't believe it. Why, she was the one who told me to stand up and fight intolerance."

"Yes, but how do you fight intolerance from your own family? That was very hard for her. It would have devastated her, family oriented as she is. So, don't be too hard on her. For what it's worth, she loved you. Perhaps she still does."

He went back home. It was there that time and Martin's counsel served to erase the hurt and disappointment. Eventually he returned to college and finished his education....

HE HAD, INADVERTENTLY been looking at Jean as the memories had come and gone. Now she had become aware of his gaze.

"John, is something wrong?"

"Sorry, I wasn't aware I was staring. I was mentally far away, reminiscing."

"Was it, no, never mind."

He smiled. "Some things are best left up there, in some pigeonhole marked 'memories.'"

"Yes, I know. We can't escape them no matter how hard we try."

"And have you tried?"

"There was a time, then I saw there was no need to hide what is only in the private corner of your mind and invisible to all but the inner self. They are the lovely and the sad memories that won't stay pigeonholed. Sometimes, that's all there is."

"I know. Memories help tide you over those black days when the whole world has gone wrong."

"Yes, but sometimes memories don't make it any easier. Has it been hard?"

"Truthfully? Yes. But time has made it more tolerable. And Indians have to maintain a stoic appearance," he smiled. "Life on the reservation helps maintain that."

Her eyes glistened, and he thought tears might come. He reached over and clasped her hand. "Please don't take it that way. One has to be truthful or lie. Neither is guaranteed to be the right approach. So, let's enjoy this week and build new memories that will make the old ones more tolerable."

She laid her other hand on top of his. "We will do that, together."

"Let me have your attention. Please, everyone be seated," Dorothy called out over the public address system. Dorothy, Linda, Sylvia and Esther had moved to the stage at the end of the hall. Dorothy had the mike and the others were seated behind her.

When the caterers left, the tables had been cleared and moved out of the way. The chairs were rearranged in front of the stage. The small group of fifty-four people seemed lost in the cavernous hall.

"On behalf of the school and faculty, I want to formally welcome back our classmates. I know a reunion was unexpected by many. The question often asked is: Why a fifteen-year reunion? To which I say, why not? My close friends who know me, know I need no special reason for many of the things I do. I apologize for the hall. I was not allowed to use any of the regular school facilities because it might disturb classes. So it came to this. And it's cheap compared to any downtown halls. This is almost like home to those of us on the stage. It is the Civil Defense Shelter for the school which we were responsible in putting together."

"Fifty-four of our classmates have responded. Who knows when or ever we shall be together again. Do you remember one another? Earlier Jim Fenzer said that, 'Jim who?' was the most likely question to be asked when identifying our class president. Is that true? Have we changed that much? Well, let's look at some of those faces out there and introduce some of them."

"We have the Longleys, Susan and Sherman. They have their own law firm. How is that for togetherness?

"There is Tom Wadley, Stonecliff's representative to the NFL. Of course, according to the newspapers, he wants lots of money to continue playing. Hope you make it, Tom.

"The medical profession is represented by Dr. Walter Heerlson and Ellen Service and Stella Mundick. The last two being old friends who went into the nursing field.

"Then we have two other buddies, Helen Tessler, now in the military and Jane Sestos who recently made the six o'clock news with some controversial statements.

"Helping to keep the peace locally, we have one of Stonecliff's finest, Joe Hingle.

"Then we have the beautiful Susan Gilbert who has made a few fashion covers.

"Speaking of glamour, we also have a representative from the entertainment industry, Joan Sandry.

"Of course, in the teaching profession, there are the four of us here on stage, but down there is another who chose the unglamorous life of a teacher, that happy fellow. Carl Umbrall.

"There are many more out there. Forgive me if I don't mention all. Roy Worlee, Howard Manabell, Margaret Stanton, Anna Esparto, George Perez..."

She stopped. She felt a shaking under her feet, a rumbling noise started to build up. Then she heard screams all around her and realized hers were mixed with the others. She felt herself falling backward, then she was sliding on the floor, a blow struck her head, then....

CHAPTER FIVE

May 10, 2020
The storm raged on. It had been the seventh of May when the catastrophe hit. It was now the tenth. During this time the wind had not abated. The ferocity of the storm was aptly demonstrated to the group as every now and then, objects, mostly rocks, came crashing down the stairway and careened into the shelter. This, along with a rivulet of water that steadily came down, step by step, kept most of the class away from the doorway. There were three more minor shocks, but no major damage was sustained. The group subsisted on food and drink from Dorothy's storeroom.

Jim had hobbled to her storeroom to inspect her supplies. He was amazed at the amount of food stored there. He saw cans of all sizes and contents, boxes of powdered and pasta products and sealed bags of various type chips. There were also canned sodas, cooking utensils, soap and other toilet articles. In one corner was a huge pile of blankets and next to them, several dozen folding cots. Also in view were boxes of flashlights and spare batteries. He examined the titles on a shelf full of books. There were many other items including a box of seeds for various plants and vegetables.

"Now that I see it, it's still hard to believe. I agree with you. I don't think all of this is what is prescribed by the Civil Defense people."

"We have the basic requirements. Two weeks supply of food for 1000 people, that's what we originally planned for. The food, the water, blankets, radio, flashlights, batteries, first aid kits, shovels, rope, all of these are standard for these shelters. However, the kids got over-enthusiastic. You'll notice there's lots of games that someone thought absolutely essential for survival. From a child's viewpoint, I can't blame them."

"And how much of this reflects Dorothy Walters AM?"

"AM?"

"Yes. After Martin."

"Quite a bit. The books, the seed, implements, toilet articles, many others."

"But, the safe place was the cave of the tablets, not here."

"Why not here? Hasn't that just been proven? Besides, I wanted the people of my town to have a chance too. Only there wasn't any warning. My son, the other children, they didn't get the chance after all the years of planning starting with my grandfather and down to me. Can you understand how that hit me?" There was a mixture of anger and sorrow in her voice.

"Yes, I can," he put his arm around her shoulder. "You've held up very well. I don't know how you do it."

"It's been hard. But I've taken the attitude that I can't do anything up there when I'm stuck down here. But I'm about convinced everyone up there is gone. Else why haven't they come after us? Everyone knew of the reunion. It's the Frontier Days celebration. There should be a lot of activity up there."

"Because of you, fifty-three people have survived. They may not have been the ones you had in mind, but the Fates have provided a different ending. With your supplies, we can last for six months if necessary."

"I wonder if fifty-three was Martin's magic number."

He turned to leave the storeroom, swaying a little and she put out a hand to steady him. "Thank you, you've been a big help at the risk of incurring a lot of loose talk."

"As the old saying goes, 'talk is cheap.' That's why there's always a lot of it being dispensed."

He nodded. "A wise and truthful observation."

DAVID WAS SITTING WITH his River Road group and Nancy when Jim and Dorothy walked by. "There's two really fine people," said David to no one in particular.

"Do you suppose they're in love?" Thelma asked. "She has been so solicitous over Jim since he got hurt. She's been with him constantly. You can't tell me that isn't love."

"You've been reading too many romance novels," said George. "And probably nibbling when you shouldn't."

"Don't try to read something that isn't there," said Jean. "But what if it is? Maybe we should take what we can, since we don't know what's coming next in life."

"I've heard of romances developing or re-igniting at reunions," said Thelma. "But Dorothy is married."

"Do we really know that?" said David. "I think we should be prepared to expect the worse up there. I'm afraid the quake and the storm have taken their toll."

"I've thought about it," Jean was staring at the ceiling, eyes half closed. "So has everyone else. It dominates your thoughts. And Edna won't let you forget."

Nancy sat quietly next to Jean. She had silently been accepted as part of the group ever since Margaret's outburst. And she seemed at ease with everyone, even David.

When John and George had joined them, David had been afraid George would make with one of his tactless remarks. But George had been subdued. David, on the other hand, had been experiencing conflicting emotions about Nancy. He was excited about her presence in the group, but miserable over that invisible barrier of long ago.

"Unless they managed to find shelter somewhere," he continued, "the chances of survival are very slim. Just look at what that wind did to Jim in just a few minutes. It must have blown houses away. Masonry structures weakened by the quake were probably knocked down. Who has seen or heard what we've witnessed? No, Edna is going to have to face some harsh realities."

"Poor dear," said Nancy. "I know how hard it was with just one, but five?"

She turned to Jean and saw her biting her lip. "Oh, I'm sorry, Jean. I shouldn't have brought it up..."

She put her arms around Jean. John sprang up and knelt before her, grasping her hand. "I think we should all stop commenting on the situation. It's all speculation," he said.

"No, no, don't blame anyone," Jean managed between sobs. "I know they're gone. They were all in school. This basement is where they should have been if there had been a warning. But there was no warning because we all thought in terms of a nuclear attack not natural disaster."

"Nature does give its warning," said John. "We just don't look for them or if we do, we refuse to heed them because they're far-fetched or unscientific."

"I think we should all lie down and get some sleep."

88

IT'S STOPPED! THE STORM is over!"

Jim hurried to the door. He saw Carl Umbrall at the opening. He had given the alarm that now galvanized the rest to their feet.

"Let me go first and check what's up there. John?" he looked at him.

"You're a glutton for punishment, Jim," John smiled.

The two advanced cautiously up the stairs. Water was still coming down the steps, only more so, it seemed to Jim.

He was still wary that something could come crashing down the stairs. But that seemed unlikely with the cessation of the cyclonic winds. At least the wind had done one good deed, clearing the stairs and freeing them from suffocating.

They came to the top and it was raining, hard. Revealed was the debris of civilization. Mounds of rubble with rivulets of water running in between surrounded the opening to the basement. A haze hung over the ground, no longer stirred by the departed winds. The sky was dark to gray with visibility limited to about a city block.

There should have been a two-story building above them. Except for a scattering of brick and stone, it was as if a giant hand had swept a table top clear. As far as the eye could see, nothing had been left standing. There were no lights, no sound except for the rain hitting the ground and causing ripples on ever-widening puddles. It reminded him of a primeval setting at the dawn of time as he had once seen in a movie.

His hair plastered down and water dripping over his face, he gave out a sigh. "What does one say at a time like this? Something for the history books?"

"Jim, I don't think we have to worry about putting words in a history book. No one will be around to read them. History may have come to a crashing halt four days ago from the looks of this."

Jim stared at the view. "Yeah, I wonder why the media didn't report this on the evening news. Well," he continued, "it looks like we can't get rid of this place and the real estate market has collapsed. We still can't get out of here. There's no shelter out there."

"They're not going to like it."

"I won't stop them. Let them get wet."

"They need you," John looked at him. "They're a helpless bunch in this environment."

"You could do just as well."

"Now who is out of touch with reality? They wouldn't take orders from me."

Jim grunted. "How do you transfer out of this stinking outfit? Who do you tell to take this job and shove it?"

"I don't know, Jim. I do know I'm getting wet and down there is the only dry spot."

They went down to meet the inquiring looks from the others. "It's wet and soggy up there. No sign of life. I suggest we wait. There's no available shelter that we can see. If you don't believe me, go take a look."

Several of them accepted the invitation and scrambled up the stairs. Disgusted he turned away.

"So much for having confidence in this leader," he groused to Dorothy.

"Don't be too hard on them. They've been cooped in here for four days. They've gone through a horrendous experience and most important they don't know the fate of their families."

He nodded. "You're right. Maybe I can't understand it because I don't have anyone up there for me. But you have. Why don't you join the crowd?"

She grasped his arm. "First off, I happen to know you care, perhaps too much. As for me, I think I know what's up there. Sadly, I don't have anyone either. And neither do the others."

"I'm afraid so," he agreed. "I couldn't see too far, but what I did see is probably a sample of the rest."

They came trooping back, not looking at him. Thelma, however, came up to him. "Jim, I hate to be the one to tell you. It's Edna. She went up there, saw what it was like, gave out a scream and took off."

"Oh damn! That's all we need." He bounded up the stairs followed by John, Oscar and David. She wasn't in sight. He couldn't even see any tracks so heavy was the rain. He stepped out of the stairwell and sank to his ankles. Attempting to take several more steps, he stumbled over some unseen object and went down to his knees. He just stayed there, angry and disgusted until John and Oscar pulled him up.

"It's no use," he told them. "She could have gone anywhere, and we can't track her with this rain. Damn! Doesn't she know there's no one out there? She could get killed."

"She was obsessed with her children's fate," said David. "No one could have stopped her from finding out."

"Yeah, I know. It's just frustration," Jim felt his eyes starting to water and knew it wasn't the rain.

He returned to the shelter and saw Dorothy waiting. She looked at him, saw the tears, but said nothing. She longed to comfort him, but with great effort restrained herself.

May 11, 2020

The following morning it was still raining. Using two of the tables, they made a makeshift shelter at the top of the stairs. This provided some cover for a shift of guards to maintain a vigil for Edna.

Dorothy started the day with bad news. "Jim, I know we can't get out with this rain, but it's still coming in. If it continues, it may damage our supplies, not to mention any discomfort to the inmates."

He nodded. "I know. I heard the dripping all day yesterday and last night. And since we're below water level, it doesn't take much smarts to know water rushes to the lowest level available."

AFTER BREAKFAST HE told them of his plans. "It's been raining hard for two days that we know of. Before that we had a hurricane type storm with possible tornados."

"It's got to stop," said Charlie Durian. "It can't go on forever."

"How about forty days and forty nights?" replied Sylvia.

"The thing is, it's getting bad out there," continued Jim. "If we wait too long, we face several possibilities, none of them good. Flooding will occur up there and pour in here, trapping us all. And if we wait till the last minute to get out of here, we'll have to jump right into a roaring river. So wait here and drown or up there. The third choice which I propose is to go out there and look for a high dry place. Finding one, then we all move there, taking our supplies with us."

"Huh, that was easy, wasn't it?" groused Oscar.

"Glad you agree, old son, because you and I are going searching. I'd like to have two more two-man teams helping out, preferably men with outdoor experience. It won't be easy up there. You'll be bucking running water, dangerous and unknown footing, poor visibility and little or no landmarks to guide you."

"I'll go," said John.

"Will I do as a partner?" David asked.

"You always have, David," John patted him on the back.

Josh Kendall got up, "I guess I have as much outdoor experience as anyone."

Aaron stepped out from the shadows. "Guess I'd better start pulling my weight before a rumor gets started that I ain't," he looked at Linda.

"Okay, get some lights, rope, anything you think will help you. I don't know how far we have to go. You've got watches, don't go out any farther than what four hours will get you. Try to come back a different route. Keep your sense of direction. Mark your trail with something that won't be wiped out by the rain. Tom, I want you to maintain a watch at the entrance here, not only on the water but also for any signals from the teams. Two blinks from a flashlight means 'come help.' So, come. Any comments?" There were none. "All right let's get our equipment and meet at the second landing."

"DAMN! WE'VE BEEN OUT here for over an hour and still no sign of anything that can help us," said Jim.

"Well, you said four hours, so we have quite a ways to go."

"Yes, but the farther out we find shelter, the harder it will be to move fifty people and all those supplies."

"Do we need all those supplies? Surely someone will be coming for us."

"Damn it, Oscar! No one's coming. Five days of hell couldn't have left anyone alive up here."

They were slogging through mud and water, the water sometimes reaching their knees. It didn't help they were wearing dress shoes and business suits and top coats.

Their line of search had been southwest measuring from the basement entrance which faced west. John and David had gone southeast. Aaron and Josh had chosen north.

"Look, Jim, off to the left, high ground."

"High ground, hell, that looks like a good size hill.

Come to think of it, I don't remember one that close to town. It must have sprung up from the earthquake."

They climbed high and made faster time although their shoes were clogged with mud and they were wet and miserable. Suddenly Jim stopped, and Oscar almost ran into him. "Look!"

Sticking out of the side of the hill were two concrete slabs, connected, like an inverted 'L' with the angle some-what obtuse. The top of the 'L' formed a roof and the leg came down as one side. Jim saw it must have been part of a ceiling and wall from one of the downtown buildings.

"Wow! What is that? How did it get here?"

"The wind, the force, whatever it was," Jim was shaking his head. "It gives you an idea of how much power and energy was raging over our heads. They're part of a building that was slammed into the side of the hill, like a spear thrown at a human."

"God! And you volunteered to stick your head out those stairs? Proves what I always thought, volunteers don't have any sense."

"Hindsight, Oscar. Hindsight. But you know what? I think our search is over. There must be seventy or eighty feet of slab sticking out that hill. Notice that it's dry underneath."

"Yeah, but can you stick fifty people and a ton of supplies underneath? And how strong and stable is that thing?"

"Easy to find out. We'll climb on top. Together we should weight about four fifty. Both of us jumping up and down on it ought to create a bit more pressure."

"Now I know you're crazy. Why do you always volunteer me for these nutty schemes of yours?"

"Because I remember a roommate who was fond of practical jokes."

"So, you're getting back at me? I think you and Dorothy belong together. You two are always getting involved in something then dragging everyone else into it."

"You really think so, Oscar?"

"Hell, everybody but you two know it."

"Are we that obvious?

"Damn right! Now are we going to stand in the rain talking about your love life?"

"Let's go, you old grump."

They climbed above the slab, not without slipping down several times in the mud and Oscar swearing a blue streak. Gingerly they stepped out on the slab and finally all the way to the end. It held. It felt solid. Jim jumped up and down several times before Oscar reluctantly followed.

"Well, you pessimist, what do you think?"

"It will hold, but what if we have another quake or hurricane or rockslide. We don't know what's normal in this world."

"There's no hurricanes this far inland. At any rate, it's our best bet unless the others found something better. C'mon, we're heading home."

"Okay, but what is home now?"

"Oh, shut up."

DOROTHY CAME TO THE top of the stairs to find Tom and Jane Sestos standing under the table shelter. Everyone had been taking their turn coming up for a look. They were bored. They had too much time to think.

"Any sign of them?" she asked.

"Nope, Too early. They've been gone just over four hours. That's their outer limit, always assuming they had to go that far."

"It's scary up here," said Jane. "Nothing out there. How could a whole town disappear?"

"You read in the history books about civilizations disappearing," observed Dorothy. "Now we know it's possible and how it can happen."

"Water's getting higher," said Tom.

"You think it's something like the Flood?" Jane asked.

Dorothy smiled. "Don't listen to Sylvia or she'll have you putting square blocks in round holes."

"There's someone coming," Tom reported. "From the southwest. That's Jim and Oscar."

"That's good," said Dorothy. "They're returning early which means they found something."

They had to wait another twenty minutes for the two men to slog through mud and water. When they finally dropped into the stairs, they were a sight to behold. Wet, their clothes covered with mud and clinging to their bodies, a five-day beard covering their faces, they would have thrown strangers into a panic in normal times.

"You've got to get out of those wet clothes," said Dorothy.

"You and Jane want to get your jollies?" Oscar grinned.

"Don't be silly. Jane and I will go downstairs, and we'll send one of the men with blankets. Get out of your clothes, wash out the mud as best you can and wring them. We'll get a fire going and you can dry out."

They did as she directed and thirty minutes later, they were standing over a fire built by the basement entrance. Jim narrated what they had found.

"Pending on the others finding something better, we can start moving out tomorrow. Right now, we should spend the rest of the day packing."

"How are we going to protect these supplies from the rain?" asked Sylvia. "Noah had his Ark, we haven't even got a dinghy."

"You mean you didn't get one?" said Esther. "I remember seeing it on the list and you were responsible for getting it here."

"Since Sylvia screwed up on the dinghy," Jim smiled, "we'll have to improvise. Seriously, we'll use the cots to pile on the supplies and cover them with blankets. I know this will get the blankets wet and we need them, but we have no choice."

"We can afford to ruin a few blankets," said Dorothy. "I have three hundred of them."

One hour before their time limit, Aaron and Josh returned and went through the same 'delousing,' as Oscar called it. They had found nothing. By six o'clock, the end of their eight hours, John and David had not returned. Jim directed two men with flashlights be stationed at the top of the stairs and to shine their lights into the sky. The lights only reflected back because of the overcast, but it served the purpose.

They came in after seven just as Jim was contemplating sending out a search party. Dorothy noticed the hugs given John and David by Jean and Thelma. She also noticed Nancy hanging back of the others. She had known Nancy for a long time although they were not as close as she was with Esther, Sylvia and Linda. They were the two rich girls of the class, at least that's how most of the other students had looked at them. Nancy's family owned extensive timberlands while Dorothy's were in commerce.

Nancy had come home during her junior year in college, a California school. She had been followed by a young man, apparently a classmate. Shortly after that they got married and several months later she gave birth to a son. In the few instances she and Nancy had talked, Dorothy had sensed some family problems. However, the marriage seemed happy until five years later her son was killed falling into a ravine while on a hunting trip with his father and grandfather. A year after that, her father died and shortly after her husband disappeared. A divorce was granted and Nancy, with her mother, took over the running of her father's business.

Now, since the disaster, Nancy had been spending her time with the River Road group. That was like mixing oil and water, socially speaking. Not that the River Road group was bad. Dorothy had gotten to know Jean and found in her a kindred spirit. John she knew and liked. And Thelma and George were amiable and happy types albeit unworldly and sometimes naive. She like them all. Nancy was part of that group now and apparently accepted by the others.

She saw Jim and John heading in her direction. "Is this a conference of the First Children?" she asked lightly. "Perhaps we should include Thelma."

"I don't think Thelma is ready for a First Children revelation," said John. "What I wanted to tell you both is what I saw."

"I thought you said you found no shelter, Jim frowned.

"That's true. I wasn't talking about that. You know I deliberately chose the southeast route because that's the direction to the cave."

"You didn't seriously think you could make it there in a few hours, did you?" Jim looked at him.

"No, but I wanted to explore that route for future reference. I found our way blocked by a mountain chain. I couldn't see how high because of the haze. I followed it east along the base and found a notch that seems to go southeasterly. I didn't go any farther because I didn't want you sending out a search party."

"Even so, that pass may not go all the way. It could angle off in another direction. That cave could be anywhere now, if it still exists."

"Jim, I doubted the old man for a long time, but not now. Everything he said has come true, the catastrophe, our survival and the cave is where it should be. Martin was stocking it with food and implements, even livestock. I just know it's still there and so is he."

"I have to believe it too," said Dorothy.

"It's not that I disbelieve," Jim replied. "Everything I've heard and seen certainly suggests some changes have taken place. Stonecliff is gone, but is it only local or widespread? Some changes have been disturbing and I can weave a scenario of sorts based on several theories I read about."

"You think you know what happened?" Dorothy asked.

"I think I can come up with a good guess, but I would rather not say now. Anyway it doesn't have anything to do with our present problem, which is moving fifty people and supplies in wet and soggy terrain."

"Well, you folks excuse me," said John. "I have to finish drying so I can get wet tomorrow."

"I don't know what the new monetary system is in this new world," she said after John departed, "but a penny for your thoughts."

"You wasted your penny. Tomorrow's trek is the pressing problem."

"I would have thought Martin and his cave would be uppermost in your thoughts."

"Later. After we move this bunch, then John and I will make a try through that pass."

"What about me? I've been in it from the start. Why are you leaving me behind?"

"You know that's not it. We wouldn't know where to find Martin. It might take weeks, even months, perhaps never. You couldn't wander around with two men facing unknown hardships."

"Chauvinist! What kind of hardships do you call this?

"Are twenty-one men going to carry thirty-one women all the way to this shelter? We are all going to pitch in tomorrow, both men and women. We've lost everything. What's in this basement are the survivors of yesterday's world. This new world was born with a big bang. If we survive the aftermath, we will indeed, be the 'Chosen' of Martin's legend."

"Come here," he took her by the arm and led her to the library stairs, dim and deserted. Everyone was congregated by the door and the fire where the returning men were telling what they had seen.

"Look, I know it's not proper, Hell! What's proper in this crazy world? I've seen and walked that empty void up there. Nothing could have lived through that. Your son, your parents, I'm sorry. You won't see them again. No one down here will see their loved ones again. I don't know about your husband. It depends how widespread this is. Damn! How do you go about saying what you want to say without screwing up and making things worse?"

"Why don't you say it and let me worry whether you're screwing up," she gave him a long look.

"Maybe I should just forget about it until later. Oscar said something to me which brought this up. But we have enough problems and you have a mourning period to occupy your mind."

"I've got news for you. Long ago I figured my loved ones were gone. While you were gone I got a good look up there. Granted, you couldn't see too far, but my son's school was nearby. It couldn't have survived. My father was in the hospital with a broken leg, probably mother was with him. Short of being in this shelter, that was the next best place. But if that storm could sweep aside the brick and mortar of a school, it could do the same for a hospital. So, I could break down like Edna, but that's not me. I refuse to act like a helpless female especially over events I cannot control. I ache for my family. I always shall. But I've got to shove those feelings aside for the time being. Now is the time for those alive. Later will be the time to mourn and to place flowers on graves."

He took both her hands. "Yes, I know. You're that kind of person. That's why my saying anything at this time makes it sound selfish on my part."

"Well, try me," exasperated.

"Last summer, fall really, we parted with hurt feelings. And all my fault. But at the time I thought I was doing the right thing, and it was the right thing, considering how things stood at the time. Now everything has been turned upside down."

He paused, and she filled in the gap. "So, what has changed? And I don't mean the catastrophe."

"Truthfully? Your status. Last fall I drew back, and intentionally made you see it so you could too. Perhaps I assumed too much, but there it is. I was smart enough to know you don't butt your head against a stone wall. We had our lives mapped out and headed in different directions."

"Jim, this isn't like you. When it comes to making decisions, you're more direct."

He groaned. "I can't help it. Everything depends on your reaction when I say, I love you!"

She stood there, quiet, what seemed like a ball stuck in her throat, swelling to burst forth. Then she saw his look, crestfallen, disappointment.

"Oh no!" she pulled him towards her. "No. I'm not rejecting. I'm..." She embraced him and then she gave her lips to him, the ball in her throat suddenly gone.

"Oh God! Dorothy, you don't know how much I've wanted to do that, especially in the last few days. I've wanted to put you in an envelope to protect you against the world, however it may be."

"I'm glad, for something good happening to me after all the tragedy. You were right, about last fall. There was a husband and perhaps an old girlfriend between us. I don't know where he's at now. But even then, we lived in the same house with a valid marriage license, but it didn't produce love, peace and harmony. He had already mentioned divorce several times. He may even have a lover somewhere since he made many trips out of town. So there is no longer a roadblock in my mind. But I agree, society looks at this with stern disapproval."

"Just look at us," she said as they separated. "How I must stink. I haven't showered since the seventh."

"I'm one up on you, but you can use my private shower upstairs. I'll be glad to hold the towel for you."

He reached for her again, but she pushed him off. "No, we'll be missed soon. They can't find us like this."

He got up, pulling her with him. "This bearded, disreputable looking man wants one last long kiss from his stinky, disreputable looking girlfriend."

She didn't deny him. Too many years of longing and unhappiness with her husband would not stand in her way now. Did she really care what anyone else would think? She never had before, and she was not in the mood to start now.

CHAPTER SIX

May 13-17, 2020

It took over three days to move. Jim assigned two men to a cot. For the women, he assigned four. There were thirty-nine cots available, only eighteen were utilized for carrying the supplies. Ten cots were carried by twenty men.

The odd man, the smallest was given to help the women and this group carried eight cots. The distance was approximately a mile which Jim and Oscar had marked as best they could on their return trip. However they couldn't avoid two low spots which had become raging torrents. They stretched rope across the two streams for use as handholds. As it was, they still lost one cot and its contents. But that was the only material loss. Of human cargo, there the usual cuts and bruises, not to mention exhaustion and the misery of wet clothes and the presence of mud on every square inch of human skin. They finished by noon of the fourth day. They threw themselves on the ground as they had for every day of their trek.

It had been a constant battle, not only with the elements and terrain, but with the running complaints of the disgruntled. Before they had completed the first trip, they had questioned the necessity of moving and the transporting of the supplies. It had taken tongue lashings by Jim, aided by Oscar and Tom to keep them moving. Dorothy and Jean, aided, surprisingly by Nancy, had shamed the slackers by pitching in without complaint. At one point, the three had shoved aside two men and picked up their cot, much to the men's chagrin, followed by ridicule from the others. From then on, no one dared let down for fear of being put to shame in front of the whole class.

"I may never move again," moaned Sylvia as she threw herself on the ground at the completion of the last trip.

"Those of you who can't hack it, go ahead and rest, but there's still much to be done and there won't be any food until we finish." Jim took in the tired group. "We're soaking wet. We need to dry out and the same applies to our belongings. I want a detail of the women to pick out some firewood. Dig underneath those trees and rubble out there for dry wood and build a fire near the edge of the overhang. I need some of the men to help me. We're going to provide some privacy, especially for the ladies."

Several of the cots were set up on end, vertically, so they provided a wall about six feet high. A rope was run through the top of the cots and anchored at each end. Then blankets were hung over the rope to cover the gaps in between cots. Thus a wall of cots and blankets divided the shelter in half.

"Okay, ladies. All the men will sit down so the tall ones can't peek. You go ahead and wash, rinse, then set your clothes to dry. Use a blanket to cover up. Let me know when you're through so we can take our turn."

"When it's your turn, do we have to sit down too?" asked Sylvia innocently.

It was late in the day when both groups finished. The substitution of blankets for clothes was certainly not for the fashion conscious, but there was no alternative. Already, ten days had taken their toll on what clothes they had. No one had dressed with outdoor activities in mind, much less what they had experienced.

The majority of the women had worn cocktail dresses, from above the knee to just below. A few had slack suits. All had worn high heels. Luckily, with the uncertain weather, they had also brought coats. All had managed to retrieve their purses from the basement so they had the basics to repair their appearance.

For the men it had been business suits and topcoats and dress shoes. Aside from a comb, most had no accessories to match what the women had in their purse. And ten days growth of facial hair didn't make them look appealing. The rain did afford all to have their first shower and they took advantage, even to using some of the soap in their supplies.

So all were now refreshed as much as one could be under the circumstances. For the men it wasn't too hard to keep their blankets in place since they could use their belts.

For the women, problems developed since they had a larger area to cover and not all had worn belts. It remained for Dorothy to solve the problem. Sorrowfully she cut holes in the blankets to make ponchos. Another blanket was cut into strips and these served to tie up loose ends, and that's a pun, she told Jim.

The next morning, they woke up late. The hard work of the last four days had provided a good night's rest for all. After breakfast Jim gathered them all together.

"I think it's time for all of us to talk about the situation, the realities which we must face. Water is no problem. As far as Walter can determine, it's drinkable, but we can boil it to be sure. At any rate we still have Dorothy's bottled water. She also tells me we have enough food for approximately six months for the lot of us. Originally the shelter was supposed to house a 1000 people for two weeks. So that is not an immediate problem but one we have to address sooner or later. Clothes are just about the top in our priorities. That trek has just about ruined everyone's clothing and there's nothing in sight but blankets to replace them. And we may need those blankets to keep warm because we cannot trust the weather. It's wet and damp right now, but otherwise passable. Some of you might have read about the 'greenhouse effect.' What you see above us is a good example. If that cloud cover persists, it will lower temperatures, so we will need all the cover we can get, on us and above us."

"You're talking permanent," this from Sherman Longley. "Are you saying, It's like this all over?"

"I can't prove it, beyond a shadow of a doubt, to put it in language you're familiar, but I can build circumstantial evidence. The first and most damning piece of evidence is that radio, that silent radio. Ten, eleven days with no music, no voices, just static. How many places could you hear before?"

"It varied, depending on reception in these mountains," said Sylvia. "But you could get Phoenix, Tucson, Vegas, Salt Lake or Denver. I could go on."

"Exactly. Where are they? Communication is out. And these cities Sylvia mentioned are no longer in touch, at least with us. Of course, it could be the overcast that is preventing reception, but even so, we should at times be able to hear an occasional word through the static. The radio has a short-wave band, but that too is mute."

"Preposterous!" exclaimed Charlie Durian. "What you're intimating is that we're all that's left. I can't believe that."

"It's a possibility. As I said, I can't prove it conclusively. My background is in archaeology with some knowledge in geology and anthropology. What could have happened? I think we can rule out nuclear attack. Our instrument does not register any significant radiation other than what we would ordinarily see on a normal day. All indications seem to point to an earthquake, An earthquake of immense proportions. Perhaps one of such magnitude as never before registered. But even that boggles the mind for it to have such force and energy to cut off all communication, possibly worldwide.

There is yet another possibility. The magnitude of this disaster suggests such a great amount of power and energy that can only come from an outside source. You may have heard or read the debate this past decade about the extinction of the dinosaurs. That a comet struck the earth and caused the loss of all living things. A cataclysmic event of that sort would cause earthquakes, volcanic eruptions, tidal waves and gigantic wind storms."

"The comet!" exclaimed Carl Umbrall. "As science teacher at the high school, my students were following the progress of this comet, the Century Comet, as the media dubbed it. It was supposed to pass between Jupiter and the Asteroids sometimes Saturday."

"Why weren't there any warnings?" asked Esther.

"Perhaps because it wasn't expected. For it to hit the Earth means it was probably deflected from its course by the pull of the larger planets and the Sun as it came into the Solar System. We had an overcast on the day of the reunion. We were deep in the basement. We don't know if there was a last-minute warning on radio or TV. It probably wouldn't have made a difference. Where could anyone go to escape the collision?"

Jim nodded. "All this is speculation and conjecture. I have no proof to present to you except what we see around here. In the past there have been literally thousands of articles written by learned people and an equal number of quacks that address such happenings. Consider, for instance, that this planet is some five billion years old, yet we can only date civilizations back some six or seven thousand years. Think of the great strides made in the last fifty to one hundred years. If a civilization can flourish and advance to such great heights in such a short time, are we to believe it took five billion years to reach that point?"

"Was nothing there before us? There were always the persistent rumors of great civilizations that flourished in the past. There were legends of great battles in the sky among the gods. Keep in mind that in the dim past, heavenly bodies were regarded as gods. Gods resided in the heavens above, so obviously such bodies as the Sun, the Moon and other planets attained god-like status. Then comes an intruder into the system. The head of the intruder, or comet, may appear to the observer to look like an animal. For instance, horns are attributed to such a body and are therefore named after an animal that fits the description. There is no end to the myths, legends and speculation about the past. That is the end of my lecture on the history of the End of the World theories. I'm sure there are more. My main purpose in telling you these things is my hope to impress you with the seriousness of our situation. Whether you believe it or not, we need to go on the assumption this is a most serious situation and that it is up to us to look out and care for ourselves."

"We have a cloud cover up there. There's a lot of water in those clouds plus dust, volcanic ash and God knows what else. It will all come down. All that will tend to hide the sun for a long time and possibly lowering temperatures."

"The temperature doesn't seem too bad," observed Esther.

"True, we may be in a more tropical climate. And that could come from another type of disaster, a pole reversal. But I won't go into that."

"You're painting a picture that calls for our extinction," said Aaron.

"Perhaps that could be our ultimate fate. But my point still is that we have to do for ourselves to survive. People survive, otherwise we wouldn't be here. We didn't evolve from an acorn," replied Jim.

"Don't you remember, a stork dropped us off," cracked Sylvia. "It's what I always said, The Flood." She looked around to the others in triumph.

"Was that the DeMille production?" Esther asked.

"All I know is that Charleton Heston was in it."

"You're thinking of 'Earthquake' and that sounds very appropriate," Esther responded in a serious vein.

"Will you two shut up!?" Charlie shouted.

"Having told us all this, and mind you, it doesn't mean I believe it, what do you have in mind?" asked Sherman Longley.

"We are now a community, of sorts. It means we have to organize. There's been some grumbling in the past about my 'self-elected' leadership. I suggest that now is the time to elect one of your own choosing, so we can go about the business of surviving. Does anyone want to make any statement or throw their hat in the ring?"

There was some fidgeting and looks given each other before Walter stood up.

"As the only one in this bunch with job security, I have no axe to grind. Jim, is there any reason why you couldn't continue? It seems to me you've done a damn fine job so far."

There was a murmur of agreement and several clapped their hands.

"Charlie, Aaron, you guys have any comments?" Oscar boomed.

"As one of those who was on the receiving end of some scathing comments," said Aaron. "I'd like to say that I have no ambitions to 'take over.' My only concern at the time was that Charlie was the only duly elected official present. It seemed only logical that he took over. I have no objections to Jim continuing the job."

"You're wrong on one count, Aaron," Dorothy broke in.

"A majority of this class elected Jim as class president, long before Charlie made councilman. That election has never been rescinded nor does it say for how long he can hold office. Technically, Jim is still president of the Class of '05. Moreover, a good number of those present are no longer citizens of Stonecliff so they owe no loyalty to a councilman who no longer has a constituency."

Aaron smiled and bowed. "And you should have been the parliamentarian. You've got my vote at the next election."

"I vote for Jim," Oscar announced. "Any more Jim votes out there?"

There was a resounding 'yea' that left no doubts.

"Very well. Thank you for the confidence, but..."

"Are you going to cut taxes?" yelled Sylvia.

Jim nodded. "Don't forget crime. We're all against that. But we'll leave the easy things for later. For now, there are some necessities that can't be put off. First, we have to build what was known in the service as a latrine, two as a matter of fact."

"In this rain? It will fill up before we can use it."

"We'll have to sacrifice two more of our cots to cover the site."

"It's about time," said Sylvia. "The traffic gets pretty bad at night. You don't know whom you will bump against or what you will step on."

Jim laughed. "We'll make it private, so you can walk about in broad daylight and avoid unpleasant obstacles. Now, Dorothy has told me that her father had a basement running underneath his supermarket and the Western

Post. If our basement survived, then it's possible, that one did too. This would solve our food and clothing problems for a long time."

"You're not asking much," said Tom. "Walk about in this perpetual rain looking for a heap of rubble that looks like a million others, then with only two shovels, dig up several tons of dirt and rock and maybe, maybe, we'll find the pot of gold."

"That's exactly what we'll do. Either that or we'll be using those two shovels to pat six feet of dirt over your face.

"That's all for now. We can start today with the latrine. Tomorrow we start looking for the right heap of rubble."

LATER THAT EVENING he sat with Dorothy at the edge of the shelter. "Did that little talk mean you're giving up looking for Martin?" she asked.

"No, but I couldn't walk off leaving them with so few supplies. I don't know how long the search will take, so I have to secure their future, and yours." He took her in his arms and kissed her and she responded in turn. She was wearing her poncho, not very glamorous, but it did expose enough thigh to raise his ardor. The fire was in back of them and to the side, so they had some privacy, but anyone walking about could still stumble over them. However, the light was sufficient for him to see her and be aroused by a poncho that refused to cooperate.

She broke away from him. "What about us? Are we going to limit our love life to stolen moments like this? It won't take too long for the others to notice your hands all over me."

"And they won't blame me. I never thought these blankets could make you look so sexy. Believe me, I'm not the only one who's noticed. So sooner or later we'll be joined by others in the same situation."

"I don't care to be joined by others and neither will I allow you to have a harem just because you're the leader. But if this is permanent as you say, how do you go about making our union permanent?"

"That may be a problem. Unfortunately, we don't have a clergyman or judge in the bunch. We'll have to live in sin, but of course, in the eyes of God we can declare our love."

"You're the leader. You can assign duties to the rest of us. We're a new community, you said. A new community could use a judge. So, why don't you appoint one of those lawyers a judge?"

"You are a sly one. Come to think of it, I'd better marry you before you lead a palace coup."

He reached for her again. "No," she said. "I don't think we can trust our emotions." But she was only halfhearted in her rebuff and he bore her down to the blanket.

"Oh, my darling, I can't, I won't hold you off, yes, yes. Whatever you want, I want too." Once more the blanket poncho refused to cooperate.

CHAPTER SEVEN

May 18, 2020

They woke up to a silent world. The heavy rains had stopped, replaced by light drizzle. The clouds still hovered, menacingly overhead, threateningly to erupt again. There was a light increase in visibility that also revealed the enormity of the catastrophe.

"Don't let it fool you," Jim told them. "There's still a lot of water up there, possibly a good part of the Pacific ocean."

What they saw around them was something, heretofore seen only in TV news clips of the aftermath of a hurricane, tornado or flood devastated landscape. Now it was personal. They were the victims now.

Jim had assigned four men to dig into the back of the shelter in an attempt to extend their living area. The others he had sent out to scavenge the area for anything that could be useful to the survivors. This elicited various comments ranging from mud pacts for the women to shoeshine for cleaning muddy shoes.

For himself he took the task of locating the basement of the supermarket. To this he had recruited Dorothy. Then almost as an afterthought, he added John and Jean. When the four were out of earshot of the others, John spoke up. "I know why Dorothy is along. It's her Dad's store plus it's a good day for strolling with a pretty girl. But why are we along?"

"You just said it. It's a good day for strolling with a pretty girl. But actually, I need two teams. Jean and Dorothy are familiar with the town, you and I provide the muscle and outdoor experience. You two are friends from the old River Road days. Dave and George are not outdoor types. Then too, I always heard you two women were the go-getters of the class. It would be interesting to see you two working together."

"You are going to great lengths to explain your reasons," smiled Jean. "I must have heard at least four. Further, how can Dorothy and I work together if we're going to be split working with you fellows?"

"Ah, well, you see..." Jim stammered.

"Never mind," laughed Jean. "I accept your arguments and the arrangement."

Dorothy joined Jean in the laughter while John smiled at Jim's discomfort. "Okay, I've learned my lesson. Stick to business.

"Let's get oriented. This shelter is southwest from the school basement. The basement door faced directly west. So we should be south of the city facing north. Based on that, can you ladies get a bearing on the supermarket and the Post?"

"I'd say if we're facing north, it's somewhat off to the east. Northeast? Jean?"

"Yes, looking west from the school, the supermarket was on Morgan which is one block south of Main which led straight to the school."

"All right, then, John, you two go to the right, align with the basement entrance, then swing west with Jean checking for landmarks. Dorothy and I will go left a ways, then circle and head east. We should meet somewhere in what's left of Stonecliff. We'll both call out to locate each other as we get into town. Okay? Then good luck."

John and Jean left, carefully searching for solid ground before they put a foot forward.

"Since when have you gone into the matchmaking business?" Dorothy glanced at him.

"I guess I haven't," he laughed. "You must have noticed how lousy I was. I like John. I thought I would do him a favor."

"I wasn't scolding you," she took his arm. "You're like the reformed drinker who wants to tell everyone the joys of sobriety. Only in your case, it's love. But oddly enough, I think your plan shall be successful. Those two have something for each other that goes way back. I suppose next you'll be getting David and Nancy together."

"David and Nancy?"

"Never mind. Let's get on with this, whatever devious plan you had in mind. You know, to get us together?"

"You suppose right. Keep an eye out for any dry spot that two people in love can fit into."

"Mr. President! Are you neglecting your duties? And what of John and Jean? We're supposed to meet them. They might get alarmed if they don't find us."

"I was hoping they would find a dry spot for themselves. We've got all day, although who knows how long the rain will hold off."

She rushed into his arms. "Then let's not waste time."

"I'M SORRY ABOUT THAT," said John. "Jim means well, but I don't know why he presumed as he did."

"River Road buddies. Isn't that what he said?" She arched her eyebrow.

"I guess Thelma knows the town as well. She could..."

"John," she stopped and faced him. "There's no need to go through this charade. I don't know that I can believe all that Jim said, but I can see with my own eyes what's happened here. Everyone I loved in this town is no more. I can't forget them because I had a lot of love for them and that just doesn't disappear overnight. I know I have to start a new life without them. That is, if we're going to have anything to live for in this mess. As for us, we can't go on walking on tiptoes or fencing with words. So let's be honest with each other. I hurt you very badly, for which I'll never forgive myself."

"No, no. It was..."

"Hush!" she put her fingers to his lips. "I said we would be honest."

"Okay, I was hurt. But I was young and naive. With time I've learned to accept that one doesn't always get one's desires."

"I was a hypocrite, Let's get that out. I couldn't practice the ideals I preached to you."

"Thelma explained your family's feelings. You cannot condemn those you love."

"Quit making excuses for me. I don't deserve them."

"All right, but that was yesterday, A whole life ago. This is a different time and situation. Do we let what happened then separate us now?"

Her eyes filled with tears, but he repressed any tenderness. She was a strong-willed woman. She had to make the decision, to break that barrier she had built between them. "No, but I don't know what is right anymore."

"If we survive all this, we're going to form a new world. This group is the nucleus. My feelings have never changed in fifteen years. You have always been in my thoughts."

"Oh John, John. I have deprived you of happiness all these years. It's my fault, I..."

"No, I don't want you on those terms. That you pity me or feel you owe me a debt. I want all debts, gratitude, whatever, to be forgotten. We start all over, in a new environment. I love you, and if you love me, this is the way we begin. Will you take me on that basis?"

"Oh, my dear, I'll take you on any basis," she rushed into his arms. They kissed and held on to each other as if it would make up for the lost years, "But give me some time to get over my losses," she said, as she disengaged from him. "I cannot shut them off like turning a switch."

"I won't rush you. Get over your sorrow with me to help you. Just knowing you'll be there for me is enough."

She gave him a quick kiss. "Just one more thing. Let's go by the River Road. I know it's useless, but I have to see for myself. I already saw the school. Nothing could have survived that; the children are gone."

TOM DROPPED DOWN BESIDES Linda at the noon break. "Mind if I eat with you, pretty girl? You said you still owe me, remember?"

She looked at him with a frown. "That was at the reunion, a million years ago."

"This is still the reunion. The class is still together. Till death do us part."

"Is that supposed to be funny?"

"Wasn't meant to be. Irony, perhaps. It was used to bind man and women on one of society's ancient rituals. Now it describes our situation and we don't even get the pleasure of connubial bliss."

"Tom, not only are your semantics way off, but you're pushing your innuendo at the wrong person. That little flirtation at the reunion was just that. It wasn't any long-repressed longing, finally realized, that led me to invite you as my escort. I like you, but I am not one of your football groupies that's thrilled by your attention."

He got up. "Well, that's direct and to the point. I guess they were right when they said you were trying to get at Jim through me."

She sighed. "Just go away, Tom."

"All right, but there's the irony again. Jim and Dorothy are off together, and I'll bet they're not just holding hands. They were all over each other last night. I guess they thought no one could see them. So, the 'plans of mice and men' don't always work. Is there some 'semantics' there?"

She turned away and didn't answer, so he walked.

Now it was Aaron's turn to move in. 'Are you all right? I thought I detected some harsh words."

"What is this? Is there a line out there waiting their turn at me?"

"Look, I was just concerned. I remember that day in the basement when I regained consciousness and you were there to assure me. I know how hard it is for you, the loss of your family. Rest assured, I have no intention of forcing myself on you." He got up and left.

She shouldn't have snapped at him. Tom had been the one to set her off. His comments had been better suited to accosting women at a singles bar. However, his last remarks about Jim and Dorothy had infuriated her. Why? Why should she care? She had not made things easier with her performance at the reunion. Had she expected him to come home after fifteen years and fall at her feet" If so, she hadn't given him a chance. So why was she surprised that Dorothy had moved in. Or was it the other way around? That storm or quake had cleared the way of all ties. There were no husbands or children to hinder the new lifestyle. Where did she fit in this new environment?

May 19, 2020

The next day Jim led the group to the site of the supermarket which they believed they had located. In one of the freak incidents so often found in such disasters, the cornerstone of one of the buildings had been left standing. Using this, Dorothy and Jean had marked the approximate location of their projected dig.

"You expect us to dig that up?" complained Charlie.

"I still think there's someone out there. They'll come for us," said Don Butins.

"Don't you think they would have shown up by now?" Jim asked. "And what if we just sit and wait and no one ever comes?"

"It's the water," said Charlie. Rivers must be at flood stage, blocking roads. Might even have a bridge or two out."

"There's ducks, caterpillars vehicles, might even get a copter flying low," Jim was disgusted. "Even the old fashion way, horses and mules. And if they are somewhere close, why don't we hear radio traffic, any noise like rifle shots to get our attention?"

"I just can't believe we're the only ones left," sniffed Margaret Stanton.

"There may be others out there, but where or how many, we don't know. And if so, they're just as bad off as we are. Even worse because they don't have the food and supplies we did at the shelter.

"We can't take any chances. We have to go on the assumption there's no help coming. Everything we do has to be oriented towards survival. It's been twelve days, wait long enough and you don't eat. I can't guarantee you anything. We may not find anything. We may be a few feet off. What we find may not be edible. There's too many 'ifs' in our new life."

Dorothy looked at Oscar who was carrying one of the shovels, "Well, if you're not going to use that, give it to me. I'm not afraid to use it."

Jean stepped forward. "I'll use the other one."

"Who said I wasn't going to use it," snapped Oscar. "Don't lump me in with those whiners."

The others joined in, some reluctantly. Most approached their task as if afraid of getting their hands dirty. And with only two shovels, it was obvious more than hands would have to get dirty.

May 20-22, 2020

At the end of the day, it was a tired and filthy group that trudged back to camp. All they had to show for their foray were aching backs and raw calluses on their hands. That day and the ones that followed seemed to produce no effect on the small mountains of rubble. It had produced two bodies and a horrid smell which stopped work and sobered the survivors. The bodies were buried. Then to add to their misery, the rains returned, although intermittently. After two days a total of seven bodies had been uncovered and buried. By the third day, bodies no longer aroused emotion. Everyone was too tired and numb to care.

"Tomorrow we'll shift a little to the west to be sure we're covering all possible sites," Jim told them.

"Oh, what's the use? We'll never find it," Margaret groused.

"Susan and I have to get out," said Sherman Longley. "We have commitments that..."

"My God I can't believe you people," Jim threw up his hands. "Don't you have eyes to see? Don't you have minds to reason? Look around you. Quit living in the past. You can't survive if you do. You give up and you die."

"I guess I'm just bewildered," said Ruth Libwort. "I don't know who's right. I can see what's happened, but I can't believe that, that everything out there is gone. Where do we go? What shall we do?" Jim shook his head wearily. "Where are you going and how? How many of you have experience traveling in the wilderness? Sure, you live in the West, but you don't get out there and do without the luxuries of civilization. There are no landmarks out there. You can only carry so much food and water with you. When that gives out, you die. The best thing to do is to stay here if anyone is coming, and I don't believe that, this is where they'll come. This is the logical place to look for survivors, in the remains of the town, not out there."

"Here's what I propose. All of you continue with the digging. John and I will attempt to find help within—say sixty to eighty miles from here."

"Are you going to Flagstaff or Phoenix?" from Sylvia.

"I don't know. John says there's a pass in the mountains, heading southeast."

"Southeast!" exclaimed Charlie. "There's nothing in that direction except Indians."

"They're my people," said John. It would be more likely for them to survive than people in buildings."

"Why can't we all go?" asked Linda.

"There's too many of us. We don't know what's out there. Look at the problems we had just moving one mile from the school basement. John and I can travel faster. We should make the trip in two to four weeks. If we can't find anything in that time, we'll give up and return."

"And I might add, you women are in no condition to travel in those clothes and shoes."

Later he was accosted by Dorothy. "You and John are to try for Martin's cave, aren't you? And you're leaving me behind."

"The reason I gave the others are just as valid for you. What's more important, I need you here to bolster their spirits. You've always been out front leading the cheers. We need your cheerleading abilities more than ever. All of us have responsibilities now and you are no different. John and I have to concentrate on finding the cave with the least amount of distraction. And you, my lovely, are a distraction."

"I should have known you would wiggle out of taking me along. Why do men always want to take off by themselves, like my late husband?"

"So, our women will appreciate us that much more when we return."

She whacked him on the arm. "So, go on if you must. I'll have you know I'll, miss you very much."

He took her in his arms. "I'll miss you even more. You had someone these past fifteen years. I didn't, and now I have to give you up if only for a short time."

CHAPTER EIGHT

May 23, 2020

In the morning the two men made their preparations for their departure. They had already improvised duffel bags from a blanket to carry their rations. Each had a canteen from Dorothy's stores. For clothing they had their coats and topcoats which they had worn to the reunion because of inclement weather. In addition, each carried a blanket.

"We'll be somewhat overloaded to start, but it will lighten as we eat our rations.

"Oscar, I'm leaving you in charge. Have Tom and David back you up. Keep them digging. We need whatever we can salvage out of this mess, but it should also keep them out of mischief. We should be back in four weeks at the most. If not, don't go looking for us. Don't let anyone leave the area. It's a sure way to get lost."

He got Dorothy by the arm and took her aside. "We have to say our good-byes. Would you object to a public display of affection?"

"I'd love it," she threw her arms around him. They held on tightly in a long kiss.

The class had gathered to watch them leave. Now there was a murmur as they watched the two lovers kiss.

Then Jean stepped up to John. "I guess I can do no less. I've held back fifteen years."

He swept her up. Both couples stood in deep embrace with the whole group in attendance. Then one or two started clapping, then others joined in, some added whistles.

Dorothy caressed him as they drew apart. "But I won't forgive you for not taking me along. I'm one woman who doesn't mind following her man. 'Wither thou goest...' that sort of thing."

"No one regrets it more. Be careful. Don't wander too far. Good-bye," he gave her one last kiss. He shouldered his bag and was joined by John. They waved and trudged off.

Dorothy remained watching until they disappeared in the distance. She had kept back her apprehensions, and tears. The chances of finding the cave in this new terrain were slim. Both had known it but refrained from discussing it. They had known a try must be made because the rest of the group had to know some effort was being made to find help.

The group was still in a blue funk. Some just stared into space. Some suddenly broke out into tears. They need some assurance. So, to please them Jim was gone with no assurance of his return.

"My, my, what a tender love scene that was," smirked Charlie Durian behind her. "Looks like Fenzer, our high and mighty leader has been engaging in a little hanky panky on the side."

She whirled. "You, you sneaky little bastard!"

Sylvia and Oscar joined her at this point. "You heard her," snapped Sylvia. "Get lost!"

Red-faced, all Charlie could do was sputter. "I'm not forgetting this, all of you. You've interfered once too often."

"Yeah, yeah, Charlie, you'd better get yourself a secretary to keep track of all the people on your shit list."

Sylvia looked at Dorothy. "I wouldn't put it as crudely as Charlie, but that was some show you and Jim put on."

"I'm glad you liked it, Sylvia. Too bad it can't repeat on the late show."

"It was our way of showing how things stand between us. Of course, the Charlie Durians and Sylvia Remners can choose to interpret it to suit their purpose without knowing the true facts."

Sylvia put her arms around her. "Honey, I'm with you. I always shoot off my mouth, And I know your husband is gone," she waved at the surroundings. "But what about Linda?"

"Linda? What about Linda?" Dorothy was exasperated. "Everyone talks about Linda as if she had planted a flag on Jim and forever after it's her territory. How ridiculous! I love Linda like a sister, the same as you and Esther, but I am not going to seek permission from any of you on how to run my private life. She may have had him years ago, but no more. I've planted MY flag."

Oscar shook his head. "Ah, me, you women, how you carry on over us poor fellows. I envy Jim having all these women panting over him."

"Correction, Oscar," Dorothy shook her finger at him, "It's only 'one' woman now."

A GLOWERING CHARLIE, his pride still smarting, rejoined Aaron, Don and Larry.

"I can't stand that bunch, especially that jock and that Walter's hussy. I'm going to cut them down to size."

Come on, Charlie," Aaron smiled. "You went over and stuck your nose where it wasn't wanted."

"Whose side are you on?" Charlie snapped. "I might have known you jocks would stick together."

"The only side I'm on is my side. Get that through your thick skull. If Jim and Dorothy have a thing for each other, that's no business of ours."

"Sort of clears the way with Linda," smirked Don.

"Linda isn't the subject of this discussion, or any discussion," Aaron glowered at Don until he turned away.

"As I remember," Charlie looked at him, "you weren't too particular about discussing her before the reunion."

"Linda is not anyone's business here and I would advise everyone to leave her out of any talk."

"Well, I can't forget it," pouted Charlie. "Fenzer, Walters and Bonococci, the whole bunch is on my list."

"Charlie," interrupted Larry.

"What do you want, Wilk? What are you hanging around here for?"

"Well, hell, Charlie. I was going to do you a favor, but if that's the way you feel, then the hell with it."

"Don't mind Charlie," said Don. "He's got female problems. What did you have in mind?"

"Well, I don't know. I don't like being talked to that way."

"Come on, Larry. Charlie's been pushed around, and he doesn't like it either. So, what is this favor?"

"I was going to say that Joe Hingle carries a gun."

"So, what!?" snapped Charlie. "He's a cop. All cops carry guns."

"Yeah, but that's the only gun in camp, and I can take it away from him."

"And how is that going to help me?"

"Well hell, you want to cut down those jocks, don't you? What better way than the old equalizer."

"You're a blood thirsty bastard," said Aaron.

"Look, where do you come off calling me names. I don't see you doing anything but bitch. At least I've got an idea."

"I don't remember asking you for ideas," replied Aaron, sternly. "Killing people has never been a good idea unless it's the last resort. What are you going to do? Shoot them all? I doubt Joe is carrying that many rounds."

"Maybe if we kill a few, we'll have that much more to eat," grinned Larry.

"I think it best you forget that idea," said Aaron, glancing at Don. "Food is not yet a problem."

Don nodded. "I agree with that. We're getting all worked up over nothing. Right, Charlie?"

Charlie just grunted. "We'll see."

DOROTHY WALKED BACK to the makeshift kitchen and stopped as she saw Linda watching her. Her outspoken remarks to Sylvia went out the window. Linda was one of her best friends. Why did she feel like a back-stabbing traitor?

No! She had no apology to make to anyone. She remained standing unable to decide whether or not to continue. Linda made the decision for her.

"Far be it for me to criticize, but isn't it too soon for that sort of thing?"

"What is too soon? The world changed in a twinkling of an eye. It can do that again. In the meantime, what do we do? Wait around for society to change its mores?"

"Well, for sure, no one can accuse you of waiting. You put on quite a scene in the basement slamming Aaron and Charlie. You and Jim have had your heads together, and God knows what else, since the day of the brunch. Apparently, you haven't been very discreet in your nightly activities. Someone has already made remarks in that regard. And now, necking in public. May your husband rest in peace."

Dorothy colored, her gorge rising. "Necking in public?"

"How archaic. But you're wrong, Linda. You're making it sound sneaky and dirty. I'm not ashamed of anything. I apologize to no one for my actions. My husband is dead. So is yours."

"Let's face up to that. We did not know the private lives of other people unless they chose to tell us. I was one who chose not to make mine public, not even to my closest friends. My marriage was over a long time ago and on its last legs at the time of the reunion. I'm sorry he's dead, but I don't feel disloyal for loving another man especially when my husband was with another woman. Frankly, I don't understand your attitude on this. Your remarks seem catty as if you resent Jim and I getting together. You know, that day at the brunch, you and Tom, Oscar and Esther paired off, so I was left with Jim. I didn't set that up. I recall you started the ball rolling with that 'escort to lunch' business. Not that I'm sorry. It's the best favor you ever did for me. I'll be forever grateful. However, since that time, I've been made to feel like I was transgressing on Linda Storey property. Why am I made to feel like I'm defacing a monument or spitting on the flag? It seems people, and you, are set on maintaining the status quo of fifteen years ago. Was that relationship set in concrete? Is there supposed to be a 'hands off' sign around, Jim's neck? Even Sylvia was dressing me down as if I had been caught with someone else's husband. Good God! Why?"

Linda was red-faced and on the verge of tears. "I'm sorry I spoke out. I had no call to act that way. The last thing I want is to be classed as a part of Charlie's bad taste set.

"For what it's worth, my husband was no better than yours and like you I kept quiet about my private life. I didn't want to seem a failure like Esther or a loveless type like Sylvia.

"I have no hold on Jim. We parted fifteen years ago because neither one of us were headed in the same direction. Neither one was willing to change for the other. I can't explain what happened at the brunch. Perhaps there was some rancor left in me to strike out, to think I could hurt him. It was a subconscious thing I guess. Done on the spur of the moment. I'm not proud of it. So, I end up being judgmental, another spur of the moment observation. Come to think of it, I've been subjected to some of that myself. So, the least I should do is keep my mouth shut."

"Things happen that aren't planned," said Dorothy. "They just happen, by chance or fate, call it what you want. I met Jim last summer at my father's store and later saw him several times at the reservation. I was attracted. By now I knew my husband was having an affair. Jim was also attracted although

I didn't learn that till later. Nevertheless, we respected convention and went our separate ways, until fate intervene with this disaster. So, in my mind I've done nothing wrong and I don't have to explain myself. But I just did, didn't I? Maybe because I want you to know how it is. That it wasn't spur of the moment or aimed at you."

"There's nothing to explain. I'm not in the picture. He's yours."

May 28, 2020

"Oh no! Another turn? We're going to zig again, Jim. Are you sure we're still heading in the right direction?"

"We can zig and zag but generally we've been heading south, southeast or east. I think I have a good sense of direction. As long as we remain in that quadrant, we're all right."

"How far do you think we've come?"

"I'd say close to fifty miles. We've made good time."

Jim stopped and pulled out a small notebook from his topcoat pocket. He had made a life-long habit of jotting down items of interest and he had never been without it. Now he was attempting to map the terrain they were traveling. In addition, they had set up markers on the trail to find their way back. John had gone on, so Jim had to hurry to catch up, but John was already stopped, staring at a dead end.

"This is it, Jim, no zig or zag here."

"Damn! Go fifty miles to hit a dead end."

"It's too far to go back. Let's try climbing."

"Easier said than done. You can't even see the top of this mountain because of the haze line."

"I'd say we're looking at some five hundred feet. How much more there is above that is a guess."

"But it's that or go back," John waited for an answer.

"Yeah, you're right. But it's drizzling so it's slippery and muddy. We've better tie a rope around our waists."

It took almost three hours to reach the haze line, or rather to look down and not see the bottom of the canyon. It was not so thick that you couldn't see ahead, but the top was still not to be seen.

"John, we're not going to get over this thing before dark."

"Hell, it's been dark for quite a while as far as I'm concerned."

They continued their climb, slowly, practically feeling their way. The wind had picked up and Jim felt raindrops on his face, or was it sleet? It felt cold enough. They must be at least a thousand feet above the canyon floor, but how far above sea level were they? He saw a light scattering of snow on the ground. What did that signify?

They spent the night on the mountain. It was cold but not freezing. They burrowed into the ground and covered with the two blankets. Even so, they had a restless night. In the morning they had a cold breakfast, then set out. Climbing higher, the snow became thicker.

"Damn it, John, we could be climbing the equivalent of the Himalayas for all we know."

"I know, but what can we do? Turn back?"

"We've come too damn far. But you've got a vote. What do you think?"

"Frankly, I don't know. We can set a time limit and turn back if we haven't reached the crest. Or we might be making it worse by continuing, a-a-ah..."

Before Jim could determine what had happened, the rope around his waist tightened and then he was jerked up off his feet. A moment later he was plunging down, his body sliding on the snow and into the unknown obscured by fog.

LARRY WILK TOSSED AND turned, but not because he couldn't sleep. He was avoiding sleep and he was tossing from impatience. He was waiting for everyone to go to sleep.

For the group, going to sleep was an easy thing now after the unaccustomed labor. It hadn't been that way after the quake, when worry and fear occupied their minds. Now they labored day after day on the supermarket dig. And as each day failed to see success, weariness and apathy set in from which only sleep provided escape.

Of course, Larry had been doing as little as possible. He had sneered as Aaron had pitched in, keeping pace with Oscar and Tom. He had been right. Those jocks always stuck together. Jane Sestos was the guard tonight. Sleeping close by was Helen Tessler. Larry scowled. Those two have to be dykes, always together. They might fool the others, but he knew.

When he had received his invitation to the reunion, he had laughed and tossed it aside. Later, as the day got closer, he had experienced second thoughts. Maybe he could get one of those out-of-towners to give him a break.

Larry had no skills to speak of, unless it was getting into trouble. He had finished high school and had gone straight to work, mostly unskilled jobs. He was bigoted and envious. He had taken to drinking and getting into fights that had landed him in the drunk tank. Fifteen years later, he was no better in character or station in life. His lack of skills had forced him to work alongside the people he scorned.

Nearby a figure stirred and he saw a white limb thrust out from underneath the blanket. Larry groaned inwardly, thinking of all the women working at the site, their dresses torn and disheveled and resisting all efforts of girlish modesty. He had made it a point to work, or simulate work, behind or below the shapeliest ones. When discovered, there were glares and frantic efforts to cover up. Which proved futile since most clothes had reached a point where they afforded little cover. He would smirk and wave at them.

Boldly, he got up and nonchalantly walked within a few feet of his target, Joe Hingle. Dropping to the ground, he arranged his blanket and laid down. Joe was lying somewhat apart from the others, probably because of his snoring. Larry waited ten minutes before he lifted his head and looked about. No one stirred. He stared in Joe's direction, attempting to discover if he was awake.

"Joe!" he hissed.

No answer.

Satisfied that Joe was asleep, Larry rolled over several times until he could reach out and touch Joe. He could see the edge of the holster sticking out from underneath the coat which served as Joe's pillow. Slowly he reached out and got his fingers on the edge of the holster and tugged gently. It didn't move. He applied more pressure. It still didn't budge. Larry cursed silently. If he pulled any harder, it was certain to wake the man. He reached out with both hands and started to pull. It was coming! But as he pulled the holster, it also pulled the coat from under Joe's head. The holster had snagged on the coat. Joe's head came up with a snort.

"Uh...Um... Whas that? Hey...Hold on there!" his hand reached out and caught Larry's ankle. "You trying to steal my coat...Who's there?" Joe had risen to a sitting position, one arm on the ground supporting his body, the other still holding Larry's ankle. Larry was trying to push away with his free leg. He tried to pull the gun out, but there was a safety strap on the holster.

"Larry Wilk! You little bastard...Give me that..."

"Keep away, Joe! Or I'll shoot," Larry had freed the gun from the holster and pointed it at Joe. With one hand and one foot, Larry attempted to push away, but Joe kept his hold on the ankle. Larry kicked out with his other foot and knocked Joe back, temporarily loosening his grip. Larry scrambled up, but just as quickly, Joe was up and coming for him.

Larry pointed the gun and shot.

"You...You shot..." Joe went down to his knees, his eyes wide open in astonishment, his hands clutching his side. Then he toppled over.

CHAPTER NINE

M ay 28, 2020
People sat up, awaken by the shot. Most were too sleep-ridden to understand what had awaken them. A noise, a shot, a clap of thunder? What was it? Where had it come from? Oscar was of a like mind. "What was that?

"Could have been a shot," said Esther.

Oscar grunted. "The only one with a gun is Joe Hingle."

"Where is he?"

"He usually sleeps over there," said Ruth Libwort, pointing.

"Get Doc Heerlson!" someone shouted. "He's been shot!" Oscar hurried in the direction of the voice. It was Carl Umbrall, holding Joe's head in his lap. "He's bleeding. Anyone got a light?"

David came running and shone his light on the scene. Walter knelt down, pulled up Joe's bloody shirt. He checked the wound, low, just above the left hip. He ran his hand around, feeling back of the body.

"It's not good," he frowned.

"Why?, What is it?"

"The bullet didn't exit," he looked at Oscar. "You know what that means?"

Someone brought a cot and they lifted Joe into it. They took him by the fire. It was now brightly lit.

Walter and Oscar followed slowly.

"It should come out," said Walter. "But there's no equipment, only first aid kits, and I'm not a surgeon."

"We can't let him die," Oscar exclaimed.

"An attempt at surgery could very well kill him. We have no X-ray equipment. I don't know where the bullet is lodged. What has been damaged? Hell! I don't even have a scalpel. It's lack of equipment and expertise. Stella's an operating room nurse and that's about the only ray of sunshine. Oh, but I forgot. The sun doesn't shine anymore."

"We have plenty of knives."

"Yeah, butcher knives. That's about the kind of surgery we'd get."

"So, what are you going to do?"

"For the time being, nothing. There's a slight chance he can get by. People have been known to survive with a bullet in their body."

The two nurses had already applied sulfa to the wound and bandaged it. There was a moan from Joe and he started to turn. Walter caught hold of him.

"Hold still, Joe, you're hurt. Oscar, give me a hand. All right, Joe, don't move."

"I...I always wondered what it was...what it was to get shot...felt like a big fist punched me in the stomach...it knocked my breath out...started to hurt..."

"Joe, how did it happen?" Oscar leaned over him. "Did you shoot yourself?"

"I didn't...think he had the guts."

"Who? What are you talking about?"

"Don't you know? It was Larry...Yeah, Larry...didn't think he had the guts."

"Larry!" Oscar exploded. "Larry shot you? Where is he? Anybody seen him?"

"Larry's gone. I don't see him around."

"Aaron! You and your bunch know anything about this?" Oscar boomed. "He was always hanging around with you guys."

"He was talking about Joe's gun the other day, but we thought we had talked him out of it. I didn't figure he would pull a crazy stunt like this."

"What does he hope to gain by taking Joe's gun? There's no one around but us," said Esther.

"Old Chinese saying," said Mary Tseu Tu. "Like 'power comes out of barrel of gun,' or something like that."

"Fat lot of good power is going to help him around here," Oscar snorted.

"If it comes to a question of 'survival of the fittest,'" said Dorothy, "a gun would make him more fit, at least in his opinion. Such has been the history of mankind. And dear God, in spite of our plight, it seems to be no different here."

"We'll soon know," said David. "He'll have to come back. He has no food and he can't go far without getting lost."

"He's got five bullets left," said Tom. "Walter, search Joe's pocket and see if he's got extra shells."

Walter went through Joe's clothes. "Nothing here."

"His coat," said Carl. "I remember seeing it on the ground."

"I'll get it," said David.

He returned shortly, Joe's coat on his arm. He extended his hand to Oscar, a small pouch in it. "There's six more in there."

"Throw it in the fire before he comes back for it," cried Jane Sestos.

"Too dangerous," said Oscar. "They can explode and hurt someone. David, take them and bury them. That way only one person knows where they are."

"But why make David do it?" exclaimed Nancy. "He might come back and threaten to shoot someone if the bullets are not turned over to him. Then some of his friends," she looked scornfully at Charlie and Don, "will tell him David has hidden them."

David looked at Nancy in wide-eyed wonder as she directed her anger at Charlie's bunch.

"No!" he said. "I'm as expendable as anyone else. Thank you, Nancy, but I'll take my chances."

"If David comes to any harm because of you," Thelma scowled at Charlie, "I'll personally skin both of you, and I know how to do it."

"With my help," added Nancy.

"And mine," said Jean.

"Look, you people have us all wrong," complained Charlie. "We had nothing to do with Larry's scheme. Like Aaron said, we tried to talk him out of it."

"All right, there's nothing to gain by arguing the point," said Oscar. "He got scared off. After a while he's going to calm down and figure that with a gun, he's got nothing to worry about. So, let's play it by ear. Try to get some sleep. I'll stay up with Walter and Stella."

The next morning Larry returned. He came sauntering in, the pistol openly stuck in his belt where everyone could see it. He walked up to a detail of four women preparing breakfast. One of them, Susan Longley, saw him and stopped her preparations.

"Well, Mr. Wilk, I'm glad to see you're turning yourself in. As an officer of the court, I can tell you it's a point in your favor."

"I ain't turning myself in, counselor," sneered Larry. "As usual you shysters have it all wrong. Nobody tells me what to do now. See this?" pointing to the gun. "This makes me ten feet tall."

"It makes you a murdering little skunk," called out Oscar, walking up to Larry.

Larry pulled out the pistol and stuck it under Oscar's nose. "I've been waiting for this. You want to repeat that, Jock?"

Esther rushed in between them. "Stop it! Both of you. Oscar keep quiet. Larry, take what you want and go."

"Well now, who said I was going anywhere. I like it here, with all my friends. As for taking what I want, I'm gonna do that anyway. I'll just start with breakfast. I worked me up an appetite last night."

"Yeah, running like a scared jackrabbit," spoke up Dorothy.

"Well, another smart mouth heard from, the head jock's girlfriend. I owe him and maybe you'll have to do since he ain't here. You know, I'm going to enjoy this. The old equalizer is gonna cut you jocks down and I don't care if your girlfriends get in the way."

"If Joe dies, you're a murderer," replied Dorothy. "There's fifty of us. Are you going to spend the rest of your life holding a gun on all of us? And there's nowhere to go and you don't know how to take care of yourself out there. I believe you acted recklessly without thought of the consequences. So now is the time to correct that. Hand over the gun to us and we'll be fair in our judgment."

"Nobody ever gave me a break," snarled Larry. "All of you, you always thought I was dirt, talking about me like I was some low life. So, what if Joe dies? He was always hassling me. I don't need you, I don't need nobody. But this gun is my power over you. So, who wants to be next?"

"Larry, you want to play king of the mountain, okay," said Oscar. "But we're going to have breakfast, then we're going digging."

"Didn't you hear me? From now on, I tell you what to do."

"Well what do you want us to do? Sit here and stare at you?"

"Why, Old Lar wouldn't keep you from digging that old dirt. You have my permission, of course."

"Thank you, Simon," replied Oscar, his sarcasm lost on Larry. "Everyone fall in at the diggings after breakfast."

"Of course, that doesn't include me. Right, Jocko?"

"Oh, perish the thought, Lar. Up to now only the sick and attending nurse have been excused. We'll miss you, Lar, but we'll struggle along without you. After all, rank has its privileges. Right, Lar?"

"Hey, you're learning," laughed Larry. "Maybe I'll let you stick around. I like having a big dumb jock waiting on me."

Oscar turned to his breakfast, his mouth grim, jaws tightening as he struggled to restrain his temper. There was no further comment from the others as they kept their eyes glued to their food.

JIM PLUNGED DOWN THE slope, held captive by the rope tied around his waist. It didn't protect him on his downward journey as every obstacle on the slope seem to position itself in his path. He tried to protect his face but was only partially successful as he felt a stunning blow to his head. Then his breath was expelled in one long woosh, as he came to a sudden stop, the rope around his waist squeezing it out.

He hung there for a moment until his head cleared and he caught his breath. Then he dug in his heels and pushed back to get some slack in the rope only to feel it pulling him sideways.

"John! John! Can you hear me? Where are you?"

"Over here!"

The voice came from his left, the direction the rope was pulling him. He inched his way toward him, careful of the footing. His head pounding from the lump that felt like it was still growing.

He made out John, sitting on the slope and holding his ankle. Looking up, Jim made out a large boulder, the rope sliding off its top as he approached John. The rope had snagged on the rock bringing the two men to a sudden halt, one on each side. He untied the rope and knelt by John.

"Is it your ankle?"

"Yeah, I think it's twisted."

"Sure it's not broken?"

He shrugged. "I'm no medic, but I don't think so. Up there, I thought I was taking a step forward, only there was nothing but space. I came down on it the wrong way, I guess. I went over and you came tumbling after."

"Well, my crown ain't broken, but it's the next worse thing to it. That rope caught that boulder otherwise we would be down on the bottom."

John shuddered. "One or both of us could have hit that rock head-on."

"What matters is getting you down with that gimpy leg."

"I can make it with a little help. If you can find a stick for me to lean on, it would help."

There wasn't anything suitable in the immediate vicinity, so Jim gathered their belongings and with John's arm around his neck, started the descent. In about thirty minutes they emerged from the haze and made out a valley below.

"Is that a new one?" asked John. "Or did we make a circle up there and we're back where we started?"

It was after three in the afternoon when they reached bottom. Jim decided to camp there to give John a rest. The ankle was swollen but not too much. They bandaged it as well as they could from a first aid kit. Then Jim foraged for a tree limb John could use as a crutch. He finally found the right size limb from the plentiful supply of trees covering the ground. He also found the marker. It was in the form of an arrow made of rocks, pointing to the left from where they had come down the hill. The rocks were laying on top of the ground, so it wasn't an oddity that had survived the recent cataclysm.

He hacked out a crutch with his knife and returned to John. "Here, try this for size. He helped John up and watched as John tried to move with his crutch. The point sank into the damp ground as John put his weight on it.

"We'll have to put something on the end to blunt it. In the meantime, do you think you can hobble a short distance? I found something interesting."

John whistled in surprise as he saw the marker. "Martin! It's got to be Martin."

"It could be someone else marking the trail as we were doing."

"No, It's Martin. I know that. He's been right all along. This marker is for us. It's pointing the way to the cave."

Jim looked at him. Even at this late date, the whole thing was still preposterous to him. That one man could foresee all this and now out of nowhere there was this sign pointing to their destination? They had climbed over a fog-shrouded mountain and tumbled down the other side. No one could have anticipated their coming down at this point. Still, what else could it be? Other survivors?

"I still see your look of skepticism," said John. "After all that's happened, you still don't believe?"

"It comes and goes, John. You'll have to admit its stretching belief to think he put that marker at almost the exact spot we came down. Explain that to me."

"I can't, but, we can follow it and let him explain it."

Jim sighed. "Well, not today. Let's get something to eat and a good night's rest before we tackle it tomorrow."

The next day John's ankle felt better and they started out although not at full speed. After two hours they spotted another marker. By the end of the day they had found two more.

"Have you noticed that every time we hit one of those markers, it's at the intersection of another canyon or branching passageway?"

"Then it's guiding us to a specific place."

"Yes, but where?, And how far?"

The next day dawned brighter and dry and that was probably why they were able to see the column of smoke rising far down the trail in the direction of the arrows.

"Jim, there it is. There's old Martin showing us the way with smoke signals."

"Don't tell me you read smoke signals?"

He laughed. "No, but I don't need to. The fact there's smoke means there's other people alive besides us."

"We might consider that if it isn't Martin, it might be someone else and they might not be friendly. There were several survivor groups in this state. Some could have made it. They weren't known to be friendly to outsiders."

"Start a fire. If we can see theirs, maybe they can see ours."

Starting a fire had not been easy with the intermittent rain. However, brush and debris had so picked up, that by digging into the rubble, they had been able to find fuel for their fire. Some of it was still damp and it produced heavy smoke, but this suited their purpose.

"How long should we keep this up, Jim?"

"Until we finish our breakfast. Don't pile on too much. We don't want to leave a smoldering fire when we go.

"I hope it's not too far off. We have to get results in the next five days or turn back."

"We'll make it, tomorrow for sure."

They made another day without contact. That night they built their fire until they had a miniature bonfire. With the low overcast skies, the glow of the fire reflected from the clouds. It reminded Jim of the incredible glow of the Phoenix area seen for many miles. On a camping trip into the mountains as a young boy, he had seen it for the first time. He couldn't believe it was Phoenix since it was some eighty miles away.

Next morning, they went through the same procedure with the fire. They were eating breakfast when they heard the click. Jim recognized it immediately, the cocking of a rifle. Turning around, they saw a rifle barrel pointing at them from the brush.

"Don't anyone move!"

DAVID KNELT BY THE river and ran his hand through the water. It was the same river that ran by his old neighborhood on the River Road. Only now it was three times as broad. Which meant that the homes there were flooded or washed downstream. Now it was some two blocks from their shelter.

It was six o'clock in the evening. In other times six o'clock this time of the year would still have afternoon sunlight. Now it was dark, and he could see a thin mist over the water by the light provided from the campfire in back of him.

He had taken to going by the river when he wanted to think. It brought back memories. Sad ones because his family was gone. And also, those somewhat happier, although, they too were intermingled with the sad moments of youth. Life had never been easy then. Just living in the River Road area was enough to place a stigma on its inhabitants. He laughed, thinking about it. Now all the surviving citizens of Stonecliff were in the same boat as the former inhabitants of the River Road, the poor and the homeless. And now you couldn't separate the minorities from the elite.

The strain was still showing on the survivors, especially at times like this when they had time to think.

They were alone, most had begun to realize this. Even so, it was not uncommon for some to stop working and go into fits of sobbing. Some just stared into space. At first, they were comforted by the others, but after a while they were left alone. What could one say, day after day of the same? Everyone was in the same fix.

It was getting late, so he started up the path from the river. He heard a rustling and saw a figure outlined against the distant campfire. "Who's there?" he flashed his light. A startled face was caught in the light.

"Nancy, You shouldn't be out here by yourself."

He came closer to where he could see her better. Even the torn and dirty clothes could not detract from her beauty. Her lovely red hair was pinned up. Her face was freshly scrubbed. All had taken advantage of the nearby river to bathe. Digging in the supermarket left everyone in need of washing. And the only change of clothing were the blanket ponchos.

This was the first time they had been alone. They had talked to each other, but always in the presence of others.

Now he was tongue-tied, wishing to continue the conversation but unable to find a fit subject to talk about.

"You shouldn't be out here alone. I can't vouch for all the men over there. Who knows what they might try, especially that Larry Wilk."

"You really think one of them might try to attack me? Or one of the other women? We come from the same town—went to the same school together."

"We're no longer in a civilized society. People can quickly revert to savagery if they feel their personal interests are threatened or if they want something bad enough. Look at Larry. There was no motive or sane reason for what he did."

"I don't think I can spend the rest of my life adjusting to types like him, but, thank you for thinking of my safety."

"Well, I owe you thanks for standing up for me after, after..."

"Yes?" he could feel her eyes on him even in the dark.

"I don't know, perhaps we should return. It's getting dark."

"David, After all these years, The situation we're in. Don't you think we should clear up some things? Like, why did you humiliate me in front of Gwen?"

His head snapped up. "Humiliate? You? I didn't...Well, is that what you thought?"

"You went right by me after I had called you. Gwen was there. What else should I call it?"

"But it wasn't..." he took a deep breath and then expelled it. "I saw you and Gwen laughing and looking at me. It wasn't hard to figure why. I had made an ass of myself that Saturday night, a stupid idiot. I saw you laughing at me. Why should I..."

"No!" she exclaimed. "It wasn't like that at all. Did you really think I would make fun of you?"

"I don't know, I didn't know then. I had screwed up our date. Me, the dumb kid from the River Road. What was I doing dating the rich girl when I didn't know the first thing about how to act at an exclusive club. Yes, I guess I was supersensitive that Monday morning when I saw you and Gwen laughing and giggling. What a jerk! I could almost hear those words coming from you and Gwen."

"You didn't think much of my character if you thought me capable of saying those things."

"You must understand. I didn't know you very well. For all I knew then, I was just another challenge, going out with the kid from the River Road. But I was sincere. I thought you were the most beautiful girl in school, And I still do."

She was quiet for a few minutes before she replied. "I guess you were different, and you were right about the challenge. Oh, not the way you thought. I never put myself so high above everyone else, although, I'm sure many thought that of me.

"I saw a shy young man, working and studying hard in contrast to those boys in my crowd. My crowd thought of nothing but having fun. Just get by. Why worry about the future? Putting down adults and those peers they believed were weird because they didn't act as they did. So I was intrigued by a boy who was different. I knew who you were, your background, your friends. I dated boys that I liked and not with regard to the social standing of their family. And yes, I was guilty of helping you at the restaurant. I knew you weren't familiar with classy, snobbish eating places."

He sighed. "It was so long ago and yet never forgotten by me. How could I have been so wrong? Too many personal hang-ups plus an enormous inferiority complex. Ready to believe the world was just looking at me. Ready to pounce on me when I slipped or goofed."

"I never thought that, then or now. You have worked hard to get where you are. And now in this crisis, you have shown your true mettle. Contrast that with Charlie, Don and Bill who are supposed to be from the so-called better families."

He swallowed hard. "Can you forgive my stupidity of fifteen years ago?"

"How can I refuse you when you still think me pretty, looking as I do."

"You don't know how relieved I am to have you as, as..."

"Your friend?" she laughed. "We've been that these past few weeks. What were we fifteen years ago?

"No, Forget that. We never got a chance to find out what we could have been. I've gotten to know you better out here. That's why I can forgive what happened then.

"So, do you need another friend besides Jim, Jean, John, or Thelma?"

"Yes, I want that, and more. But I don't know if I have the right to expect..."

"David, we face an uncertain future. Perhaps a lifetime measured in days. Can anyone afford to wait?"

"Fifteen years ago I sat in front of a girl that I adored. I don't know how I ever got the nerve to ask her out. You know how that turned out. You and that night and the days and nights to follow have never been out of my thoughts. I can see now that my actions were silly and immature. I regret how I acted. Youth and inexperience are my only excuse. But I won't use them because you can't change the past. There is so little left to us...I love you, Nancy."

She reached out to him. "It took so long to get that from you. How much time have we wasted?"

He pulled her into his arms. "I never thought I would experience this moment." He crushed her to him, kissing her lips, like a starving man. He moved on to her cheek, her hair, her throat. All the pent-up longing of fifteen years overcame them both. A release that left them limp. She returned his caresses. "I love you too, my darling. I followed you out here, you know."

"I'm glad. I never would have had the courage to say what I did. I thought you were unattainable. "Come on. We have to get back, but from now on, I think we'll find many reasons to walk back this way." Arm in arm they returned to camp.

CHAPTER TEN

HURRAH FOR THE CLASS OF 05

June 2, 2020

The two men looked at the muzzle of the rifle pointing in their direction. "Martin? Is that you?" John called out.

There was no immediate response. Then slowly a figure rose up from the brush. "John?"

It was Martin. Wearing jeans, boots, denim jacket and the Arizona U cap, he had a wide grin on his face. He came running, in turn, embracing both men.

"Damn! I'm so glad to see you both. I thought I was going to spend the rest of my life having no one to talk to but that young snippet, Daniel."

"Daniel?" John asked. "Someone else is with you?"

"Daniel is one of the young men that was helping me haul supplies to the cave. Two others were killed."

"Then the cave survived?" Jim asked.

"Of course," Martin beamed. "I told you it would."

"Why were you holding that rifle on us?" John asked.

"I saw the bonfire last night. I knew you had seen my smoke signal. However, I didn't know whom it was. When I crept in this morning I saw two bearded strangers. I didn't recognize the faces."

"That brings up another point," said Jim. "We've been following these stone arrows for the last ten or twelve miles. Did you set them up?"

"Yes. As soon as I realized that everything had changed, I knew you would never find your way back. So, I went up and down every canyon, gulch or pass that could lead to the cave and set markers pointing to it."

"It certainly helped. For a time, we were attaching all sort of supernatural explanations to it. Of course, that was silly. It's like predicting a great catastrophe, the survival of a cave and a bunch of people called the 'chosen.' Silly, wasn't it?"

"Ah, Jim, sarcasm is a poor substitute for admitting I was right. You haven't told me about your own adventures and the fate of my children."

John explained what had happened from the first day of the reunion up to this morning. Martin seemed particularly interested in their crossing of the mountain.

"That's going to make it difficult to bring them over. Unless we can find a pass or a notch in the mountain chain. Meanwhile I suggest we go back to the cave. John, since you have a bad foot, you can ride back."

"Ride?"

"Yes, on a horse. Oh, didn't I tell you? We have five horses, two mules, three cows, some pigs and chickens. That's just the live stuff. Wait until you get there, and I'll show you something that will knock your socks off."

Jim shook his head. "I guess we're lucky you aren't the archetypical medicine man of the old days. Your ancestors must be turning over in their graves."

"They turned over in their graves long ago when the tribe incorporated."

IT HAD BEEN ANOTHER hard day at the diggings, and just as fruitless as the previous ones. They had switched locations for the third time. Many had already lost patience and were ready to give up. Dorothy figured it was up to her to lift their spirits. That evening, after dinner, and with Larry departing for his nightly refuge, she took up the cause.

"Look, I'm responsible for having picked the location. I never said I knew the exact place. It was approximate. You've all seen the mess out there. You lose your sense of direction. We had a parking lot four or five times the square footage of the stores. They are in there. I feel it. We're going to hit it. Just don't give up."

"We're into our fourth week," said Oscar. "Every day that goes by makes it imperative that we find it."

"I still find it hard to believe," said Don Burins.

"We've been talking about it. If we build a raft, that current could take us to Phoenix. All our troubles will be over."

"Yeah, that sounds so simple," Oscar grunted. "Wonder why us dummies didn't think of that."

"There's a lot of 'ifs' in that plan," said Dorothy. "The condition of the river, here and downstream, the stability of a raft with that current and whether Phoenix is still there. If you're so interested in living, then get those ideas out of your head. You're asking for trouble if you leave here without knowing where you're headed. One month is just about gone and no one has come looking for us. Doesn't that tell you something?"

"You and your boyfriend seem very concerned about our staying here," said Charlie.

"Good God! Charlie, why do you persist in seeing conspiracy behind everything we do? We're trying to preserve human life, ours."

"What do you call Larry Wilk?"

"Oh, Now Larry is our fault? Larry is an unfortunate aberration. Who knows what pushes him to do what he's done. We had those kinds of happenings in everyday life before this came along. Did you run off to Phoenix every time a crime was committed?

"We have to start thinking the unthinkable. That this may be permanent. I have some seed packages from the shelter. We can clear a small area here and start a garden. When we finish with my father's store, we can try the Sears place. There may be other stores we can try to salvage. I'm trying to make the best of it because I have every reason to live. You saw that when Jim left. There are others out there. Ask Jean. Living is worthwhile to all of us, as it shall be for you. I have every confidence Jim will have a solution when he returns."

David stood up, "I agree with Dorothy. I too, have found a reason to stay alive. And here she is," he pulled up Nancy to stand next to him. "Just so there won't be any misunderstanding, we go way back. Only recently did we resolve our differences. We love each other. And since there is no clergyman or judge, there is no way to make it legal. From this day forth, we consider ourselves to be husband and wife."

He put his arms around her and kissed her. The class was silent for a few seconds, then they started to clap and whistle. Several got up to congratulate them, kisses for Nancy, claps on the back for David.

Dorothy held up her hands for silence. "I'm very happy for two fine people. But in regard to what David said, perhaps we can make accommodations. Jim and I discussed this because of our own situation. People got married by minister or judges. We cannot ordain a minister, but we can appoint a judge. Judges were appointed by the chief executive of a governmental entity. Jim is the elected leader, ergo. Jim could appoint a judge. In fact, since Oscar has been appointed to lead in Jim's absence, he could appoint an interim judge to serve until Jim made the appointment permanent."

"Dorothy," Sherman Longley gave her an admiring look. "It seems you would have made a good attorney yourself. You just made a very brief and eloquent opinion which I cannot fault. Susan and I are ready to cooperate in any way we can."

Dorothy was now in her element, making things happen. David and Nancy's situation whetted the curiosity of the group, especially the women. The Longleys, two of the most vocal complainers, were now getting enthused and willing to participate. She sidled up to Oscar and pulled him down to whisper in his ear. "What are you waiting for, you big lug. Now that we're getting some enthusiasm from the crowd, it's time to strike. Make an announcement on our new judge." Oscar grinned and nodded.

"Okay!" he waved his arms. "Hold down the noise so I can hear myself talk. I agree with Dorothy. Since some fellows want to get entangled with members of the opposite sex, I'll give you legal permission."

"You big oaf!" yelled Sylvia. "You just say that because you're afraid to commit yourself. Big macho man, you make me sick!"

There was laughter from the men and loud support for Sylvia from the women.

"Miss Remner's views on spinsterhood are well known, but we must give the majority the right to make their own mistakes. So, with an eye on what's good for the community, I shall appoint a judge subject to Jim's later approval. The full scope of the judge's powers shall be defined at a later date by, shall we say, the elders of this community. But specifically, the judge shall be empowered to officiate at any marital..."

"Will you shut up with the flowery speech and get to the meat of the announcement." Sylvia yelled.

"Yes, Oscar," Jane Sestos exclaimed, "you're very obnoxious with that anti-female talk. Remember that when it comes to elections, the women outnumber the men."

"If the ladies will please let me finish," Oscar smirked, "I shall continue. I am appointing, as judge of this community...Mrs. Susan Longley!"

Everyone was silent. Sherman's face fell, then he recovered and hugged Susan. Then the women exploded in a loud yell. All crowded around Susan to congratulate her.

Esther cornered Oscar. "So that was what it was about, running down women and bad-mouthing matrimony."

"How quick you were to condemn me. I love women. I really do."

"That's not news to me. Too many of them, as a matter of fact. I've known that for a long time."

She walked off leaving Oscar with his mouth open.

"Walter!"

The loud exclamation silenced everyone. The cry had come from Stella Mundick, one of the nurses. She had been checking on Joe Hingle whose cot had been placed far back against the side of the mountain. Walter hurried to her side.

He bent over Joe to examine him. He spoke in a low voice to Stella who replied in a similar manner. They were joined by the other nurse, Ellen Service. After a few minutes they stopped their ministerial efforts. They stood up and looked at each other. Then Walter pulled the blanket over Joe's face.

"He's dead, isn't he?" Oscar faced Walter.

Walter nodded. "There's nothing we could have done for him. Not with him carrying that bullet in his gut."

"That makes Larry a murderer," said Dorothy.

"For God's sake!" cried Walter. "Don't start on him about that. He's liable to go after somebody else if you keep pushing him about Joe. I can't help. I may as well be a butcher. I can't be a doctor operating under these conditions."

He strode off to the edge of the shelter and sat down, facing the darkness.

Dorothy too, walked slowly to her bed space, the party broken up. She had been congratulating herself on raising the spirits of her classmates. For a while, the camaraderie had returned. The joshing between Oscar and Sylvia allowed everyone to laugh and relax. Then Joe's death had turned everything around again. Once more they were reminded that anyone of them could be in Joe's place with a blanket over their face.

"I DON'T CARE WHAT THAT Walter's woman says," exclaimed Charlie. "She and Fenzer are up to something. They don't want us to leave here. Why?"

"Ssh!" cautioned Don. "You want them to hear you?"

"Why did you ask me here?" Aaron asked, looking at the three men, the third being Bill Miles. They were gathered almost in darkness. Aaron could barely make out their faces from the campfire light.

"I'm all for going ahead with that idea of the raft. Are you with us?" Charlie stared at him.

"You're going to build a raft?" Aaron chuckled. "You've been having trouble raising a shovel, but now you're in the raft building business. Just like that. How many rafts have you ever built?"

"How much does it take?" bristled Charlie. "Bill and Don will help me. I was hoping you would have sense enough to join us."

"Come to think of it, it doesn't take much. There's enough trees out there already cut down. Find the right size, pare them down, and then tie them together with rope or wire. Piece of cake! Of course, if you plan to keep this secret from the others, you'll have to work at night and far enough from here to keep them from finding out."

"You don't have any confidence in us, do you?" said Don.

"Now that you mention it, No! I doubt the three of you have ever gone camping without taking along all the finer things in life as provided by Sears's catalog of outdoor fun," said Aaron.

"And I suppose you're an expert?" said Charlie.

"Never claimed that. That's one reason I won't go with you guys. In my business I hire experts to take care of those little details. Jim, Oscar and John are the outdoor types. So far I can't fault them for what they're doing."

"Aha!" exclaimed Charlie. "I knew you would end up siding with them."

"I side with no one. You and I had a business deal. It's all gone now. Real estate, it's all there for the taking and dirt cheap. My having been in a deal with you doesn't put me on your side. I survive because I don't tie myself down with anyone, for business or sentimental reasons."

"All right. So you're not with us," said Don. "Are you going to tell them about our plans?"

Aaron shook his head. "Not at all. You want to kill yourselves, that's your business. In fact, I think you ought to take Larry with you. I'm sure he's dumb enough to go for your plan. He's out there in some rabbit hole. If you're going to build this raft in the dead of night, you're liable to step on him. And scared rabbits fight, especially if they have a gun to give them courage."

"We'll find some others that agree with us, including some of the women."

"I'd advise you to leave the women alone. You're going to have enough trouble navigating a flooded river with unseen obstacles without the added burden of women, always assuming you build that raft."

"Are you afraid your Linda might come with us?" Charlie smirked.

"Charlie, to quote Larry, how has a guy with your smart mouth managed to survive this long? I don't beat up on little people, but don't keep betting on it." He left them on that note.

CHAPTER ELEVEN

J une 4, 2020
  Jim and John arose refreshed and had a dip in the pool. It was cold, but not as much as they had imagined. Martin had brought straight razors and for the first time in a month they were clean cut. Most important they got a change of clothes. Martin had brought their bags.

"Umph," Jim leaned back, eyes half closed, a satisfied smile on his face. "All I need is Dorothy at my side and I could die happy."

"You can't die on me now," smiled Martin. "Not after I said you'd be a survivor. You want to make me a liar?"

"Well, I'm happy about my foot," said John. "What did you put on it, Martin?"

"Old Indian secret," Martin smiled. "I asked you once to let me make you my successor. You turned me down. You could have had all the smarts."

"What are you going to do with them, now that you are the last in your line? Daniel?"

"John, John, Daniel is just a child."

"I remembered I was twelve when you wanted me. Even then, you said I already had too many preconceived ideas."

"All right. When we get settled, I'll get to work on you. But you're going to have to be a bigger believer than in the past."

"By the way," said Jim, "you said the chosen would be the only survivors. How do you explain yourself and Daniel? And fifty people back there?"

"I can't speak for the fifty people since I haven't seen them, aside from Dorothy and Thelma. But Daniel is not, and neither am I, as far as I know."

"How do you know you aren't? You said you could see an aura, feel a force when touching. Is it something like a person being unable to tickle themselves? If you cannot see yourself or independently feel your own force, how do you know you aren't? Wouldn't it make sense that the last shaman of the tribe, the keeper of the secrets, would be a survivor, as you surely are?"

"I can't give you an answer, Jim. Perhaps surviving is more than surviving a cataclysm. After all, I'm sixty-one. That's why I must pass on my knowledge to John. Enough of this, the job at hand is getting those people here. I've stocked the cave with food, clothing, implements, plus the stock, so we're ready for them."

"The only obstacle is a whole mountain, a mere trifle," said John.

"That's right," replied Martin. "A mere trifle. We'll blow it down."

"Do you want to explain that?" said Jim.

"I have three boxes of dynamite."

"Dynamite?" Jim looked surprised. "Why in the world did you bring dynamite as a necessity for survival?"

"Elementary, my boy. We would be holed up in a cave. What if we were trapped in there?"

"Of course, the dynamite," smiled Jim.

"I think we ought to scout the area before blowing down mountains," said John.

The two younger men had finished putting on their boots which had come along with their clothing.

"I guess there's nothing more to be said," John glanced at Jim. "Shall we take the horses?" Jim nodded. "Let's try to complete this in three days at the most. I want to get back."

"We'll make camp where you two came down and explore from there, although my own explorations haven't found a cut in the mountains," Martin added.

... Back at the Camp ...

They buried Joe first thing in the morning. Oscar said a few words over the grave, then they trooped back to camp. Larry was waiting for them.

"Where have you people been? I'm waiting for my breakfast."

"We were burying Joe," Dorothy told him. "You know what that makes you?"

Larry shook his head. "I swear you smart mouths just won't learn. Joe got his because he was too damn stubborn. If he hadn't put up a fight for that gun he wouldn't be dead. He got what he deserved. Now let's have that breakfast."

The group had been listening and now they encircled the speakers.

"Get it yourself, punk!" snapped Dorothy. "No one's going to get near you or give you anything. The food is there, help yourself. But from now on, you're a leper. You're no longer a member of the group. God! I'm sorry we ever invited you. You're going to need eyes in the back of your head. You won't dare turn your back to anyone. It might be a shovel aimed at your head. Maybe a rock will come out of nowhere. You won't know what's in your food.

When you go to sleep, you may never wake up again. We'll be coming after you."

Larry stared at her. "You're crazy! I could kill you."

"Sure, why not. But look around you. When you take your first shot, your back will make a broad target. How many shots will you get off before you go down?"

A startled Larry whirled around to face those behind him. Then Dorothy laughed, and he turned again, realizing he was entirely surrounded. The gun was in his hand, waving it, although not at anyone in particular.

"Yeah," Dorothy continued. "Five bullets and then you're history. See Larry run. See the people run after Larry. See Larry die. Good-bye, Larry. Nobody's sorry about Larry."

Dorothy turned away leaving Larry to stare after her. The rest of the class drifted away.

"ALL RIGHT NOW. LOOK at this map I made. You'll have to bear with me. This small notebook was all I had, it's continued from one page to the other." The two men leaned over to get a closer look as Jim traced a path with his finger. "This is the canyon we followed from Stonecliff. As you see, it curved around and back, but its direction was generally eastward and southeast. Here is where we ended and where we went over the top, And as far as we know, the only way to connect the two canyons.

"But is it? One possibility may be that if we follow this canyon westward, there may be a cut or notch that we missed because of the haze on top. And that assumes it continues to parallel the one to Stonecliff.

"The other possibility is that if we had gone over the other side of the canyon, we might have found another passage to the cave."

"Even two possibilities are two too many," said John. "I'd say we need one or two days to explore this canyon westward before we even think of the other possibility. Even then, I would be more inclined to go back the way we came rather than go over the other side of the canyon in hopes of finding a better route. While we are under no timetable, the longer we stay away from the group, the more restless they will become. You know what that can lead to."

"There's always the dynamite," volunteered Martin.

"Have you ever handled that stuff?" Jim asked.

"No, Except for some tree stumps. But in this new world we have to do things we never did before."

Jim shrugged. "Let's wait until we see what we can find before we consider that route. John has a good point. There's a lot of restless, frightened people back there. They don't know about their immediate future and unless they've uncovered that cache of food and supplies, their future may be numbered in days.

"We'll separate. I'll go westward on this canyon. John, you search northwest from the cave. No farther than two days on horseback. We'll meet back at the cave no later than four days from now."

June 6, 2020

Oscar assigned the three men to the wood detail. Since he didn't care for the three, he figured it was a good way to get them out of his hair. Besides being chronic complainers, they were poor workers. He didn't think it would detract from his work force's productivity by assigning them to forage for wood.

He spotted Esther working on the rubble. Squatting next to her he picked at the dirt and rock. "I'm glad I have this opportunity to speak to you," she said. "I don't want you to antagonize Larry. Let him say whatever he wants. It doesn't hurt you and the rest of us know better."

"What if he wants you? He's made no secret that he'd like to take some of the women. He'd like nothing better than to take one of the jock's girlfriends."

"I'm not your girlfriend. I doubt he sees very much in me."

"You carry my name. That would be enough for him."

"Just the same, you leave him alone. If what you say is true, about him eyeing the women, then all the more reason not to bring attention to yourself."

"I guess you're right. But just the same it's galling to know there's a killer in the group and we can't do anything."

"One consolation, ever since that run-in with Dorothy, he's taken off and left us alone. Although he does make his daily stop to pick up food."

"If we could just find out where he holes up, we could set a trap for him."

"No, Oscar. It's too dangerous. Wait till Jim gets back."

"What does that mean?" he boomed. "What can Jim do that I haven't done?"

"Be quiet, you two," shushed Sylvia, who was working nearby. "We can't afford family squabbles. Our only cop is gone."

"You big baboon! I just don't want you hurt. Larry is just itching to use that gun after Dorothy tongue-lashed him."

"Aw, you love me," he smirked. "You know, I've been meaning to ask you...Will you marry me?"

"Quit horsing around. First you're getting feisty about Larry and now you're acting silly."

"Who's being silly? I made an honorable and decent proposal to the woman I love."

Esther stopped digging and looked at him. "No, you're not joking, are you? You realize that in the eyes of the Church we are still married?"

"There is no Church anymore, no rules, no laws except how we choose to live. However, I defer to your beliefs. Consider us still married or we can have Susan do it over again. Why do you think I appointed her?"

"After Dorothy pushed you into it."

"Well, what about it? Will you forgive a fatheaded fool? I love you. I always have."

Esther looked at him, then threw her arms around his neck. "Yes," she whispered in his ear. "Yes, yes, yes."

He kissed her hungrily. "Those many nights without you. I was slowly dying."

"No more, my dear, no more," she eagerly returned his kisses. "Tonight, we'll be together."

Sylvia whooped.

"Damn that Sylvia!" Oscar growled. They withdrew from each other and looked in Sylvia's direction. But she was not looking at them. She was staring at a hole in the ruins.

"There it is!" she yelled.

Oscar and Esther joined the others running to the site of the exposed opening.

"Can you see anything?"

"Ugh! What is that smell?"

"Okay," said Oscar. "We've broken through. We still have a lot more to clean up. As for the smell, there's probably bodies in there and decaying food. You're going to need strong stomachs. Remember, all we want is canned foods, toiletries, hardware items and such. Ready?"

They all moved in and debris started to fly, but it didn't last long as one by one they retreated, gagging from the stench. They gathered at a distance where their noses could get relief.

"Okay," Oscar instructed the others. "We'll put any bodies we find in those holes we dug, then pile on dirt and rock to fill them up.

"Carl, Pete and Frank will each form a team and take turns digging. Tom, Aaron, David and Josh will help me drag off any bodies and decaying food."

There were the usual protests and grumbling, but they fell in to their tasks. Bit by bit, stops and starts, gasping and gagging, each team took its turn. Sylvia, egged on by Dorothy, kept a running commentary on everyone's shortcomings, especially the males.

It was thus they finished out the day, pulling out two bodies and perishable items which they quickly buried. On the plus side they had a pile of canned foods which Walter ordered them to clean up. He explained his concern to Oscar.

"We're playing with fire. We could all be wiped out if an epidemic got started. I would be helpless to do anything."

"Walter, we need that food to survive. We chance an epidemic or eventually die from lack of food."

"I know, I know. It's just that I have that feeling of inadequacy. I'm supposed to heal the sick. Instead, I have to stand by and do nothing. I should have tried to operate on Joe."

"Don't blame yourself," Oscar put a hand on Walter's shoulder. "You could just as well have killed him if you had operated. You're not a surgeon and you had no equipment or facilities. Place the blame where it belongs, Larry."

"All right. I won't endorse it. If you insist on going ahead, I suggest they cover their nose and mouth, take a bath in the evening and change clothes."

"We can do all but the last."

"Oscar, if I might suggest. Why not send a small party to explore the residential area. Tell them to concentrate on gathering clothes. They might not find too much, but it's worth a try."

"Well, if it will ease your mind, I'll assign three people to do as you suggested."

"Don't do it to ease my mind. I should think it would ease yours. I doubt it would make you happy if they all came down sick because you didn't take precautions."

"Okay, Doc, you made your point. In fact, I'll appoint you to head the detail. Get a couple of the women to help you."

The group returned to camp laden with booty from the dig. Besides the canned food, there were toilet articles and some small tools. They had not yet broken into the Western Post which was the priority because of the clothes it held.

The camp was deserted. Oscar and the others stopped, their good-natured and happy exchanges turned silent.

"Where's everybody?" he exclaimed.

"Maybe they're out by the river," Dorothy speculated.

"They should be preparing the evening meal, but there's no fire."

"Something's happened."

"What could it be? There's no one around, except Larry."

"He couldn't have shot four women without us hearing the shots."

"The wood detail should have been in by now. Where are they?"

"David!" Oscar boomed. "You and Frank take a look by the river. Esther, you'd better round up a crew for kitchen duties if we expect to eat tonight."

"There's no sign of a struggle here," said Tom. "Larry didn't have enough bullets to shoot seven people, and even if he did, he wouldn't trouble himself to drag off the bodies. No, wherever they went, they went willingly."

"You had Charlie, Don and Bill on the wood detail?" Aaron looked at Oscar.

"Yes, why?"

"By now, I'd say they're somewhere downstream on a raft."

"A raft? How do you know that?"

"Several nights ago they tried to rope me into some scheme to build a raft and float all the way to Phoenix. I told them they were crazy and to forget about it."

"That's the second time you've known in advance and chose to keep quiet. How many are we going to lose this time?"

"Look, Oscar, I thought both ideas were crazy and I told them so. I didn't think either idea would be carried out, they were so dumb. I'm sorry about Joe and I'm sorry about those women if they bought Charlie's scheme, but you're better off with those three gone. They were out for themselves and of no use to the group."

"And you?" Dorothy looked at him. "You're not out for yourself?"

"I've always had to look after myself. Have I shirked my duties here?"

"No," Oscar shook his head. "You've done your share, and more. But, why do I get the feeling you're not with us?"

David and Frank returned. David held up an axe. "We found this, but there's no one out there."

"There were footprints and signs of activity at the edge of the river, but it could have been any of us," said Frank.

Oscar explained to them what Aaron had said. Frank nodded. "That would explain what seemed to be logs dragged into the river."

Oscar concurred. "The damn fools built a raft and took the women with them. Shows how dumb they are, leaving the axe. They could have used it."

"And they almost cleaned out our food supply," said Esther. "It's a good thing we hit pay-dirt today else we would be in bad shape."

"Are you going after them?" Dorothy asked.

"After what they have done to you?" Aaron snorted. "If I know that bunch they'll pile up on the rocks or drown."

"No thanks to you," Oscar growled. "It's too late to go off in the dark. Besides, with that current, they're pretty well downstream by now. We'll search in the morning.

"Maybe they'll be on the rocks," he looked at Aaron.

CHAPTER TWELVE

June 7, 2020

Jim pulled up on the reins of his horse and gazed up at the unbroken wall of mountain range. It was midmorning of his second day on the trail. Starting from the point where they had come over the mountain, Jim had followed the canyon westward. It was desolate, broken country that offered no passage through the heights on his right. The haze hung low and there was no way to gauge the height of the mountain short of climbing it.

It was now fifteen days since they had left the others and a month since the disaster. A month out of one's life, but what a month. Setting aside the tragedy of the cataclysm, they had really accomplished a great deal in such a short time. By now they should have uncovered the super-market. He and John had accomplished half their task, finding the cave. That alone was something he had expected to take a long time, if ever.

The horse perked up its ears and snorted. Jim turned around and surveyed the area around him. But there was nothing to see that could have alarmed the horse.

"If you were human, I'd say you're putting me on, but I know animals are not devious. You heard something."

He continued following the canyon, trying to go slower so he could check the reason for the horse's alarm. The horse, on the other hand, never hesitated, even seemed eager to continue. Evidently, whatever had attracted the animal's attention was not threatening to keep him from advancing.

A few minutes later Jim saw the probable cause for the horse's reaction. Water! A rushing roaring river that carried so much water that an overflow had seeped into the canyon like a tributary. It also blocked his path.

The trail ended here. The river was too broad and the current too fast to cross. Unless there was a ford downstream or even upstream. He rejected that immediately. With so much rain in the recent past, it was unlikely there was any safe place to cross. It seemed that all the rain north of here was rushing through this one river.

North? Was this the same river that ran by Stonecliff? The one close by his classmates? It could be. The distance he had traveled, some fifty miles, should put him directly south of Stonecliff. It couldn't be more than twenty miles, possibly thirty miles away from here. That made the river his cut in the mountains. The drawback was the torrent of water going in the wrong direction. It was pointless anyway. Navigating that stream, even with the current on your side, was suicidal.

Not favorable, but why cross? He was already on the right side if it was the same river. Was there stable footing on the banks to allow travel upstream?

He decided to investigate. Jim tied his horse and proceeded on foot. He skirted the edge of the water that had flowed into the canyon. The water was not as swift, and even stagnant in some places, along the bank. His doubts started as he encountered debris piled on the edge of the bank, making it difficult to walk without climbing over trees and branches. They looked like logs that had been sent downstream to a lumber mill. Looking upstream, that was all he could see. The pressure of the raging torrent had pushed and piled up brush and trees on the banks and they resembled a box of toothpicks haphazardly thrown on a table, the ends pointing in all directions. The mountain rose straight up from the mess. The river gap was clogged. There were no banks. The footing would be treacherous.

He also saw the body, a woman, judging by the bright print dress. Her body had been caught at the edge of the stream and was floating face downward. The dress caught his attention. He was sure he had seen it before. At the reunion! At the camp! She had to be one of the women from the group.

He returned to the horse and brought him up as close as he could. He got the rope from the saddle and found a place close enough to tie one end to it and the other to his waist. Then he slowly edged towards the water. The last few feet he had to crawl over brush and trees.

Using a small branch he attempted to snag her by her belt. It took several tries before he succeeded. He floated her closer, feeling the tug as the river tried to reclaim her. He finally got her close enough to touch, but lying down as he was, he had no leverage to pull her up without endangering his own safety. He exhaled, resting his head on his arms. After a few minutes he resumed. He attempted to dislodge a tree trunk next to him while holding on to her. After much effort, swearing, his arms tired, the tree came loose, almost floating away. He managed to hold on to it and adding more scratches to his arms. He maneuvered the tree until it was at a ninety degree angle to the body.

Then taking a chance of falling in the water, he half rose and pushed the tree into the water while still holding on to her. The tree went down and under the body, then floated upward bringing the body clear off the water. Letting go of her belt, he pulled at the floating tree with both hands and got it against the debris on the bank. He fell back, exhausted, his arms and hands shaking from the tension of the last few minutes. He rested on his back, staring at the gray overcast sky. After a few minutes he sat up. He got a firm footing and turned her over. A purse flopped between his feet, her belt looped through the handles of the bag.

My God! It was Betty Leye! What could have happened? Did she fall in and drown?

Jim finally made himself examine the body. He noticed bruises on the arms and legs; her dress was ripped just below the rib cage. Carefully he pulled aside the cloth and saw a larger bruise.

He sat back and speculated. The bruises didn't seem to be the cause of her death. The skin was not broken. Only a doctor could tell. He felt her head. There were lumps, but again, no sign of penetration. Most likely the lumps and bruises were caused by hitting or bumping into objects on the river. The most probable cause remaining was drowning.

The puzzle was why she was here. And why she was carrying her purse looped through her belt. She was dressed and her purse secured in order, for what? Ordinarily a woman would hang it over her shoulder. It suggested a more strenuous undertaking.

God! Did she get out on the river on purpose? Suicide?

But why the purse if she was going to kill herself?

There were too many questions and the answers were not to be found out here.

He dragged the body towards more solid ground, mentally apologizing to her for not being able to treat her remains in a more decent manner. He dug a grave of sorts. He had no tools. Then he said a few words which he hoped were appropriate.

He mounted his horse, gave one last look at the river, then at the grave. The river was not the way to go. He headed the horse back to the cave.

"CARL, AREN'T WE GOING to do any digging today?" asked Sylvia.

"Well, since Oscar's leading that search party for the runaways, I guess we can take a break."

"We can't sit here doing nothing. We have to finish that supermarket and then search for the Post."

"People aren't exactly in the mood. The attrition rate has taken its toll. First there was Shirley, then Edna and Joe. Larry has gone wild. Now seven more are gone."

"They're gone, not dead," said Sylvia.

"I wouldn't give much for their chances. Even Aaron knew well enough to stay out of it. Then there's Jim and John. Who knows if they'll return?"

"Fifty-four little Indians," Sylvia mused.

"What?"

"That old rhyme 'ten little Indians...' It ends with '...then there were none.' They even made a movie based on that."

"Naturally. Trust you to know that significant fact. Poor Sylvia, stuck in this new world, deprived of all the niceties of the old, especially the late, late movie."

"How do you know what I do at night? Have you been peeking in windows?"

"I think it's ghoulish to think we're going to die one by one," said Jane Sestos, who was sitting nearby.

"I can tell you one thing. If we don't keep digging, we're going to die," Sylvia glared at them. "And not one by one but of mass starvation."

"You're getting to sound like Dorothy, push, push push," said Carl.

"Sylvia Remner, the new cheerleader of Stonecliff High," cracked Jane, then immediately was contrite.

"Sorry, Sylvia. I didn't mean it to sound as if she was one of your little Indians. It wasn't supposed to be offensive."

"You mean bitchy," said Carl. "Hmmm, You know, Sylvia, you might not make such a bad cheerleader at that. The legs are good, figure could use a little more meat, but you have to smile and laugh. You need a lot of practice in that department."

Sylvia colored. "Quit talking about me as if I was a piece of meat hanging on a hook. I can laugh. I laughed myself silly when the principal had you on the carpet for stinking up the school with that, that, compound."

"Sulphur dioxide," Carl smiled.

"Whatever, So, my legs are good, huh? Is that all you have to do, look at woman's legs? You're getting like Larry."

"Pervert!" said Jane.

"I can hardly help it," smiled Carl. "What with the condition of your clothes. Everywhere you look-legs."

"All the more reason you should get off your duff and dig us up a clothing store."

"What! You want to spoil the only good thing left to us boys, girl watching? I notice you do a bit of watching yourself. When we bathe in the river."

Sylvia flushed again. She couldn't remember when a man had caused her such discomfort. But inwardly she was delighted with the direction of the conversation. She liked the give and take in the battle of the sexes.

She studied Carl more closely. Besides being a classmate, he had been the science teacher at the school. A married man with children, he was a pleasant person, very well liked. He was of medium height and build and with an almost perpetual twinkle in his eyes, as if he were laughing at the world. He had been the class clown and prankster. She had immediately stuck him with a Hollywood tag, a young Burgess Meredith. Until the disaster, the extent of their relationship had been occasional exchanges of greetings on the campus. The conversation usually pertaining to school business.

"Why shouldn't women look at men if they want to," interjected Jane. "You men are always gawking at women's legs, why shouldn't we?"

"Why not indeed. You want to gawk at my legs? I can assure you they're not as pretty as yours or Sylvia's. Whom do you watch, Jane? Tom Wadley? I notice your eyes following him."

Now it was Jane's turn to blush. "Damn you, Carl! Why don't you stick to women's legs and leave my eyes alone. Besides, if you watch his eyes, you'd know they only see Linda Storey."

"Aha! So you do watch him," taunted Carl.

"Oh shut up!" snapped Jane. "Why don't you drop in that hole we dug."

Carl smiled and reached over to pat her hand. "Forgive me. I was trying to get our minds off the tragedy. I didn't mean to hurt you."

Sylvia saw that Jane was miserable. My God! She's in love with Tom, and Tom's mooning over Linda. That's all we need, another triangle.

Jane smiled wryly at Carl. "Yes. I should have known. But sometimes your clowning can hit a vulnerable spot."

"I guess I should direct my humor at those that can understand me. How about it, Sylvia?"

"Oh yes," Sylvia grimaced. "By all means, try it on me. I don't have eyes for anyone. I suggest you continue watching women's legs. The worse that can happen to you is a slap on the face."

She whirled around, her skirt flaring out revealingly and left them.

Carl whistled, appreciatively.

The search party returned in late afternoon, empty handed. "They're gone," said Oscar. "We found no trace of them except where they built the raft. God help them. I hope they reach their destination safely, wherever that might be."

"As far as we know, they got off all right," said Aaron. "Which may not be too far. That raft could break off very easily in that current, not to mention any obstructions on or under the water. If it did, we'll never know because any evidence will be swept downstream. As far as we know, they're no better than Edna or Joe."

Oscar gave him a sour look but said nothing.

"Look," said Dorothy. "Let's not lose sight of the fact all this could have been prevented. Edna let her grief overcome her good judgment. Those seven could be sitting here safely if they hadn't questioned Jim's motives.

"There's forty-four of us now. Let's not make that any less by dying of apathy or self-flagellation. We're survivors. We're special people. If we can survive a world-ending catastrophe, these other problems are a piece of cake. We've got food, a shelter over our heads and pretty soon the shirts for our backs from Dad's store. You never had it so good, and it's all for free."

There was a long groan from the crowd, but she noticed there were a few smiles at her attempted humor.

Tom, who had been in the search party, made a beeline for Linda.

"I'm glad to see that all of you made it back," she said. "No one defected, and no heroic efforts to save that worthless bunch and endanger more lives."

"No chance of that since we never laid eyes on them. How about you?"

"Why, I'm fine. If it weren't for this dampness I might even forget the surroundings. Sometimes I think there's fungus growing on parts of my body."

"Well, What I meant, You know, by now we're all that's left. We're starting new lives. People are, making commitments. Jim and Dorothy, David and Nancy, Oscar and Esther are back together. I thought, you and I..."

"Yes," she sighed. "I guess I know what you mean. However, my feelings haven't changed since the last time I talked to you."

"What about Aaron?"

"Well, what about Aaron? Am I supposed to account to you for his actions or mine?"

"No, no, but, shouldn't you, I mean, have you thought about, you know, a choice?"

"A choice!" she burst out. "Just why am I supposed to make a choice? Has some rule been formulated that says each woman has to choose a man? Have I been singled out as 'most eligible' unattached woman?"

Tom suddenly felt like a little boy asking his mother for a piece of candy. Her outburst had dampened his ardor and he saw himself in a way he didn't like.

"I apologize for bothering you," he said stiffly and walked off.

After dinner, Linda wandered off in the direction of the river. There wasn't much to see that she hadn't already seen, and it was getting dark. She was seeking privacy not scenery. It was quiet except for the murmur of voices from the camp and the rush of the current. Even with forty four people, no, forty one, since Jim and John were gone and Larry was hiding somewhere. Yes, even so, there was little privacy to be had because their world was so small.

She wanted time to be alone and think. She sat on a bluff overlooking the stream and stared into the darkness of the river and beyond, seeing nothing of course.

She felt alone even though surrounded by her classmates. At night there was that blink of an eyelash before you went to sleep after a hard day's work.

In the morning there was that little time before you arose to face a new day. Then all your thoughts were centered on the day's work and the filth and stench, the sweat and discomfort that went with it. Who ever said that ladies don't sweat?

Not that it was unendurable. The others were bearing up and she prided herself that she would not whine or complain. The luxuries of life were gone, but they were gone for everyone. One could even say that some good had come out of it. The hard work made everyone forget and sleep better.

Their enforced diet had made everyone lose weight, even dumpy Thelma Rattling. It was her personal life that bothered her. She had made a fool of herself that day of the reunion, taunting Jim with Tom. What had caused her to do that? To get back at him? She hadn't even taken the time to find out how Jim would react at the reunion. No, she had plunged right in to embarrass him using Tom. Now Tom thought he had acquired territorial rights. Meanwhile Jim had taken up with Dorothy.

Did he really love her? Was he, in turn, trying to make her jealous? No, she had to be fair. Jim would not do that. As for Dorothy, she was a beauty in her own right. Moreover, her go-go character, her drive fitted their new environment. She made a fitting companion for Jim. She had lost him fifteen years ago because she couldn't accept his outdoor life and long absences. Now here they were, living under the very conditions she abhorred. There was no return to yesterday for her and Jim. It was all in the past and buried, and she had helped nail the coffin with her spiteful performance at the reunion. She heard a crunch behind her, a step on the brush. She whirled, expecting to find Larry behind her. She saw a form outlined by the campfire.

"Linda?" It was Aaron.

"You scared me. You shouldn't sneak up behind me that way. Not with Larry still at large."

"Sorry. I thought I was making enough noise so you could hear me. You shouldn't be here if you're afraid of Larry."

"Really, I wasn't thinking of him until I heard your step. Were you looking for me or just walking?"

"I was concerned about you being out here by yourself."

"I needed to be alone with my thoughts. Even with so few of us, it gets crowded sometimes."

"Then I'll honor your need and leave."

"No, Stay. I'm not having much luck with my thoughts. Besides, it seems others want to get a view of the river too." She nodded towards another couple headed for the river. It was David and Nancy.

Aaron glanced at them. "Yes, why not? This is the only time of day you have to socialize."

"Is that what you call it?" she sniffed. "It looks to me like they're headed for a heavy necking session."

He looked at her. She could tell he was exasperated. "I believe they made their feelings quite public the other day and I heard no clucking from the hens. Those two come from opposite sides of the track, but they seem to have hit it off. Nothing will ever be the same."

"Well, the rich could always afford to dabble, to indulge their little lives with some escapade."

"No one is rich any more, at least in terms of money. You can love someone for themselves."

"Is that what worried you before? Did you think that every woman that showed an interest in you was after your money?"

"It never bothered me. If I returned the interest, then so much the better. My comment was in regard to David and Nancy. Her money would have made a difference to him."

"I'll bet it wouldn't have made a difference to you if you were poor and the girl was rich."

"Of course not," he replied. "Because whatever she had, I would have doubled. I have that much confidence in myself."

"Well, Does it really matter? As you say, no one is rich any more. Nancy's timberlands have no more trees. Dorothy's supermarket is flattened and whatever food was salvaged, no one paid a penny for it."

"Ah, Finally we get to the crux of what makes Linda so unhappy these days."

"What are you talking about?"

"I'm talking about the eternal triangle, Dorothy, Jim and Linda. The problem is that it exists only in your mind."

"And yours, apparently," she snapped. "Everyone seems to know how I feel. Is my mind such an open book?"

"Are you going to carry a torch for the rest of your life? Face up to it. You lost Jim Fenzer a long time ago. He seems to have gotten over it. Ironically, you are the one that got married while he remained single. That's hardly the way to get him back. Always assuming you both wanted to. Do you think he would remain faithful to you and someday come back to claim you?"

"Oh shut up, Aaron. What business is it of yours how I feel?"

"I made it my business because I love you."

She made no reply for a few seconds. "Revelations do abound, don't they. First Tom and now you. How many more are out there?"

"Not Jim," he said. "Dorothy has him. She always wanted him. Just like Tom and I wanted you."

"I don't like that. You talk as if I were an object to be bought over the counter. Besides, as far as I know, I'm still married. There's no corpus delicate or whatever those lawyers say about missing bodies."

"Oh for God's sake! When are you going to stop hiding behind that excuse? Your husband is dead. Everyone is dead except us. And if you're still married, why the long face because Jim and Dorothy are in love?"

"I don't have to explain myself to you or anyone else."

"Maybe not to the rest of us, but surely you need explaining to yourself."

"Just go away, Aaron. Leave me alone."

"All right, But I meant what I said. I love you."

"Just like that? You put as much emotion in that as if you were ordering a cup of coffee."

Aaron flushed. He closed the distance between them and took her in his arms and crushed her to him. He kissed her hard on the lips. She put her hands on his shoulders to fend him off. Then she relaxed. She made no further effort to resist or encourage him.

Frustrated, he let her go. "I guess the rumors are true. You are the ice princess. I'm not your type. I apologize for taking advantage."

"Oh, Aaron, it's not a question of type or coldness. What is right, anyway? It's just that, that I'm confused. So many things have happened, one right after another. I don't know where I stand. I can't be like the others, so quick to jump into someone else's arms."

"So quick? It's been a month. No one's spouse has shown up to claim their partner. As for others jumping in someone's arms, as I understand it,

David and Nancy, John and Jean go back a long way. Oscar and Esther were married. Tom once had a date with Dorothy and all she wanted to know was about Jim. I would hardly call it something that sprouted overnight. So let's face reality."

"How I hate that word, 'reality.' Everyone wants to use it as an excuse to justify their actions. It's just frustrating."

"Come on," he caught her arm. "I think you'd better go to bed. You have a bad case of nerves and I helped cause them. I'm sorry for that, but not for saying I love you, or kissing you."

She looked at him. "Perhaps there were a few revelations tonight. I need to sort many things out in my mind. For what it's worth, my husband and I were having problems. Maybe its guilt I feel. As if I were responsible for all this," she waved her hand around.

"Things happen all the time," he said. "Ranging from the trivial to a disaster like this. Who knows whether it is by design or accident? It happens and people get caught in it and it further complicates their own problems, or sometimes solves some of them. Shall we go?"

She didn't reply, but started back to camp, brushing off her dress. He followed a few steps behind her.

CHAPTER THIRTEEN

June 8, 2020

Dorothy arose out of the water, dripping and reached for a tablecloth being used as a towel. The water, at least that part close to shore where they bathed, was murky but everyone had overcome any aversion in their efforts for any semblance of cleanliness. Then too, Walter was very strict in enforcing the bathing rule.

But even Walter had not been too happy about using the river to bathe, or drink, for that matter. He had explained to Oscar it was the lesser of two evils. There seem to be less chance of contamination from the water than exposure to the ruins.

Ordinarily, all the women took their baths in groups with one standing guard to ward off peeping Toms. Only the men took their baths with carefree abandon, not caring that anyone might see them.

Today she was the last one. She had tarried at the shelter while the other women made a dash for the river. She was exhausted, more mentally than physical. As always, she was deeply involved in the daily activities which included the ups and downs of their existence and their subsequent effects on the mental attitude of the group.

"Ups and downs" was truly descriptive. From the joy of the reunion followed by the disaster. The breakout from the basement to Edna's death. The miserable search for shelter to its discovery. The happiness of Susan's appointment to Joe's death. Now the supermarket discovery followed by the disappearance of the seven classmates. It had been one "up" followed by a "down.

What was next? Jim had been gone over two weeks. Was the jinx still working? Would the next downer be Jim's failure to return?

She toweled herself, feeling more relaxed and at ease after her bath. She should have done this right away instead of letting apathy and worry take over. She put on bra and panties, rinsed her feet, dried them and then slipped into her shoes whose heels had been knocked off. She stepped to the water's edge to soak and wash her towel.

Faced with a shortage of cloth, they had cut up the tablecloths salvaged from the tables at the school shelter. These had substituted for towels and all had agreed they should be washed, rinsed and hung up to dry after each use.

Only Margaret Stanton had been snotty and refused to comply. Whereupon, with much enthusiasm, the others had seized her and snapped a wet towel across her bottom. Thereafter all obeyed the rules.

As she crouched over the water, she heard heavy breathing behind her. She turned to face a leering Larry Wilk.

"Isn't this a pretty sight," his eyes running over her body.

"What are you doing here?" she exclaimed. "You know the rules."

"Why can't you people understand? The rules are not for me. I make my own. And right now, here is where I want to be. I figure you need some company, understand me?"

"Oh, I understand you, you creep," she was furious. "You ought to hear yourself. You don't even make a good third-rate villain. My God! To think that at the end of the world I have to listen to that drivel from a little shit like you!"

The instant she let out the expletive, she knew it would have its consequences, but her anger knew no bounds. Larry flushed. He took a step forward and slapped her face, knocking her down into the mud at the edge of the river.

"That's your first lesson in manners," he snarled. Dorothy was seething with anger. The slap had brought tears to her eyes. Sitting there in an undignified and immodest position, she could feel the water and mud on her bottom. Feeling degraded, she struggled to regain her wits.

"Now for lesson number two, you're going to like. You've been pretty free with that jock, but now he ain't here. I guess I'll have to be the man you need."

"You little jackass! You're not even half a man, much less the man I need."

"You're really going to get it, bitch. I owe you and that..."

She shifted her eyes to look behind Larry and yelled. "Oscar! Look out! He's got his gun!"

Larry cursed and turned around while pulling out his gun.

Dorothy sprang up and started running for the river, but the treacherous footing was her undoing. She slipped and went down to her knees.

"You lying bitch!" screamed Larry, finding no Oscar in sight. He turned to confront her only to see her back as she ran for the river. He raised his gun and fired as she slipped on the mud.

He came up behind her and pulled her by the hair. "You don't have a choice now. You're getting it."

"Shooting at me gave you away," she gasped. "They'll be coming after you."

"And I've got the gun!"

"You can't shoot them all. They won't let you get away with harming a woman."

He hesitated, then pulled her away from the edge of the water. "They can't do anything if we're not here."

He let go her hair, got her arm by the wrist and twisted it behind her.

"Now you just march," he ordered.

"Wait! My clothes!"

"You won't need them. Move!" He pushed her along the water's edge and away from camp.

The suspense was over. The "downer" had arrived.

The group came running to the river in response to the shot, Oscar in the forefront.

"Larry? Is that you? What are you shooting at?" There was no answer and Oscar could see no one.

"Do you think it could have come from elsewhere?" David asked as he and the others crowded behind Oscar.

"It sounded close to me," said Tom.

"Oscar, look!" cried Linda. "Here's someone's dress. It looks like..."

"That's Dorothy's dress!" shouted Sylvia. "I recognize it."

"Oh God! Has he shot her too?"

"I don't see a body here," said David. "Spread out! And get some lights! It will be dark soon." Carl and Sylvia returned to camp for the lights.

However, even with lights, they could find no trace. After an hour of searching, Oscar call them in. "It's no use. She's not around here. In the morning we'll take a closer look. At least there's no body."

"Maybe he threw her in the river." offered Jane.

"Don't presume the worse," said Sylvia. "He could have taken her with him. He's threatened her before and making advances to other women. Perhaps that's why he took her."

"May I make a suggestion?" said Frank Jaboty. "I've had some experience in the outdoors and what we've done here hasn't helped. We've trampled over the ground and made a mess of tracks. In the morning we can make a better check. Two sets of tracks in this mud shouldn't be too hard to spot."

"That's a good idea," said Oscar. "Everybody else will stay out of the way."

"You forgot one thing," said Tom. "Sooner or later he has to come back for food. If he's got Dorothy, he would have to bring her along."

"Not necessarily," replied Oscar. "He could leave her tied up in his hole, maybe already dead. He's not going to admit to harming her."

"What do we do then?"

"One thing we can't do now is to try to figure what Larry will do. We'll have to wait for our search tomorrow or until Larry comes in.

"So, back to camp. We'll eat, then pray, and worry."

June 9, 2020

"This is where we say good-bye," Jim told Martin. The three men had ridden to the base of the mountain where they had come over originally.

"Never say good-bye. I thought that was a cliché in the white man's world," said Martin.

"Maybe a cliché, but very apt in this new and imperfect world."

"Don't think otherwise. Remember, you have fifty people back there, depending on you to lead them out of the wilderness."

"Now whose talking clichés?" said Jim? "And by my count, it is only fifty-one. Betty is the third one we've lost, that we know of.

"We'll see you back here in about a week or two with the first contingent."

"I'll be right here. Daniel and I have to finish protecting the stock in the cave. You know, in addition to saving our hides and that of our animals, our cave also saved some wild life. So, we have to protect the chickens from the fox. Then we'll camp here, waiting for you. Maybe we can do something to make it easier for you to come over the mountains."

"Don't do anything drastic," said John. "Remember, you're not a young man anymore."

"John, I haven't been one for quite some time."

Both men were carrying heavy packs. Jim had picked up some clothing and shoes for Dorothy. John had done the same for Jean. In addition, John was carrying his old Winchester which he had refused to leave behind. Jim had refused Martin's offer to take a firearm.

They waved at Martin and started up the mountain.

OSCAR ASSIGNED FRANK Jaboty to tracking Larry and Dorothy.

"I'd go with you, but I'd better stay here in case he shows up for food. Think you can do it alone, Frank?"

"No problem, Oscar. I know my way around here."

"Just be sure he doesn't see you first. I don't want to write a letter to your family."

Frank laughed and left in the direction of the river.

"What about the rest of us?" Walter asked. "I think I should follow up on that residential area search. Stella and Ellen think we should locate the hospital to stock our dispensary."

"Good idea, Doc," Oscar nodded. "Take Peter and Helen along to help you.

"I want Esther, Irene, Peggy and the Longleys to stay here for camp chores. Tom, you take the rest to the diggings. I think keeping busy is the best way to forget our problems. And Tom," he took him aside where the others couldn't hear, "you might conduct a personal and private search for a gun, a hand gun. A store that caters to outdoor types should sell firearms, wouldn't you think?"

"You going after Larry?"

"What do you think? I can't afford to let Larry run amok any more. Who will be the next victim?"

"Are you two going to start blazing away at each other? The next victim could be an innocent bystander."

"That's why I want a handgun I can conceal. He won't have a chance to draw."

"You're going to kill him in cold blood?"

"I'm going to surprise him and disarm him, but if I can't, I'll do whatever is necessary."

"I gather Esther doesn't know about this."

"No. And she isn't going to find out, from you or anyone else."

Tom nodded. "Okay, I'll try to fill out your order."

DOROTHY WOKE UP. A blanket was covering her and she was bound hand and foot. She looked around. She was alone in Larry's hideaway. Yesterday's events came flooding back. Larry had pushed and pulled her through the brush, away from the river and the camp. He had made sure of leaving no tracks, by circling and twisting and turning until even she had lost any sense of direction.

He laughed. "They all think I'm a dumb jerk that doesn't know his way in the woods. Well, they haven't been able to find me."

"I've got news for you," she said. "They weren't trying to, up to now. You've kidnapped a woman. Now it's different."

"Yeah? Like, what can they do? I killed Joe and they stood for it. Not that I wanted to kill him, but he wouldn't give up his gun quietly."

"I wonder why. But you're still a dumb jerk. Don't you realize that each of us needs the others in order to survive? But no. Here you are waving that gun at everybody, and with only four shots left against forty people. Tell me if that isn't dumb."

He scowled. "You never learn. Your smart mouth got you in trouble and you're still at it."

"You didn't think I was going to beg? Did you? I won't go easy, and even if you get me, your ass will be mud. Jim or one of the other men will get you sooner or later."

"Well then, I've got nothing to lose, bitch!" he shoved her roughly.

They finally reached his hideaway, more like a hole in the ground. Apparently he had cleared out brush and debris and the result was a hollowed out space approximately six by six.

"So, for this you gave up a room at the Hotel Paradise?" she sneered. That was the name given their shelter by Sylvia. "Just about the size of a prison cell. Yeah, it suits you fine."

"I'm glad you like it," he sneered in return. "You're going to be my cellmate, oh, for, well, I haven't decided the sentence yet."

"There won't be any sentence," she looked him in the eye. "My lawyer is on the way, and I don't mean the Longleys."

"If you're figuring on your boyfriend showing up, forget it. He's gone. Maybe he's dead. Maybe he found more lost people and a new girlfriend to rescue."

"Yeah, dream on, Larry. You've never been able to plan two minutes ahead."

She peered into the shelter. "Well, you've kidnapped me from my dinner. Does a prisoner get fed?"

"Same thing you get back there, canned food. Tomorrow I go back and draw rations for two."

"Oh my brave Larry," she breathlessly mocked him. "To go back there and face all those angry people. Aren't you afraid they'll do something to you?"

"Ha! They won't dare. I'll have you here. They don't know where you are. If they harm me, you'll die out here, tied up and no food or drink. So you see, sweetheart, you need me."

The rest of the evening was an anti-climax after his earlier threats. He opened cans and started eating. She had no choice but to follow. Then he tied her up, covered her with a blanket and went to sleep.

Thinking about it this morning, she still couldn't believe her luck. She thought he would rape her for sure. What now? Apparently he had gone back to camp to extort more of their meager food supplies. Dorothy knew she had to get away, but how?

She strained against her bonds, futile, but she had to try. She looked around the small space. There was nothing that could free her. There were no knives, at least he hadn't used any. And if there were, he had hidden them. The can opener? That might do.

She pushed herself over, first her heels, then her body until she was next to the can opener. Then she saw the open can with the pushed back lid top, and the sharp jagged edges. The cans from the dinner last night.

Dorothy expelled her breath. The sharp edge of the can would make a better cutting tool, but it was also dangerous. She could end up slashing her wrists. She would have to be careful. Take it slow. How much time did she have before Larry returned?

She struggled to sit up and grasp the can, then what? She had the can, but the open lid was too flexible. It bent over as she tried to run it over her bonds. She would have to grasp the lid itself, jagged edges all around. She gasped as she transferred her hold from the can to the lid and it nicked her finger. Finally she had a firm grip on the lid. With one hand straining away to expose her bonds, she started sawing with the other. She had to apply pressure on the lid opposite where it was sawing and that in turn caused the edge to cut into her palm.

She sharply inhaled and moaned, but she didn't stop. Feeling one piece give way. Encouraged, she renewed her efforts. Between gasping with pain and straining at her bonds, it took several more minutes before the final strand gave way.

Dorothy brought her arms forward, resting them on her knees, her head resting on her arms. She stayed that way for a while, then looked at her bloody hands and scratches on fingers and wrists. Then hurriedly she attacked the rope on her ankles.

Free at last, she rubbed her ankles. She looked around, seeking something to clean her hands, but could find nothing except the blanket. Reluctantly, she used that.

Crawling to the opening she peered out. There was no one. There was only the silence of a dead world. No, there was the sound of her heavy breathing and the crackling of the brush as she move around. All of it magnified by the silence of her dismal surroundings, a forest laying inert.

Dorothy crept out of the shelter, then on second thought, reached back and got the blanket. That would have to do in lieu of any other clothing. The blanket would not only protect her from the weather, but also cover her near-nakedness. She had been very uncomfortable with Larry staring at her. She was ready, but in what direction was the camp? She stood still hoping some sound might carry and give her a clue. Nothing. She would have to guess. Then there was Larry returning. She could run right back into his clutches. She set out, knowing only she was getting away from Larry's hideout.

"HERE HE COMES," ESTHER tugged at Oscar's arm. "Don't get into a fight. Remember Dorothy."

"How can I forget her," he growled. "As for Larry, I can't promise anything."

Larry came swaggering into camp, pistol stuck in his belt, visible to everyone.

"You've got your nerve showing up here. What have you done with Dorothy?" Esther lit into him while Oscar looked at her with amazement.

"She's safe so far," he leered at her. "And her safety depends on you, all of you. You cross me or try anything funny, you'll never find her. Without me, she'll die out there."

Oscar clenched his fists. "How do we know she is all right? How do we know you didn't kill her?"

"Just take my word for it."

"Ha! Your word! Your word is as worthless as that ground you're standing on."

Larry shrugged. "Suit yourself. That's all you've got. I came to pick up food for both of us."

Oscar stared at him before answering. "All right, Larry. The kidnapper is always supposed to provide proof his victim is still alive. I'll give you enough food for one day for both of you. You come back tomorrow with proof Dorothy is still alive."

"I could take the food anyway," patting the gun.

"Yeah, and we might not cook it or hide it out there. There's a lot of things we can do. You haven't got eyes in back of your head. While you're shooting one in front of you, there will be another behind you with an axe." Larry stared at him, then whirled around.

"You don't know who might be hiding out in the brush," Oscar continued. "You pass by, someone jumps out with a spear. You turn around and another jumps out behind you. They're all over. Every time you turn there's someone behind you. Too many for what you can take care of with that pistol."

"You're all crazy!" Larry screamed. "I can hurt you!"

Oscar turned to Peggy. "Fix the food for Larry and Dorothy.

"Esther, you write a note to Dorothy asking her a question only she can answer." He turned to Larry. "You return tomorrow with that note answered by Dorothy and you'll get your food. And you'll continue to get food only if you can prove Dorothy is well enough to answer our questions.

"That's all, Larry. Get on back to her."

Peggy handed him the package of food.

Larry stood staring at them. "You can't treat me like this. I go when I'm ready."

No one paid any attention to him. They went on with their work.

"Look at me! Damn you!" he shouted. He pulled out the gun and shot into the air.

Everyone froze. They looked at him, saw no one was hurt, then resumed their duties.

"That's three, Larry," said Oscar. Then he too turned his back on him.

Larry remained standing for a moment, then turned and strode away, looking right, then left, then behind him.

There was a mass expelling of air from all of them. "Thank you all," Oscar told them. "You held up well. He's shook up now. I think he realizes he could be in trouble."

"I nearly had a heart attack," said Susan. "I thought I had been shot."

"What now, Oscar?" Sherman asked.

"We wait and see."

At the end of the day, the work parties returned. Walter and his group were very elated and pushing a loaded gurney.

"We found the hospital and it didn't take much effort to get into the basement where surgery was performed. We've got medicine, anesthetics, sheets, gowns and a book, Gray's Anatomy."

"Is that those gowns with the slit all the way to your neck?" Sylvia inquired.

"Of course," Walter replied. "You were expecting couture fashions?"

"Funny no one survived if they were in a basement," mused Oscar.

"Perhaps they did, But afterwards? They had no food as we did. We found four bodies."

"Do you think you can perform surgery now?"

"Oscar, as I said, I'm no surgeon. Ear, nose and throat is my specialty. However, with this book and my early training, I will bone up on how to treat gunshot wounds.

Especially since our Mr. Wilk is still on a rampage."

Tom's party had also come in and Oscar took him aside.

"Sorry, I wasn't able to fill your order," said Tom. "We haven't broken into the Post yet."

"The need is getting urgent with every passing day. He came back. Claims he has Dorothy and wanted food for both of them."

"We heard a shot. It was all I could do to keep them there. I don't see anyone hurt."

"No, he fired in the air. More in frustration. His way of making a point, I guess."

"Then it's one less bullet for his gun."

"Small comfort if three of us are on the receiving end of those remaining bullets."

Tom shook his head and they rejoined the others. "I think we should also look into locating the Sears store. They had a basement," Oscar told the group. "We can scrounge the area. Some of our needs may be found just laying where we can pick them up, like tools or clothing."

"Is there a Good Will Center?" Sylvia asked.

"I'm pretty sure there was a TV store," said Carl, "and video stores. Something you might want to keep in mind, Sylvia."

"Trash video, literally," said Esther.

"Isn't this apt," said Sylvia. "Sort of, like 'You Can't Take It With You,'" she looked at Esther.

"Jean Arthur, James Stewart..." Esther rolled her eyes pensively.

"Are you guys through screwing around?" Oscar growled.

Esther shrugged, turned to Sylvia. "The jock wants to say something?"

Oscar broke up.

CHAPTER FOURTEEN

June 10, 2020

"That was fast," observed John, as they scrambled down the last few feet from the mountain. Jim, without stopping to rest, took off in the direction of the camp. "It took the better part of two days to cross over that mountain the last time."

"We didn't know where we were going then. We were feeling our way...And speaking of feeling, we didn't do a great job of it as I recall."

"Tell me about it. When we were kids, we used to get banged up once a month. Now, it is an everyday affair. Your head should be a delight to those people who tell fortunes by the bumps on your head."

Jim laughed. "I hope that's the least of my injuries.

As for my fortune, I doubt any psychic could have foreseen what we've gone through."

A few minutes later he drew up short, holding out his hand to stop John.

"Look," he whispered. "There's a man ahead of us."

"I see him. What's he doing? Looks like he lost something."

The man was bending over, studying the ground. Then he walked a few paces and repeated his search.

"C'mon," said Jim. "Let's get closer. He might be one of ours."

"Then again, he might not," said John, bringing his Winchester to port.

As they got closer, actually closing in from the rear, Jim hailed him. "Hello! Wait for us."

The man started, then turned around.

"Jim!" he exclaimed.

"Frank! My God! What are you doing here?"

"Damn! I'm glad to see you fellows. All hell has broken loose since you left."

"I knew something was wrong when I recovered Betty Leye's body from the river. What happened?"

"Betty? Well, that solves one mystery. The other six probably suffered the same fate."

"What other six? Tell us!"

Frank told them about Larry, Joe and the seven who left camp on a raft.

Jim let out a curse. "Larry and Charlie, I might have known those two would cause trouble."

"Oh, Jim...That's not all. Larry kidnapped Dorothy while she was bathing in the river."

"What?"

"We heard a shot by the river. When we rushed down there, no one was to be found. We found her dress. Yesterday Oscar assigned me to track her down."

"Come on, we have to get back," Jim picked up his bag.

"Wait! There's more. I found Larry's hole, where he hides. He must have kept her hidden there, tied up. I found it this morning. It was empty. But I found pieces of rope that had been cut. Apparently she used the sharp edges of an opened can of beans to cut the rope because I found a can with blood on it. Larry must have gone to camp to get food, so she escaped. I've been following her tracks. She must be lost. She's heading away from camp."

"We'll take over from here," said Jim. "You go back and tell Oscar we're following her trail. Tell him to humor Larry till I get back. I want that son-of-a-bitch. He's mine!"

DOROTHY WOKE UP AS someone was pulling her to her feet. She saw hands on her arms, rough hands. Then she was looking into a strange bearded face peering at her. "Who are you? Where did you come from?"

The questions were coming from the bearded one, but then, there was another bearded one, although he was smaller than the first. Both men were clad in fatigues, and armed.

"I'm lost, and hungry," her mouth dry, she barely managed a hoarse whisper.

"What did she say?" the smaller one asked.

"Says she's hungry." The man who held her was big, over six feet, hard eyes and a cruel slit of a mouth almost hidden by whiskers.

"Where did she come from? She isn't carrying food, no clothes except that blanket."

"Probably ran out of food. Must have had enough to last this long. Hmm, I bet if you clean her up she'll be a looker. That's some body she's got."

He looked her up and down, lingering over the two brief garments she wore. She became conscious of his eyes devouring her body and she started to struggle. She was too weak, however. Moreover, it only gave him an excuse to put his hands on her body. He held her close, one hand lingering below her breast.

The tears came bubbling out, but they were tears of outrage and at her impotency in defending herself.

"What are we going to do with her, Curt?" from the smaller man.

"Take her along with us, of course. She's hungry, so we'll feed her."

"We can't do that. Remember the rules. She's an outsider. There were to be no exceptions."

Curt stared at the other man. "Who's going to stop me? You've got a woman. So has Jack and Harry. And now I've found me one. Christmas has come early."

"Sam ain't going to like it."

"I don't care what Sam likes. She's mine. Now let's get going."

They went in the direction she had been traveling. Though by now, she realized it was the wrong way. The fact these men were going in that direction was proof she had been lost.

The two men set a fast pace and she couldn't keep up. Curt laughed and picked her up in his arms. His eyes probed hers, flickering over her body until she felt violated.

"My, my, with those pretty green eyes, I bet you're a spitfire. It looks like I hit me a jackpot."

"I appreciate your help," she managed to blurt out. "If you'll give me a few scraps of food, I'll be on my way."

"Oh ho! She speaks. Well, now, you're in no condition to be out here, all alone. There ain't nobody out here, or is there? Is somebody else out here, huh?"

She hesitated. It wouldn't do for him to be forewarned there were other people back there. But then, no one knew where she was or whether she was alive. She bit her lip, but the tears came anyway.

"My, my man. He went to Phoenix for help."

"I don't like this, Curt. We could get a whole mob in here if they came looking for her. We've been lucky so far, but it's been over a month now.

That's enough time for some people to be making it out of the cities and start foraging the countryside for food. I don't trust her. I think she's lying."

"Shut up, Cal. You let me do the worrying."

They kept going. Curt had a hard chocolate bar which he gave her. She munched on it ravenously as the two men watched her.

"She wasn't lying about being hungry," said Curt.

The chocolate bar gave her enough energy so she could walk. Curt led the way, then Dorothy. Cal brought up the rear. She lost all track of time and soon began to lag, the weariness creeping back. The farther they went, the more she despaired. She was being pulled away from everything and everyone she knew. No one would find her now.

"You go ahead, Cal. I have to help my lady friend."

She tried to evade his arm, but he caught her and put her arm around his neck. She was too weak for further protest.

After a while she became aware of a towering pock-marked cliff that rose up in their path. Apparently this was their destination for she could see no way around it. A quarter of an hour later, they were at the foot of the cliff. There was an area where the debris had been cleared. Logs and brush had been piled around the perimeter to form a low barricade about four feet high. The only opening was the path they were following.

As they entered the perimeter of the camp, she noticed two more fatigued-clad people working around a campfire. Each had a belt and revolver strapped around their waists. They turned to look at the newcomers. It was then she saw they were women.

"Cal, what in the world is that?" the younger woman cried. "Why are you bringing in a stranger? You know the rules."

"Ask him," Cal motioned towards Curt. "He wanted her."

"Where did you find her?" the older woman asked. "It looks like she's been wallowing in a pig pen."

Dorothy reddened beneath the grime accumulated over the past two days. "If you have some water where I could wash."

"We have no water to spare for bathing, much less for strangers," snapped the younger one.

"You better get used to her, Ann," replied Curt. "She's gonna be around from now on. Cal, Harry and Jack have themselves a woman. Now I've got me one."

"Sam ain't gonna like it," persisted Ann.

"Sam, Sam, that's all I hear," snapped Curt. "Who appointed him boss?"

"Sam doesn't have a woman either," the older woman said. "She's going to cause dissension. We don't need that."

"Oh?" Curt eyed Ann. "Were your husbands going to share you with me and Sam?"

"Share?" the older woman exclaimed. "We're not possessions to be passed around."

"There's five men and three women. That's not very equal for Sam and me. I've got one now. Which way would you rather have?"

"Are you going to share with Sam?" Cal snickered.

"Don't you worry about Sam and me," Curt responded. "By the way, where is he?"

"He and the others are in the shelter," answered Ann. "What's your name?" she turned to the captive.

"Dorothy."

"Dorothy, Well, I like that," said Curt.

"I'm spoken for," replied Dorothy. "He will come looking for me. I belong to no one else."

"Where is this man of yours? Why are you wandering out here, half naked, without food or water?" Ann persisted.

"He went to Phoenix for help. I, I got lost."

"Then he won't know where you are."

"He'll find me. He won't give up."

"He'd better not find you or you'll be short one husband," said Curt. "And maybe that's good. That will settle who you belong to."

She had not said 'husband' and couldn't explain why. Curt had assumed, and she was not going to deny it.

"I'll never belong to you. You could never be sure of me, could you? I could stick a knife in you while you slept."

Curt's smile was wiped off his face. The older woman cackled with laughter. Cal smiled, and Ann frowned. Further talk was prevented by the appearance of two men who materialized from behind some rocks at the base of the cliff. From where she stood, Dorothy could see the space underneath the cliff. She had seen larger versions of this in other parts of the state. A legacy of nature that had been used by earlier inhabitants to make their homes, the cave dwellers of ancient times.

"What's going on here? Who is this woman?" a tall, heavyset, black-bearded man addressed the group.

"It seems Curt decided to get himself a woman, and there she is," Ann looked at Curt maliciously.

"Damn it! You know we're not taking in outsiders. It was just supposed to be our group. We did the work and made the contributions. Once it started we couldn't take in anyone."

"Hell!" exclaimed Curt. "There's only eight of us. Where are the others? It's been over a month now and they haven't shown up. She's the only one we've seen. There's plenty for us and one more won't make that much difference.

"Besides, Sam, where's your Christian charity? She was lost and starving. She could have died if we left her out there."

"Charity Hell!" snorted Sam. "When did you ever show any charity except to yourself? All I have to know is that a woman is involved to know what you're thinking. Why, I've wondered if I was going to need a guard over Ann, Elaine and Judy."

"Well, then, if I take her you won't have to worry about the other women, will you?"

"And then where do we stop taking in people?" the fourth man finally spoke up. "Any day now we can expect a horde of survivors to descend on us from the cities. We have only God and these trusty rifles to repel the invaders."

"Oh, cut the crap, Jack," retorted Curt. "I'm tired of your pious, self-righteous shit, you old hypocrite. You wave your Bible with one hand while grabbing Ann's ass with the other. Does Judith know that? Or Cal? Did you know that, Sam?"

Jack got red in the face. A silence descended over the group. Everyone was suddenly embarrassed, either for themselves or someone else.

"We won't have any more of this bickering among ourselves," Sam broke the silence. "As for the girl, we'll feed her and she'll spend the night here. Tomorrow we decide what to do with her.

"You," he turned to Dorothy, "where did you say you were from?"

"I didn't say," she replied.

The hostile attitude of the group towards her and each other gave her pause before replying. They were well-armed and ready to shoot anyone they considered an outsider. Certainly, her class was no match against them, even though there were only eight of them. She would have to be careful what she said to them. She didn't want to alarm them in case someone came after her. But, no, there was no one coming. It was up to her to save herself.

Sam caught her arm and twisted. "Don't get smart with me. I don't have time for games. Answer my question."

She pulled her arm from his grasp. "I'll answer your question, but I won't forget your manhandling me. I owe you.

"Stonecliff, I'm from Stonecliff. What's left of it?"

"I've heard of that town," said Jack. "It's some thirty, forty miles from here. Why, isn't that...?"

"What are you doing this far?" interrupted Sam. "Are there more people out there?"

"I told you. I was taking a bath in the river when I got swept away. When I made it out, I tried to get back, but I was lost. I was wandering about, trying to find my way back when they found me,"

"What of the other people?"

"There's fifty more people back there," she finally replied. "They'll come looking for me."

"We're ready for them," exclaimed the belligerent Jack.

"We knew that was the way it would be."

"Let me go," she pleaded. "I won't tell anyone where you are. We don't need your food or supplies. We salvaged enough to last us a long time. But once they come after me and see what you've got, well, I can't speak for them. They're armed too."

"Why should we trust you," interjected Ann. "This is what we prepared for. We knew we would have to fight others that survived."

At this point Dorothy's eyes shifted towards the cliff as she caught movement out of the corner of her eye. A couple came sauntering from the cliff, arm in arm. Her eyes widened. "Harry!" she screamed.

Harry stopped in his tracks at the sound of her voice. Then he slowly moved to the group around the fire, Elaine trailing behind him.

"Oh my God! Dorothy! Is that you?"

"You two know each other?" Sam looked at him.

"Stonecliff!" said Jack. "I knew I had heard that name before."

"Well, Harry?" said Sam.

"She's, she's my wife."

"Oh God!" gasped Elaine.

"Your wife?" exclaimed Curt. "She said her husband went to Phoenix. Who's right?"

"Well, uh, I did. I had business there. But...On the way, I, uh..."

"Yes, I see," smirked Sam. "Tell the wife you're going on a business trip while all the time you've got a girlfriend stashed in a motel room. Only in this case it was a cave."

Dorothy, recovering from shock, suddenly realized that no one was taking the time factor into account. She had told them her man had gone to Phoenix. In her mind that was Jim.

The husband part was their assumption. Only now it had proven true, but with what consequences? Harry had not questioned her statement because he was equally in shock at her appearance. His surprise in her appearance, Sam's snide remarks, all had contributed to passing over the slight discrepancy in the stories.

At least his presence might protect her from Curt. Or would it? She saw Elaine and suddenly Sam's remarks became clear.

"Well, well, how cozy," smiled Sam. "A wife and a girlfriend. How are you going to handle this?"

"He can't have both," interjected Curt. "I found this one. She's mine."

"She's married to Harry," said Sam. "We can't break up a marriage. Can we, Harry?"

"Okay, I'll take the other," said Curt.

"No!" exclaimed Elaine. "You can't pass me on like...like..."

"Exactly what I said," cackled Judith.

"I'd like to hear your answer too, Harry," Dorothy looked at him.

"Look...All this is so sudden," Harry glanced at Elaine. "My wife and I are estranged. I was planning to ask for a divorce. Then this happened. I didn't know where I stood. There was nothing on the radio."

"Why didn't you try finding out, Harry. If I made it here without food and clothes, you could have gone back. You have all the equipment here. Even if I didn't matter, didn't you care what happened to your son?"

"Oh God, Dorothy. Is he...Is he..."

"He's dead...Like everyone else in Stonecliff."

"I'm sorry...I loved him very much. I planned to go back later. When this was over. It's over a month now. There's nothing I could have done."

"Ain't this all nice," interrupted Curt. "But it still don't answer the question of him having two women. Not when there's some that ain't got one."

"We've wasted enough time," said Sam. "I'll make a decision tomorrow. In the meantime..."

"Who appointed you leader?" challenged Harry.

"No one did," replied Sam. "But maybe it's time we appointed one. It looks like Shel isn't coming and we need someone to make decisions.

"Not you. You can't make a decision on your personal life much less for the entire group. It's just us now. So, I'm taking over. Anybody got any objections?"

"I'm with you, Sam," said Jack.

"I'll go along," said Cal.

Judy and Ann said nothing, but they nodded at their husbands' comments. "That's five out of eight," Sam looked at Harry. "You got anything to say?"

"What's there left to say."

"Okay, then, it's getting late. It's time for supper."

"What shall we do with her in the meantime?" Cal asked.

"Get her over by the cliff. She'd have to get by us to get out."

"She might jump the barrier."

"Not likely. Take her shoes if you want. She wouldn't get far in that brush."

"We could tie her up."

"Later...Tonight."

"You'd better tie her up tonight," laughed Judy. "She said she'd stick a knife in Curt if he bothered her."

Curt glowered at her. The women went back to preparing supper. Sam sent Curt and Cal to the cave on an errand. Then he sat down, smoking a pipe, every now and then looking at Dorothy.

Harry approached her. "Will you be all right?"

"You see me. I'm alive. But I didn't bring my crystal ball."

"Dorothy, I meant to ask for a divorce after the semester was over. Who could have thought something like this would happen?"

"Harry, it's all right. It's over. Everything is over. You have your Elaine. In a way I'm glad. All I ask is that you get me away from here."

"I can't do that. I'm stuck by the rules of the group. Let's see what Sam decides."

"Are you going to let Curt take me? Even if you don't love me, you wouldn't let that happen. Would You?"

"I...Uh, let's see what Sam decides."

She nodded, looking at him. "Why is it that one of us didn't have the decency to die? It would have simplified everything. If it doesn't break any group rules, can you get me some water and a cloth, so I can wash up?"

"That I can do."

They sat down to supper as darkness settled. There was little talk. Dorothy ate ravenously, the others watching her. She didn't care. She didn't owe them anything. This might be her last meal. Tomorrow they could kill her or turn her over to that vicious Curt. She shivered.

Sam noticed. "Are you cold?"

"Well, sort of."

"Judy, get her another blanket from the cave. We'll prepare her a place to sleep. There's a tree stump by the entrance. Set blankets there and tie her hands to the stump."

She looked at Harry, but he made no comment.

Cal and Judy fixed her blankets and then tied her hands.

"This won't be comfortable," chortled Judy. "But we can't have you running about tickling Curt with the silverware."

PETER J FLORES

It was uncomfortable with her hands tied, but then, the last few nights hadn't been any better. She turned around several times as much as her bonds allowed until she found a position that felt comfortable.

Where was Jim? Had he returned to camp by now? What could they tell him? That Larry had shot her? What about Larry? Would he shoot Jim too?

It didn't take long for her to fall asleep. The long trip in her weakened condition had left her bone-tired. The hard ground and tied hands proved no obstacle to sleep.

SHE WOKE UP WITH A hand covering her mouth. A figure loomed in front of her, outlined by the fire. The blanket was pulled off and she felt a hand tugging at her panties. She started to struggle and cry out, but the man straddled her and kept her down, his hand pressed down across her mouth. She opened her mouth and parted her lips, felt a finger across her teeth. She bit down on the finger, hard.

There was a cry from the man and he jerked his hand away.

She screamed.

CHAPTER FIFTEEN

June 10, 2020

As Frank headed back to camp, Jim and John hid their packs in the brush, then took up Dorothy's trail. They took only food, flashlight and John's Winchester.

John took the lead, eyes to the ground. "These tracks are very erratic, almost like..." he looked at Jim. "Almost like she was hurt."

Mouth grim, Jim didn't reply.

In an hour's time they discovered where she had slept. John knelt to examine the ground.

"Someone else was here," he said. "These other tracks were made by boots, or heavy type shoes. No one in camp has shoes like these."

"Unless they found them in the ruins."

"Yes, but these other tracks come from the direction she was going, and away from camp." John stood up and started walking around being careful not to step on the prints. "Well, Jim, it's a good thing my old medicine man taught me tracking and to read the story behind those tracks."

"You want to tell me or do you want to string out your credentials."

"The boot tracks are all over the place. There were two men at least. One set is smaller than the other. And they were armed. At least one of them was."

"How can you tell?"

"There's an indentation of a rifle butt over by that log. Someone must have leaned their piece against it.

"They took her, willing or unwilling. They're headed back from where they came."

"Did she struggle? Is there any sign of blood to indicate she was hurt?"

"No, I saw where she slept. There were no bloodstains. I don't think she's hurt other than from where she freed herself with that can lid. More likely she's weak from the trek and not eating."

"Then let's get going. We don't have a moment to lose. One way or another she needs our help."

Sometime later, John stopped on the trail as it sloped upward. In the distance loomed a pock-marked sandstone cliff with the horizontal veins so common in this part of the country.

"Thank God not all the beauty of this land was destroyed," said Jim.

"I can see the tracks from here," said John, intent on the trail. "But we'd better go slowly. They're armed and with this much brush, they could easily ambush us."

"I can't believe they would be so belligerent. We need to make contact. There's not too many of the species left."

"They might not care to make contact," replied John.

"You know, looking at that cliff there, I'll bet these people survived in an open cave. There's lots of them. The ancient ones built their homes in the larger ones. "I seem to recall hearing about survivalist groups being very active in the state. They shouldn't be in this area, but who knows what they have done in this wild corner. It also means they are heavily armed, suspicious and very, very unfriendly. They are very likely to shoot first and ask questions later, if the victim is capable of answering."

They continued on the trail. They kept an eye for any movement and perhaps get a few seconds warning. John was cautious.

"If they're the type of survivalists I've heard about, they've had plenty of training in combat tactics. They could lie and wait for us, blending with this brush. I'd be willing to bet they're wearing camouflaged clothing and those were the imprints of combat boots."

It was getting dark now and Jim was fretting about the slow going. The cliff loomed dead ahead.

"We should be almost there," said John. "If I'm right and they're holed up in there, we'd better keep down. They'll probably have a guard close by."

They bent over, at times going on all fours trying not to outline their bodies above the level of the brush. "Look!" John whispered. "There's a fire, a campfire. I can't believe our luck. They must have gotten careless in posting guards."

"We're not there yet," cautioned Jim. "There may still be one about. One good thing, we don't have to look for them up a tree."

They proceeded even slower, looking and listening. Now they were only a hundred feet from the entrance to the clearing. They could see forms crossing the light from the campfire and hear the murmur of voices.

"Let's get off the trail," whispered Jim. "Maybe we can make it to that barricade and get a good look."

"Okay but watch your step. There's a lot of dry brush that will crack like a rifle shot. And by now they must know there's no wild life out here."

Luckily for them, in order to build the barricade, the area adjacent to it had been swept clear and piled up to form the enclosure. The two positioned themselves, keeping their heads down and conversed in low tones.

"Just as I thought," said John. "They're right at the base of the cliff. Ten to one there's some sort of shelter back there."

"John, I believe I've counted five to seven people. It's hard to tell in the dark. I may have counted the same one twice. There's two women for sure, and you're right, they're wearing combat fatigues and belts with revolvers even while they're cooking."

The continued watching. One man sat off to the side, smoking a pipe. Jim concluded he must be the leader. One of the women called out that supper was ready.

Slowly the little group assembled around the fire. Then one of the women came up leading Dorothy.

"It's Dorothy! My God! Look at her! What have they done to her?" Jim started to rise.

John pulled him down, placing his hand over Jim's mouth.

"Get hold of yourself, Jim. You won't do her any good if they discover us here. Just wait, she's alive. They might shoot her if we bust in there now."

Jim was shaking. "What have they done to her?"

"I don't think they've done anything to her. Judging by what Frank told us and the time spent in Larry's hole and on the trail, her appearance is just what you would expect after going through such an ordeal. That's the way she came."

"We've got to get her out."

"We'll do it the Indian way, Jim. We attack at dawn."

They kept watching as the people finished eating. Jim kept fidgeting, almost crying out as he saw Dorothy's condition. He raged as he heard the order to tie her up for the night.

"There seems to be only eight," said John. "Five men and three women. They must be lax. I saw no one come in to eat. So that means no one was keeping guard, else they would have been relieved for supper."

"It's going to be a long night," said Jim. "Why don't you try to sleep? I know I can't. I'll take the first watch."

"It's only eight o'clock, Jim. I can't go to sleep this early. We'll both keep watch. Later on we'll decide who stays up."

After an hour the camp quieted down. The long day and lack of food began to tell on the watchers. Both began to doze. Once Jim woke with a start and noticed John asleep, so he forced himself to stay awake by pinching his arm. He was half in and half out when the scream abruptly awakened him. He came to with a start, not sure what had awakened him.

Then another scream split the night.

Jim sprang up. "That's Dorothy!"

He shook John who was coming awake, then started climbing the barricade. John cursed, grabbed his rifle and followed Jim.

Meanwhile the camp had come to life. Pulling out guns, they stared at their surroundings. Then the second scream pinpointed the direction, and all ran towards the source.

They didn't notice Jim scrambling over the fence.

The group arrived at Dorothy's sleeping place to discover Curt on his knees next to Dorothy. The blanket was flung aside, and her panties were down to her thighs.

"Damn you, Curt! You couldn't wait. You had..."

Jim came running up. To the ones already gathered there, the sound of running feet was only natural. No one had counted heads in the excitement. No one was thinking of intruders but were focused on the tableau before them.

Judith was at the edge of the crowd as Jim came up. She was looking at Curt and Dorothy. There was a revolver in her hand but pointing downward.

Jim reached out from behind and in one quick move, jerked the pistol from her grip. Then he shoved her into Cal who was in front of her.

"Drop your guns! All of you!" Jim shouted.

They turned around, momentarily surprised at the entrance of a new actor in the drama. Jack was the first to recover. With a curse, he swung his rifle to aim at Jim.

There was a roar from a rifle and Jack was clutching his arm, his rifle clattering to the ground. John stepped into Jim's line of vision, his rifle pointing at the huddled group.

"You killed him!" screamed Judith, rushing to the fallen Jack.

"He won't die," replied John. "It's only a shot in the arm."

"Cover them, John," Jim called out.

He ran to Dorothy. "Are you all right," he exclaimed, cutting her bonds.

"Oh Jim!" she flung her arms around his neck. He pulled up her panties, gun still in hand, eyeing Curt.

"Can you stand?" he asked, pulling her up. She nodded.

"What happened? We've been waiting out there for dawn. Was it him? Was he trying...?"

She nodded. "He attacked me. Tried to rape me as I was sleeping."

"And you were tied down? Helpless? Here take this gun and hold it on them.

He gave the gun to Dorothy and turned to Curt.

"Come on, get up, or don't you take on anyone unless their hands are tied?"

Meanwhile John had piled on more wood on the fire, lighting up the scene.

"Look, friend," Curt began. "I was just checking..."

Jim kicked him on his side. "I'm not your friend. I said get up, or do you want it lying down?"

Slowly grasping his side, Curt got to his feet. Then he lunged at Jim. Jim sidestepped and kicked him on the thighs.

"Come on, dammit!" Jim jeered. "Don't you ever stand up to a man, are you only brave with helpless women?"

Curt was a few inches shorter than Jim, but he outweighed him by thirty pounds. Now his humiliation turned to rage. But he came towards Jim more slowly.

Jim was in no mood to spar. He had his own rage to expiate. He waded into Curt, taking several blows from him, but oblivious to any pain. He connected with Curt's jaw once, twice. Then he lowered his sights and went after Curt's ample belly.

Curt was still able to get a good swing at Jim's head before the blows to his stomach began to take effect. Gasping for breath, he stumbled and was a perfect target for Jim's fist to the jaw. He took three of them in his face and went down.

Panting, Jim stepped back. He took the gun from Dorothy and put his arm around her.

"I haven't had a fight since I was a kid, but I can't remember anything else giving me so much pleasure."

John stepped over to the dazed Curt and placed the muzzle of his Winchester to Curt's head. "You want me to shoot him?" looking at Jim.

Jim shook his head. "Not right now. I might still change my mind later." He turned to Dorothy. "Anyone else gave you trouble?"

"Yes," she stepped towards Sam. "I told you I owed you." She suddenly kicked out and caught Sam on his upper thigh, near his groin. He gasped, groaned and doubled over.

"Sorry," she said to Jim as she returned to his side. "But after several days of taking all that crap from these macho men, I had to get that out of my system."

Jim nodded, turning to the others. Curt was still on the ground, now joined by Sam and Judith was tending to Jack's wound.

"Why did you treat her like this? What kind of monsters are you? With the world in ruins and so few of us left, we should be working together. Instead, you've degenerated into savages. Who is your leader here?"

"I am," from Sam, sitting up now.

"If you're the leader, I hold you responsible."

"We shoot them all?" John interjected. Jim looked at him, an inkling of John's behavior beginning to form. His hesitation was misinterpreted by Sam.

Hurriedly he spoke up. "Look, I don't approve of what Curt was trying to do. Hell, I would have beat him up myself if you hadn't shown up."

"Even so, is it your practice to treat people like you treated her, tying her up, threatening her?"

"You don't understand," Sam hastened on. "We, our group, set up this place for just such an occasion. We set up rules. We couldn't share with outsiders. I told her. Fact is, Curt and Cal never should have brought her in."

"It wasn't my idea. Curt wanted a woman of his own," Cal defended himself.

"She's already spoken for," Jim put his arm around Dorothy's waist. "And if you want to put it another way, I beat Curt for her, not that I didn't already have her."

Dorothy looked at Harry who was scowling.

"I don't know what to do with you," Jim continued. "My blood-thirsty Indian friend wants to kill you."

"These white eyes have much guns and food in cave," John broke in. "I call my people and we take."

Jim had a hard time keeping from grinning as John put on his Indian act. The survivalists were now apprehensive.

By nature, suspicious, they were ready to believe the worst in others. Wasn't this why they had built their stronghold?

They had expected a mob of displaced refugees to come streaming into the countryside, killing and pillaging. In their eyes, Jim's party was representative of that mob. Having been overcome, they expected the worst.

"We have more of our people coming in any day now," said Sam. "There's thirty-six more of us. They won't take this sitting down. They put a lot of time and money into this. We'll come after you and your Indian friend."

"I hate to be the one to pop your little bubble. But no one is coming. As far as we know, we are all that's left. As it now stands, only our groups have survived in this area. What should we do now? Shall we remain enemies or join forces?"

"Why should we join you? We have more than you. You stand to gain more than us. And if what you say is true, that our friends are not coming, then what we have here will last eight people a long time. So, no. We won't join you. But of course, you have the upper hand. Where do we go from here?"

"Yes, we do hold all the high cards, don't we?" Jim smiled. "Our group has enough to last a good while, so we won't need what you have. I'm not as blood-thirsty as you are, so you will live as long as you behave yourselves."

"What about him?" Sam nodded towards John.

"John is my blood brother. He will go along with me."

He felt foolish going along with the charade, but they were already in too far with this confrontation. The truth would wreck their credibility in other matters. It was important these people believe him otherwise the class would forever be in danger from eight heavily armed people ready to strike at their imagined enemies.

"Whatever my brother wants," said John.

"We have lots of guns," piped up Jack, holding his arm but still belligerent. John fixed his gaze on him. "It only takes one gun and one bullet." There was no retort from their group.

"You will be left alone, so long as you behave. We will not destroy or take any of your supplies. The only thing I shall take is a change of clothing for Dorothy. You owe her that much.

"We'll leave in the morning. To save you from temptation, all of you shall accompany us a few miles, unarmed. We'll release you at that time. From then on, we're non-belligerents. We'll leave you alone if you leave us alone. You come into our area and all bets are off. It's open season. And if you bushwhack one of my people, I'll come straight here, no quarter given, understood?

"Do we have a choice?" said Sam.

"I just finished giving it to you. You can tell me anything you want. After we're gone, I don't know if you'll keep your word. However, you break it at great risk to yourselves. You might get one of us, but we outnumber you and, in the end, you all lose."

"What guarantee do we have that you won't do that to us?" said Judith.

"You have a better guarantee than I have. The proof is here and now. I could have you killed now, but I won't, regardless of how much some of you deserve it for what you did to Dorothy. So, I made the first concession at a time when I have control of the situation. That is your proof."

He looked at them for a few seconds. "Are we all clear on our course now?"

"There's just one thing," said Sam. "Why are you so protective of this woman when her husband here has gone along with everything I've done?"

"What? What kind of nonsense are you talking about?"

"Jim," Dorothy interrupted, "that man, Harry, is my husband."

"Your husband?" Jim looked at her blankly.

"Yes. It seems both my husband and I were under the impression the other had been killed."

"This is your husband," Jim looked at Harry, "and he stood by and let all this happen to you?"

"Well now, why am I being made to look like the villain," said Harry. "It looks like you've been busy yourself. How long has this been going on?"

"Not as long as yours, apparently. And don't try to assume the martyr's role, Harry. Your hypocrisy comes through. I found you out long ago when you didn't bother to wipe the lipstick off your shirts.

"Since we don't have anything more between us, why do you care? Does it salve your conscience to think I was cheating on you? Well, I'm sorry to disappoint you. It didn't happen until a few weeks ago, and after you were presumed dead along with the rest of Stonecliff."

"What kind of man are you?" interjected Jim. "Even if you didn't love her, how could you stand by and see her tied and left unprotected from slime like him," nodding towards Curt.

"You'd better take that up with the 'boss' there," Harry nodded towards Sam.

"Yeah, Harry," Sam glared, "not only do you not have any guts to stand up to me, but you're good at passing the buck.

"She was uncooperative," Sam turned to Jim. "We had to tie her down. Tomorrow, today, I would have made a decision."

"I'll bet," said Jim. "I can ease your mind, you won't have to worry about having to divide Dorothy between two men. She is mine. Harry can do whatever he wants except have her. He forfeited any right by his conduct here. There is no law out here. You people have shown me that. Well, my law says that Harry and Dorothy are divorced.

"That was what you intended doing, wasn't it, Harry? That should suit all parties. As they say in the marriage ceremony, if there are any objections, speak now or forever hold your peace."

"Harry?" Dorothy looked at him.

"Do I have any choice?" he said bitterly.

"What do you mean?" exclaimed Elaine. "Don't you know?"

"Harry, you're a rat, with due apologies to that rodent," said Jim. "Stringing this girl along. I'd say she deserves better."

"If I had any qualms about this," added Dorothy, "you just shot them down. You can't give up anything. Can you, Harry?"

Harry looked away, saying nothing while Elaine sobbed.

CHAPTER SIXTEEN

June 11, 2020

Jim halted the group a few miles from their stronghold.

Judith and Ann had made breakfast, but only Jim and his party had anything to eat.

"You get to eat when you return," he told them. Eating at a later time would hold them up and also, he hoped, give them pause about taking revenge.

"This is as far as I'm taking you. You're free to return to your camp. Before you go, let me repeat my offer. Join us. There's only eight of you left."

Sam shook his head. "This is the way we set it up. We'll take our chances."

"With four men and three women, and him," nodding towards Curt. He shrugged. "As you wish. I don't envy the problems you'll have."

"We've taken nothing from you except for some clothing for Dorothy and a couple of guns for insurance. A small loss compared to what you did to her. Let it end there. Don't take our compassion for weakness. Enough people have already died. I don't want to kill any more unless it is absolutely necessary. You're free to go."

They walked off slowly. Harry lingered, gazing at Dorothy. "Don't forget. No matter what anyone says, you're still married to me."

"I can't believe this," she replied. Then she called out to the departing group. "Come back and pick up this piece of slime before he fouls up the environment."

"You won't forget. I know you," Harry said, then hurried to join the others.

"He is completely changed," she shook her head sadly. "That's not the man I married."

Jim put his arm around her. "Do you really care? He made his choice. I get the feeling he's the type that hates to give up a possession, and you were one of them."

"Our son was the only tie and with him gone, there's nothing to connect me to Harry."

"Jim," John was watching the departing group. "Why don't you and Dorothy go on? I'll keep watch and see if they come back for us."

"That's a good idea, but don't wait too long. If they're coming back, you should see them in about two to three hours. We'll wait for you at the mountain where we left out packs. If they come, we'll make our stand there."

"Why can't we go all the way to our camp? As you say, we have some three hours head start and they don't know where our camp is," Dorothy asked him.

"They would find us eventually and our people are unarmed. We would be no match for them."

Walking hand in hand, they left John. "What makes people fall so in love, then end up like this?" she said.

"I presume you're talking about Harry. That's not us."

"It isn't? How can one tell? How did you feel about your love for Linda? Or hers' for you?"

"That was fifteen years ago. We were just kids. And people do grow up and see things in a different light."

"Age doesn't always improve your wisdom. People in love do foolish things."

"Are you having second thoughts about us? Are you going to let Harry haunt you with his comments?"

"Oh darling, I love you, and I know you love me. But is it possible that could change? The track record for marriages is not very encouraging."

"It wasn't in the old world, but this is a new one. We can make our own records, and for the better."

"Does marriage, being together, strip away all the mystery? Do all the warts come out and we see ourselves as we really are? Is this where hate, indifference or resentment begins?"

He stopped and took her in his arms. "It looks like Harry got to you. I don't think anyone can ever answer those questions, as I'm sure many have asked before. Men and women are still attracted to each other. That's the way we were made. Some do make it, you know. And I will try my utmost to make it so."

They reached their rendezvous point an hour later. Jim recovered his pack. "I have something here that is more feminine than those fatigues."

"Not a dress and high heels, I hope. I spent a month in that apparel and I was mentally and physically uncomfortable. Besides, what is there here that we should need to dress up for?"

"For ourselves, if nothing else. But don't worry. Slacks, blouse, some under things and flat heel shoes. Is that mentally and physically comfortable for you?"

She kissed him. "Darling, they're fine, but I don't want to put them on until I have a good bath. I need to wash off Larry and Curt."

"I understand. When we get back, I'll personally stand guard while you do. Although by then, Larry will be history."

"Strangely enough, he never tried what Curt did. I suspect Larry is all talk, trying to give his impression of a movie bad guy."

"Nevertheless, he killed. Good or bad impression is immaterial. He has to pay.

"It's sad that even here we can't escape the violent part of that last world. Human nature didn't change. Faced with this disaster and having survived it, one would think people would change. Get religion, so to speak."

"Well, enough of Philosophy 101. We'd better rig some sort of defense in case the worse happens."

They cleared out a small space and piled logs and brush, then sat down to wait, arms around each other.

She giggled. "We stink, you know."

"Me, not you," nuzzling her hair.

Sometime later they heard the crunching of brush and John burst into view.

"They're coming! We've got about an hour to get ready for them."

"I was afraid of this. Is the whole bunch coming?"

"All eight of them, and heavily armed."

"Harry would kill me?" her eyes widened.

"Who knows? We have to assume the worse if all eight are coming with guns."

Jim grasped her arms. "Dorothy, why don't you head for camp? We can get you started in the right direction."

"No! I let you go once and look what happened."

"But we're outnumbered and outgunned. We can only expect to inflict minimum damage and hope they back off."

"No," she repeated. "I don't want to seem overly dramatic, but I stay with you come what may."

Jim threw up his hands, turned to John. "Then you go. If they've broken into the Post, they should have found weapons."

"What do you hope to accomplish by staying here?" John asked.

"I don't know. Hold them off until you get back with reinforcements."

"You two are going to sacrifice yourselves?"

Jim sighed. "Believe me, I don't want to. So, hurry up and go and get back as soon as possible."

"All right. I'll take the revolver. You and Dorothy keep that Berretta and the Winchester. There's a box of extra shells in my pack. You have enough to take care of them if you don't waste too much. I'll hurry, but I don't see how we can make it back before two days at our fastest.

Good luck."

He embraced both, then took off running.

ALMOST TWO HOURS LATER, they had not appeared. "Maybe they changed their minds," she said.

"I hope so. We need all the time we can get."

"Jim, if they fire at us, it's our lives or theirs. Don't hesitate to fire at Harry. If he is with them, carrying a gun, you can't hold off."

The silence was broken by the crack of a rifle. The shot was off twenty feet to the left.

Jim put his hand on her shoulder, keeping her down while he peered through a slit in their barricade. He couldn't see or hear anything.

"They must think we're near, otherwise they wouldn't have shot," he whispered. "But I don't think they've pin-pointed our position. Maybe they're trying to get us to return their fire." He listened intently. For once he blessed the presence of all the brush. No matter how careful they might be, it was almost impossible to creep up on them without making noise. Judging by what he had seen at their camp, they were lax and divisive among themselves.

Curt's attitude towards women created suspicion. Jack's hot-headed actions promoted rashness.

"They've taken the first shot. We won't shoot until we have a target. I'll use the Winchester, it has greater range than the Berretta. Save your shots for close up work. Don't fire until I tell you."

"It will be dark soon," she said. "Will that make it worse? They can't sneak up without noise and revealing themselves." Daylight, which at best had always been equal to a dark cloudy day, deteriorated into darkness and soon it was pitch black. They dared not make a sound and spoke in low tones.

She fell asleep in his arms while he kept watch, trying to estimate the time, since he couldn't read his watch. He tried counting. That was the wrong thing to do. He fell asleep.

The shot striking the barricade just above them, woke them up. Then there were three more in rapid succession.

"They're behind us!" Jim whispered in her ear.

IT WAS MORNING AND the working parties were being organized.

"Esther, Sylvia, Linda, you three buddies take over the camp chores. Nancy, you join them. Aaron, you and Josh stay too. I need some help and you guys have the muscle.

"Tom, I suggest you concentrate on that project we talked about. I'd like to see that completed today."

Tom nodded. "I'll complete it today, even if I have to pay overtime."

"Ha!" said Sylvia. "If anyone pays overtime, I'm due a fortune. Some gigolo could be chasing me for my money."

"How much are you worth, Sylvia?" Carl cocked his head.

"What's the going currency in this dump, rocks? Why, big boy? Are you interested?"

Oscar sighed. "If you two jokers will tell me who is Abbott and which is Costello, so I can assign work under the proper name?"

"What is this special project you want Tom to finish," Esther asked.

"Oh, why not," Oscar threw up his hands. "I told Tom to locate a flower shop so I could send flowers to every female in the class."

"Everybody wants to be a comedian," Sylvia sniffed.

"What about Larry?" interjected Frank.

"I don't know," said Oscar. "He hasn't shown up. Ordinarily, I'd be worried, but you told me Dorothy escaped and Jim and John are looking for her.

"But," his eyes swept the group, "let's keep our stories straight. If he shows up, no one is to let him know about Dorothy's escape. We'll play it as if she's still his captive."

"We know nothing!" Sylvia exclaimed.

"Sgt. Schultz in Hogan's Heroes," Esther interjected.

Oscar rolled his eyes.

Two hours later, Larry appeared.

Esther saw him first.

"Well, we were wondering if you fell in a hole," she said. "No such luck, I see."

He looked at her, at the women on the kitchen detail, then at the three men who were wrestling with a log.

"Do you have the answer from Dorothy on that question I asked her?"

"Are you putting me on?" he snapped.

"Putting you on? All I did was ask for Dorothy's answer which you were supposed to return."

Oscar and the other two men joined the two. "That's right, Larry. That was our agreement."

"Your agreement. Not mine."

"Are you saying you didn't let Dorothy answer?"

"I ain't saying that," a puzzled look on his face.

"Then what are you saying? Is she all right? Have you harmed her?"

He didn't answer immediately. He was obviously puzzled, looking about as if expecting Dorothy to pop out of hiding.

"I don't have her. She left, She escaped."

"What!" Oscar had to feign outrage. "You took her. Now you say she's gone. She isn't here, so where is she?"

"You're lying to me! She's here. You're hiding her."

"Hiding her? Ha! You look, anywhere you want. If you can find her here, at the ruins, wherever, I'll kiss your ass."

Larry was clearly upset, pacing back and forth, eyes darting everywhere. The others looked on nervously.

"Linda," Oscar told her, "give Larry rations for two people. Until she shows up, we'll assume he still has her."

"I don't have her! There's something going on here. You're up to something."

Linda held out the rations to him, but he seized her arm, spun her around so that her body shielded him. He whipped out his revolver.

"Okay, so she's not here. She's not there. So this one is going to take her place. I don't care."

"You're signing your death warrant. Let her go," Oscar cried.

Aaron now came forward. "Wilk, I told you once what would happen if you messed with the women. I'm telling you only once, let her go!"

Larry laughed. "I always said you was a jock at heart. As for the woman, I know you have the hots for her. That makes it all the sweeter. I need me a playmate."

Aaron kept coming.

"No, Aaron!, Stay away!" cried Linda.

"Come on, Aaron," taunted Larry. "I'm aching to plug me a big jock."

Aaron lunged, low like a fullback hitting the line. Larry yelped, shot. It was high, missing Aaron. He reached the two, tearing Linda away from Larry with such force that she fell to the ground.

Larry backed off, trying to tear away from Aaron's grasp. He shot again.

By this time Oscar and Josh were coming towards them. Linda and Esther were screaming.

There was a sudden flash in the eastern sky, followed a second later by an explosion that lighted the horizon. Everyone froze.

Then Larry scrambled up and ran into the brush.

Linda rushed to Aaron's side. "Help me! He's been shot!" she screamed.

CHAPTER SEVENTEEN

June 12, 2020

"Get down, as low as you can!" cried Jim.

"How low is low," she grunted. "We've got on the wrong side of the barricade and left our backside exposed."

"My fault. I fell asleep."

"Maybe we can burrow under the barrier and get on the other side."

"We don't have much choice either way."

"Hey Fenzer! You let my girl come out and you can go free!"

"Curt!" Dorothy recognized the voice. "You're wrong, I have a choice and it ain't him."

"They're behind us, at the base of the mountain."

He cupped his hand to his mouth. "You giving the orders, Curt? Where's Sam?"

"I'm right here and still giving orders," Sam's voice came from the same direction.

"You want Curt to have Dorothy? What does Harry say about that?"

"Harry doesn't care. Not after the way she treated him," Sam replied.

Dorothy snorted. "I hear you, Sam, but I don't hear Harry or Elaine," she said.

"You heard right!" Harry's voice came on.

"My deepest sympathy to Elaine," Dorothy replied.

"I don't need your sympathy!" Elaine cried out.

"Let's get this over with," that was Jack's voice.

"That's five of them behind us," whispered Jim. "What are the chances the other three are in front?"

"Let's try it. What do we have to lose?"

"Try making a hole at the bottom of that barricade and we'll crawl under. Meantime, I'd better keep an eye on them. I may have to waste a couple of bullets on them."

Jim kept his eye trained on the base of the mountain, trying to distinguish movement or form. He debated whether to shoot if he did. So far, all the firing had been done by Sam's bunch with no effect. Was this on purpose? He didn't want to kill any of them, but could he afford laying off until it was too late?

"We're waiting, Fenzer!" it was Curt again.

"All right, Curt. You want her? You come get her."

"Tell him to bring along Harry," said Dorothy. "I might want to waste a couple of bullets myself."

"My, my, you're getting blood-thirsty."

"It's catching. Besides, these last few days have taught me to fight back any way I can, even with a gun."

He explained his uncertainty of shooting back, his reluctance to be the first to draw blood.

"I understand," she said. "We're being forced to do things we never dreamt of doing. We decried the violence of the last world as we sat safely in our living rooms viewing the carnage from a distance and thinking it couldn't happen to us. Well, it did."

A bullet came crashing through the brush, just missing him.

Jim had kept watch even while listening to Dorothy, so he saw the flash from the rifle. He quickly returned fire and was rewarded by a yelp.

She looked at him. "I see you made your decision."

"It was an automatic reaction, No! It was anger, damn it! Everywhere we turn, every time we think we've solved a problem, it's something else. Larry, Charlie, Curt or Harry, there is no end. I want them out of my way! I just want to enjoy our happiness together."

She reached over and kissed him. "I want that too—and we shall. C'mon, I think we can squeeze through now. That last shot was too close."

"Fenzer! You just clipped Jack!" shouted Sam.

'Good Old Jack! Trust him to be in the right place,"

Jim returned the exclamation. "I warned you yesterday. You didn't let it end there."

"Kill the son-of-bitch, Sam!" screamed Judith.

"Here it comes!" Jim pulled her down beside him. There was a crash of rifle fire that splintered the barricade above them. And it didn't stop with that one volley. Two, three, two, four, the groupings varied, but continued on for two or three minutes. Jim, holding Dorothy close, felt the debris from the shelter splattering down on them. They were firing wild, with anger, instead of thinking. He knew he couldn't count on that for long.

At last there was a lull, "Let's start inching away from here," he told her. "They'll get smart sooner or later and get their aim lower."

"Maybe they'll think they got us."

"Could be. No more talking from our side. They can draw their conclusions."

They slowly drew away from the shattered barrier above them. "Fenzer! Had enough?"

They kept quiet. They had managed to squirm some four feet away. Luckily there was no lack of cover in the debris-strewn field, but they had to keep their heads down because their cover was so uneven.

There followed a series of reports as their tormentors probed right, left, then repeated the pattern.

"Maybe I should scream in pain or you should cry out," she whispered. "Let them think they got us."

"Yeah, that's a good idea, but if we do that, they may move in. Then we have to make a decision to shoot them. Are you ready for that?"

She nodded. "What else could we do? They've constantly left us with the worse choice."

A sharp explosion interrupted them and they felt a rain of shattered limbs and dirt.

"A grenade!" he looked at her. "How can we fight that?"

"Do we give up?" she answered.

He rolled over and embraced her. "I don't like the choices."

A shrill yell reverberated, repeatedly across the canyon. Then no sooner did it die out, a flash of light was seen in the haze covering the mountain top, like a bolt of lightning. Almost immediately came the sound of the explosion and half the mountain came hurling down towards them.

LINDA WAS SCREAMING. The others stood by, momentarily stunned by the shooting and the distant explosion. Then Oscar recovered.

"Josh! Hurry! Get Walter!"

"I'll get some blankets," Nancy ran to the shelter as Josh took off.

Oscar knelt by Aaron. "Can you hear me, Aaron?"

"Yeah, my chest, is that where he got me?"

"Yes, don't move. Josh is on the way to get Walter."

"Linda, Did he get her?"

"I'm right here, Aaron," she answered, taking one of his hands. "Larry's gone."

Nancy returned with blankets and a first aid kit. They made him comfortable tended to his wound. However, it was evident to all that he needed treatment which they couldn't give him.

"It's going to be up to Walter," Oscar told Esther. "His first case of major surgery."

"Is he up to it?"

He shook his head. "I don't know, Hell! I don't know much of anything. Damn! Nothing goes right anymore."

It was at this moment that John arrived. It was evident he had been running as he stood there panting, looking at Aaron.

"My God! What happened now?"

"Larry strikes again," replied Oscar. "What happened out there? What was that explosion?"

"I don't know. I'm afraid to guess."

He told them of the survivalists, right up to the moment he left Jim and Dorothy.

"That explosion came from the direction of where I left them. It could be they are using explosives to attack them.

They need help. That's why I'm here. Have you gotten into the Post?"

"We know where it is, but as of this morning we hadn't broken in. However, Tom promised to do it today.

"But now we have this. Aaron's badly hurt. Larry is still at large although he's down to one bullet. In addition to all that, you tell me Jim and Dorothy are besieged by a bunch of wild-eyed radicals. Hell! If they've got explosives what chance do we have when we can only wield log clubs?"

"You're going to leave them out there?"

Oscar sighed. "No, I'm overwhelmed with problems and no solutions, or at least the means to carry out the solutions. Guns, John. The ultimate solution to our problems. I guess that says something about our society, the last one and the new one. Why should things change?"

John didn't have to answer because the entire class came running. Jean saw him and ran directly to him. He took her on the fly and swung her around, kissing her hungrily.

She responded with equal ardor. Thelma and George joined them, watching with wide smiles.

Walter immediately went to examine Aaron. Linda stood by on the other side until Stella and Ellen pushed her out of the way.

"Damn! Just what I don't need," Walter exclaimed.

"You're not going to let him die like you did Joe," Linda tugged at his arm.

"My God, Linda! I'm just as likely to kill him on the operating table."

Aaron weakly raised his hand and waved him over. Walter knelt by his side and put his head close to Aaron's. Linda on the other side.

"Doc, You go ahead and cut me up. You got something to put me to sleep, Right?"

"We have anesthetics. We don't have a specialist. We don't have monitoring equipment. We don't have a blood supply. Do you know your blood type?"

"O, I believe, Yes, it's O."

Walter nodded. "That helps. I should be able to find one of your classmates with that type."

"That's my type," said Linda.

"Okay. Now any operation is dangerous and those odds double or triple in this environment and with a non-surgeon like me. Stella is an operating room nurse so that will be a great help. I'll do whatever you want, now that you know your chances."

Aaron looked at Linda who was holding his hand.

"Hey, big guy," eyes teary, but smiling. "Don't you know I like you for your money?"

Aaron smiled, turned slightly to Walter. "There's your answer, Doc. Never disagree with a beautiful woman. So go to it. If I don't make it, I'll sue you for breaking up my love life."

Walter nodded. "I think we'd better move you to the basement of the hospital." He turned to the others. "Besides Stella and Ellen helping me, I need some help in cleaning and disinfecting the operating room."

"I'll do it," said Linda.

"We'll help too," said Esther. Sylvia nodded. Several others also volunteered.

"Hey!" Sylvia came to Aaron's side and took his hand.

"Did I ever tell you that you were a ringer for Raymond Burr, the actor who played Perry Mason on TV?"

He moved his eyes to look at her. "No, Why didn't you tell me this fifteen years ago, You made me feel left out."

"When could I have done that? Did you ever call me up for a date?"

Aaron laughed, then regretted it as he felt a spasm in his chest.

"Sorry about that," she said. "A comedian is allowed to die on stage, but never to kill the audience."

"The audience is supposed to roll on the floor and that's where I am," he grinned. "Stick around, I'd like to meet your friends."

She squeezed his hand. "Any friend of Linda's is a friend of ours."

As they made preparations to move Aaron, Tom took Oscar and John aside.

"I got that order you wanted filled. I brought six Winchesters and four revolvers and ammunition. There's others, but I hid them. We can get them later."

"Great!" exclaimed Oscar. "Will that make it for your purpose?" glancing at John.

"That's more than enough. Now give me three men and I'll take off immediately. There's no time to lose. We may already be too late judging by that explosion. But if the bad guys won, we still need to stop them before they get here."

"Frank! Josh! Get over here!" Oscar boomed. "Those two, you and I will go. We'll take the Winchesters. Tom, you distribute the remaining weapons. Post guards and keep an eye out for Larry or any other strangers. Protect yourselves."

Oscar explained the situation to Frank and Josh. "Get food and water and ammunition. We'll be traveling light and fast. Get moving!"

He then explained his plans to Walter. "You do what you have to do to save Aaron. Draft any of the others you may need to help."

Jean and Esther stood by anxiously.

"Why do you have to go off and play hero," Esther complained grimly.

"Let's get this straight, Esther. I didn't ask for this, but I can't dodge my responsibilities or let down my friends. They're your friends too."

"Then be sure to get your ass back here," she kissed him and went to rejoin Linda and Sylvia.

"I can't better that performance," said Jean to John. "Go count coup," she kissed him.

CHAPTER EIGHTEEN

June 12, 2020

Seconds before he pulled Dorothy down and himself after her, he saw rocks streaming down on them like a meteorite shower. Hastily he pulled the packs he and John had brought, on top of them. Even so, he heard the thuds as some of them connected. They rolled up in a fetal position, clutching the packs tighter over their bodies.

The rain of earthly projectiles ceased after a couple of minutes and they came out from under their cover. Again silence reigned, as it had when they first arrived.

"They're not shooting at us," she said.

"Understandable, if all of them were at the base of the mountain," Jim was looking at the mountain top, or rather what was left.

"My Northwest Passage," he said.

"What?"

"Surely a history teacher has heard of the Northwest Passage."

"Yes, and it was never found. At least in the manner they expected. It's at the top of the world through an ocean of ice."

"Very appropriate. Ours is at the top of a mountain. For the moment though, and more important, your erstwhile captors have been improperly buried and without benefit of last rites."

He arose but staying on his knees and keeping an eye for any sudden movements. He surveyed his notch on the mountain. Then a thought came to mind.

"Martin! By God!"

"Did you say Martin?"

"Yes, the mountain. Martin blew it down, or at least I think he did. Why else would it go off?"

"Our world has been blowing up for months," she joined him. "What's so different now?"

"Martin had three cases of dynamite. Twice he mentioned blowing up the mountain. The last time when John and I failed to find a direct route between our camp and the cave.

"And that yell, just before the explosion, was that an old Indian war cry?"

"Are you saying Martin blew up that mountain to save us?"

"I believe his original plan was to open a passage for his children. Then he might have heard all the gunfire down in the canyon..."

"And naturally he figured you and me were besieged by these bearded Castro types."

"I admit I can't prove it, but it makes sense. He had binoculars so he could have seen what was going on. He knew we had no arms except John's Winchester. It wouldn't take much to figure all that gunfire couldn't come from one piece."

"That's a lot of supposing. Don't you think he might figure that blowing up the mountain might also bury us? But assuming that you're right, where is he? He got his passage. The firing has stopped."

Jim frowned. "Yes, where is he? If he did this for us, wouldn't he come down to check?"

"Shall we?" she nodded in the direction of the mountain.

He nodded. "But first we should check on our late foes before one of them pops up from the grave like a horror movie."

"Let's hurry up and check on them."

"Harry?" he questioned.

"Well, is he or isn't he? I want to know one way or another."

The explosion had made a cut in the mountain that Jim now estimated at three hundred feet. Still a formidable obstacle to a group supplied only with limbs acquired at birth. However, it was less challenging than what he and John had faced and within the capabilities of their classmates to climb. It had also created a continuous, unbroken slope that now extended from the pass to just short of their barricade.

As they tried to climb, their feet sank into the freshly turned earth.

Jim shook his head. "This won't do. We don't have the equipment or the time to dig them up, only to rebury them. If they were at the base of the mountain, and we have no reason to believe otherwise, then they were killed immediately or suffocated shortly after."

"So Harry has left me dangling again."

"We can't prove beyond a reasonable doubt, but I'd say we can be ninety nine point nine percent sure. He was here. We heard his voice. If he ran off before the blast, where is he? Back at the stronghold? When John returns, we can go check. Perhaps Cal and Ann survived. We never heard their voices, but John said all were coming. So, I'd have to say he's here, under our feet. How much more proof do you want?"

"I'm scared that sometime in the future he'll show up with that smug, 'you're still my wife' self-righteous facade. And what that does to us?"

"It wouldn't bother me. But I can understand your concern. Especially when other women can be so judgmental.

"When we get settled, I'll find some excuse to dig them up and confirm Harry's demise."

They ate their rations, then arranged a matted area where they could lie down. They kissed and held each other, but Dorothy discouraged anything more intimate.

"Not until I have a bath. I stink."

"So do I. We're just a pair of stinkers."

So they napped than ate again. They talked and made plans until darkness came and they went to sleep in each other's arms.

TOM AND HIS CREW HAD carried Aaron to the hospital basement. A detail of the women had cleaned and disinfected the operating room. And while they were at it, included some of the other rooms.

"Ah!" Sylvia exclaimed as she plopped on a hospital bed, her eyes half closed, and a look of rapture in her face. "I never thought I could enjoy lying in a hospital bed."

"Do you mean to tell me these have been here all along?" Esther shrieked. "My aching back!"

"You know what they say about going into a hospital? You'll never get out," Sylvia locked her fingers behind her head and gazed benignly at the others.

"Yeah, The Hospital, starring George C. Scott and Diana Rigg," Esther replied from the adjoining bed.

"Don't you two ever stop?" Linda pressed her fingers to her temple.

The three women, along with Jane, Nancy and Carl were resting after their labor and awaiting news from the operating room.

"What would you have us do, Honey?" Esther got off and put an arm around her. "Shall we all sit in a circle and have a good cry, wringing our hands?"

"No, Please go on. I've heard you two for the last four years. I should be used to it. It's just that..."

Jean poked her head in the door. "Linda! They need blood donors."

Linda rushed out and Jean addressed the others. "They also need reliefs for the light holders, unless you can't stand the sight of blood."

The operation was being performed under the glow of a battery of flashlights. "Well, I can always keep my eyes shut," said Sylvia.

Carl regarded her. "Walter doesn't need distractions. More than your eyes have to be shut."

"What are you? A critic?" she stuck her tongue at him.

It was three hours later that Walter emerged from the operating room. Tom, who had been keeping vigil outside the basement, glanced at him as he came out of the corridor to the outside.

"Well, are you going to tell us? We're all immediate family."

Walter stuck out his arm. "See that, shaking, but luckily it was steady when it needed to be."

"By that, I take it to mean it was a success?"

"A success with all the usual cautions that go with all operations. The next two days should tell us how successful. But it looks good. He's in good shape."

"You and the nurses grab some of those beds in there and take a rest. Who's looking after him?"

"Linda and her friends are in there with orders to call me in case of, you know."

Tom sighed. "Okay, you've earned a rest. We'll call you if necessary. The rest of us will stay here until Aaron can be moved."

"Do you think it's wise to be divided in view of all these latest developments?" Carl asked.

"I've divided the troops equally and we've got arms. Can't do much more than that. We'll have to wait on Jim and Oscar and find out the outcome with the bad guys."

June 13, 2020

The rescuing party arrived about midmorning to find Jim and Dorothy sitting nonchalantly, leaning against the packs.

"Oh, Dorothy, we have company. Did you invite them or are they calling unannounced," Jim regarded his visitors, trying to keep a smile off his face.

"You son-of-a-gun," boomed Oscar. "We're pushing our butts to come save you and here you two are making like honeymooners."

"Believe me, less than twenty-four hours ago, I wouldn't have given much for our chances. Eight heavily armed people pitching grenades. God!"

He explained to Oscar what had happened. Frank and Josh listened while Dorothy took John aside. Jim hadn't told the others his suspicions that Martin has caused the explosion.

"We haven't seen him, if it was him. No one has been by. Of course, there's always the possibility that someone else blew the mountain. In that case Martin should have heard the explosion and come to investigate."

Jim joined them with the others. "I've told them how we found Martin and the cave. Now we have a couple of things to do before we return to camp. "John, I think you might want to check on Martin. Take Frank along with you. Then return to the Stonecliff camp.

"Dorothy, Oscar and I shall go to the stronghold and check if there are any survivors. We can't afford to have these people wandering about, armed and ready to shoot those considered outsiders.

"Josh, you return to camp and tell Tom about our plans, so they won't worry. Our party should be back in about a week, John's a little later."

Josh nodded and took off.

"John, do you think you and Frank can handle everything on your side?"

"I don't see why not. Give us a week or ten days. I don't expect any problems."

"Okay, we'll see you back home then."

June 14, 2020

"It's obvious no one has been here for some time," observed Jim. "The embers are cold. How long does it take for heat to dissipate?" he looked at Oscar.

"Don't ask me. I don't go in for such weighty questions. But the facts do seem to indicate these characters being AWOL from their camp."

"I think we can safely say they were killed in action and we know where the bodies are buried," said Dorothy.

They proceeded to the open cave. Oscar whistled. "These guys were well prepared, about as well as Dorothy's basement."

"Yes, but with an accent on the firearms," she said.

"Well, in hindsight, perhaps we should have had a few of those ourselves," Oscar continued. "Someone could have challenged Larry. It might have prevented two deaths, a wounding and a kidnapping."

Jim surveyed the contents of the cave. "Shall we take what we can? We did win the war and while we crave no additional territory, we can sure use the loot."

"We can take what we need the most, especially clothes and shoes," said Dorothy.

"Fatigues?" Jim asked.

"No, but no frilly stuff, Well, maybe one or two," she gave him a sultry look.

"I think we should take the firearms," said Oscar. "Larry is still out here. We don't want him to replenish his armory."

In the end, each made a pack containing food, medicines and clothing. Then they added what firearms they could carry. The rest they buried. Each strapped on a belt with canteen and a revolver or automatic.

June 17, 2020

The three returned to base camp in late afternoon to be greeted by David.

"Josh told us the crisis was over, but," he looked at all the firearms they were carrying. "Do you know something we should?"

"We're just cornering the market, so we can start World War I of the new world," Oscar grimaced, letting down his pack heavily.

"I sent Josh to tell Tom the good news," David continued.

"Did Aaron make it?" Oscar stopped to ask.

"With flying colors. Walter said we can move him here in a couple of days."

"Great!" exclaimed Jim. "As soon as John and Frank get back, we need to have a general meeting to decide our next move."

"Literally," added Dorothy.

"Any sign of Larry?" Oscar sat down.

"No, we kept watch around the clock. I don't know how long he can hold out without food."

"Its five days now," said Oscar. "Unless he has food stashed somewhere, well."

David shrugged. "Does anyone care?"

"I intend to mount a search for him," said Jim. "He has a lot to answer for."

"As I said, after five days," Oscar drew a finger across his throat.

June 19, 2020

The full class was united with Tom's party arriving in midmorning. John and Frank arrived in the afternoon.

The group from the hospital was surrounded by well-wishers congratulating Aaron and Walter and the nurses.

"Hey!" exclaimed Sylvia. "I scrubbed floors and walls."

"Ah, our little spinster," Oscar patted her head, "Keeping out of trouble, I hope."

"Trouble?" she gave him an innocent look. "When have I ever been trouble? Do I get in trouble?" she directed her question to Carl.

"Of course not, my dear," he turned to Oscar. "How dare you insinuate such balderdash?"

"Boy! Are YOU in trouble," Oscar guffawed?

Jim and Dorothy extended hands to Aaron.

"We're relieved you made it through our primitive hospital facilities," Jim told him.

"Yes, thanks to Walter, the nurses and a lot of others who put themselves out for me."

"Is this the same Aaron who looked out only for himself?" Dorothy smiled.

Aaron nodded. "That was me, wasn't it? But as you both have been hammering at us, this is a new world with new conditions. Besides, no matter what anyone thought, I didn't condone the actions taken by Larry or Charlie," he gave her a meaningful look.

"You have me there," she replied. "I said some things in the heat of the moment. It's my turn to eat crow."

He smiled. "Aren't you glad there's none left for you to digest?"

She gave him a hug. "I knew that when I said it. Anyway, welcome back."

He sighed, patted her back. "Why is it all the good women are already taken?"

Jim grinned. "From what I've heard, I believe there's one left."

"You know it. I know it. But does she?"

"Give it a little time," said Dorothy. "In the vernacular of the business world, your stock has risen in the last week. Don't get out of the market just yet."

That afternoon John and Frank returned, riding and leading extra pack animals. Only Jim did not express surprise at the little caravan. He waited as John was welcomed by Jean. Frank sought out Anna Esparto and shyly held hands. The greetings over, John pulled Jim and Dorothy aside.

"I couldn't find Martin or Daniel. The dynamite was missing, so we can assume they set it off and got killed in the process."

Dorothy tilted her head back, eyes closed and sighed.

"Poor Martin, giving up his life to save some white eyes that never appreciated him or his people."

"They were his children," said John, quietly.

"Really? Can you honestly tell me that someone like Margaret Stanton is worthy of salvation over the likes of Edna, Shirley or Joe?"

Jim shrugged. "A few days ago, we probably would have said the same for Aaron. Now he is a hero and a team player."

"He said he and Daniel weren't," mused John. "So, we still don't know who the true survivors shall be."

"What's next?" Dorothy changed the subject. "Do we move to the cave or bring its contents here? Do we tell them about Martin's theory?"

"I don't think we should talk about the 'children' bit," said John. "Martin doesn't deserve the ridicule."

Jim nodded. "I agree. But everything else, we put on the table, tomorrow after breakfast,"

CHAPTER NINETEEN

June 20, 2020

Breakfast was an event, fresh eggs. John and Frank had brought them. Unfortunately, there weren't enough for each person, so they were scrambled.

"I never liked scrambled eggs," Sylvia volunteered, "but today I could eat the whole chicken, feathers and all."

"I suppose that reminds you of an old movie," said Carl between mouthfuls.

"Of course, The Egg and I."

"Claudette Colbert and Fred MacMurray," Esther contributed. "The first appearance of Ma and Pa Kettle."

"You had to ask," Oscar glared at Carl.

"In fact," continued Sylvia, "just give me a word and I'll connect it to a movie."

There was a long groan.

Jim got up. "I think this is a good time to interrupt before Sylvia incites a riot. We've reached a point where we have to make choices. The remains of Stonecliff have yielded much that shall make life easier for us. We have another hoard at the stronghold. Even better, as you have seen, John and I discovered John's old medicine man who survived the disaster with a well-stocked cave. Let me tell you the story."

He told them about Martin and his belief that an old world would end and a new one begins. How he had stocked the cave to save any survivors. He did not mention Martin's notion of the 'children.'

"My first thought on discovering Martin and his cave was to move everyone there. There's fresh water, shelter, food, plus the animals. It's clean country and there are no reminders to bring back sad memories. On second thought, I decided that was pushing my opinions on you without allowing your input. So, let's talk about it."

"Well, you know, Jim, most of us haven't seen the place," Oscar remarked. "If I were to vote right now, it would be difficult to choose. God! Anything would be better than this. It's dismal, but is it better there?"

Jim nodded. "Of course, and it's dismal until we make it livable. We're better off than the caveman, but we won't see the comforts and luxuries of the old world again."

"We can go back to the log cabin days," said Sylvia.

"God knows we have a plentiful supply of logs. We can use these blankets for curtains. What a comedown."

"Yeah," Oscar muttered. "You ought to know. Just like Scarlet O'Hara in Gone with the Wind."

"Why Oscar," she cooed. "You might be saved after all. What a team you and I and Esther will make, but I won't sleep on the sofa."

Oscar groaned.

"It's true," said Martha Endosmot. "This place isn't much. It's not what it used to be, but it's what's left of Stonecliff. I spent my life here. It's not glamorous and I'm not the sophisticated type, but I was happy here. There's a tie here that I can't break. It's changed, but, it's still home. Can you understand that?"

Jim smiled. "I understand, and I respect your views. Many others feel the same."

"On the other hand," Sherman interrupted, "there's some of us that no longer had ties to Stonecliff."

Jim nodded. "We could split, but I'd rather not. We don't have to decide today. There's no rush."

"Jim, our stock at the cave needs looking after," John said. "Why don't I make a trip out there and take along a few tourists?"

"That's a great idea. You take Jean, Thelma, George and," he searched among the others, "Frank, Josh, Anna and Martha. Let's live a little, Martha. We also need to finish off the stronghold and bring in those supplies. So I'll send off that great team of Oscar, Sylvia and Esther." He waited until everyone had their laugh.

"And to keep the peace on that team, let's add Tom, Carl, Jane and the Longleys. Divide our four-footed friends between the two parties and leave whenever you're ready. The rest of us will stay here and finish our salvage of Stonecliff and by that time I hope everyone has thought it out and come to a consensus of where we will plant our roots."

June 29, 2020

The days had gotten brighter, the overcast lighter. They had noticed it five days earlier. Every day since, upon awakening, they had cast their eyes to the sky the first thing in the morning. Today there was only a light haze and as the morning lengthen, they saw the dim outline of the sun. It was greeted by a roar of approval.

"Let there be light!" screamed Sylvia. "Lo and behold, there was light."

"How blasphemous," retorted Linda.

Oscar's party had returned the day before. They had finished clearing out the stronghold except for a few minor items.

"We got everything we thought we could use, but," he pursed his lips, as if undecided, then continued, "somehow I got the impression there was more when we were there last."

"What are you inferring?" Jim glanced at him.

"That someone else had been there and taken some of the stuff."

"Damn! I thought we were clear at last."

"I might be wrong. Like I said, it was an impression. They had a lot of supplies and equipment there."

"If you're right...Who could it be? Larry? Or maybe someone survived that blast. That would seem more likely since they knew where to go."

"When is John due back?"

"I didn't give him a deadline. I deliberately paired several people in hopes of promoting a little romance and thereby easing some of the complaints."

"Yeah, I gathered as much when you gave me Tom, Jane, Carl and Sylvia."

"Any success there?"

Oscar shrugged. "Tom and Jane seemed to get along well. Carl and Sylvia?, Well, you know those two. One-ups-manship is the name of the game they play."

"Yes..." Jim was already on another track. "I don't like it about those missing items. They could signal more problems for us. We can't live like this, working and keeping watch for possible intruders. Then John's group possibly walking, unexpectedly, into an ambush."

"Maybe we'd better warn them."

"Yes, except I'm the only one that knows the way to the cave," he fingered his chin, absently regarding the others. "So, I'm elected."

Hurriedly he called the others and explained what Oscar had found. "John's party has to be warned, so I'll go since I'm the only one that knows the way."

"You're going alone?" Dorothy eyed him.

"Yes, I have..."

"No! Damn it!" she stamped her foot. "I told you once, never again. Do I have to club you on the head to make you understand? I go with you!"

Jim laughed, then took her in his arms and kissed her. "Of course, how stupid of me to believe otherwise."

Aaron observed Linda watching the byplay and a twinge of jealousy gripped him, but only momentarily. He wondered if she would ever let go of her past.

"Okay," Jim resumed. "Oscar, you hold down the fort, literally. Let's suspend any more salvage activities and keep the bunch here until we get back. There's plenty to do in camp. I want everyone armed at all times. Stay in pairs at the very least. Set up guards twenty-four hours a day. At night, stay in camp and away from the light of the fire. Well, as much as possible. Those on guard keep your eyes on the surrounding darkness not on the fire.

"Come on, Tonto," he took Dorothy's arm. "We've got to head 'em off at the pass."

"Who is 'we,' stranger? I don't recognize you without your mask," Dorothy deadpanned, looking at Sylvia.

Sylvia rolled her eyes. "Oh brother. Those ad libs will kill you."

"That's what I've been telling you all these years," said Esther, "and you're still in one piece."

Later, all preparations finished, Jim and Dorothy were ready to leave. They had decided to take the horses which he figured would save them a couple of day's travel.

"How long are you planning on staying?" said Oscar.

"Not too long. They can't have much more to do. They might even be on the way. We'll play it by ear. Meanwhile you keep your guard up."

July 2, 2020

"What kind of celebration are you planning for the Fourth, Oscar?" Carl inquired.

It was late afternoon and preparations for the evening meal were in progress. They had all quit early. Taking heed of Jim's warning, they had stayed together and confined their duties to camp housekeeping.

"What's there to celebrate?" replied Oscar, without enthusiasm.

"Well, we're here, alive."

"You've got your holidays confused."

"Yeah, it's called Thanksgiving," Sylvia offered.

"Can we get off the crowd-pleasing amenities and tackle the serious and unpleasant problems?" Aaron interrupted.

"Oh? I thought this was our long-delayed reunion picnic," Oscar grunted.

"This is no time for sarcasm, Oscar. Pete and I heard what sounded like the engines on a chopper."

"A helicopter?" Oscar perked up. He looked at Peter Sourenson for confirmation and was given a nod in return.

"And what else? Did either of you see it?"

"No, it was off in the distance. I don't know how far."

"Where were you at?"

"We made a circle around the hospital. A place I know well," replied Aaron.

"Gil and Ralph relieved us," he continued. "I told them we had heard something but didn't say it sounded like a chopper. I didn't want to implant a suggestion in their heads. If there is one, we want separate confirmation."

"Good idea," said Oscar. "How long before they come in?"

"Another two or three hours. Howard and Roy will relieve them.

"And speaking of relief, Oscar, I think we should be putting some of the women on guard rotation. There's thirty-three of us and only eleven men. We should at least have two or three helping out."

"I'll vote for that," said Jane. "You can even put two women together. We can do our share."

"All right," agreed Oscar. "Aaron, you're Sergeant of the Guard, set up a schedule.

"The important thing is the possibility of a chopper. We aren't alone after all."

"Yeah, but whose chopper is it?" Sylvia said. "Our sky is almost clear now, but they haven't appeared overhead. Why? Maybe it was an invasion after all and they're just now getting to us."

"Ridiculous!" Sherman cut in. "Who would want to invade Stonecliff, or what's left of it? There never was a military facility larger than a recruiting office in the whole county."

"Yeah, that makes sense," said Carl. "But it's still strange they wouldn't fly over."

"Because they couldn't see anything worth seeing with that overcast," said Oscar, holding up his hand for silence.

"Until we find out who or what they are, we stay alert. Except for the guards, we'll stay here. We'd best be making some sort of a barricade, just in case. I want all water bottles filled in case of siege."

"We've always kept them filled," said Esther. "There's only a few empties."

A party was dispatched to the river to fill the empty bottles while the others formed a barricade around the shelter.

After the evening meal, Aaron called the relief for the guard detail. But before they could set out, the guards came running.

"There's a large party of armed men approaching. They're right behind us!"

"Everyone take cover!" Oscar shouted. "You women take shelter in the back!"

"What do you mean, 'take shelter in the back?'" cried Esther. "You think we're prissy, drawing room types?

"Girls!" she turned to the others, "grab a rifle or shotgun and man the barricades!"

"Shouldn't you have said 'women the barricades'?" Sylvia grinned.

They got armed and took their place at the barrier, keeping watch on the surrounding area. It was just past seven, but there was plenty of daylight left. A couple of weeks ago it would have been dark by this time.

Then they saw them, strung out in a skirmish line and advancing towards their position. They wore dark clothing and masks and carried assault weapons. Oscar's heart sank. Too much firepower. And the masks? Did they have chemical weapons too? Who were they? He groaned. No way they could prevail against them.

"All right!" he shouted. "Show them we have fire power too!"

Rifle barrels were shoved over the barricade. There were a series of clicks as pieces were cocked.

July 2, 2020

Jim and Dorothy had been riding steadily and at a good pace following the trail they had traversed before on foot.

Even so, they had to be careful because the brush-strewn ground could easily cause a spill or a leg injury to one of the horses. Every now and then, Jim stopped and using binoculars, surveyed their surroundings.

"Larry is still out there. There's a possibility some of your captors survived," he explained to her.

"God! Will we ever reach the point when we aren't threatened by something or someone?"

"Yeah, I'm beginning to believe the only way we can achieve peace of mind and body is to mount an extensive search of the entire area and make sure we are the only two-footed animals remaining."

They were almost to the base of the mountain pass when Jim uttered an exclamation. "There's John and his party. They're at the crest of the pass."

"Oh good, I wasn't looking forward to climbing that mountain."

"We might still have to. However they decide to go, it will take them almost an hour to come down. Shall we wait for them at 'our place?'"

She pulled up on her reins. "'Our place?' We almost got killed there."

"A weak attempt at humor," he smiled.

They dismounted as they reached what was left of their shattered barricade and were greeted by three rifle barrels pointing up to them. Lying prone behind them were Harry, Elaine and Judith.

"Just stand there and act natural," Harry instructed.

"We don't want to alarm your friends."

"My prayers are answered," cackled Judith. "We were going to take that bunch coming down the mountain, but to have you two drop in, Jack will be avenged."

"My dear wife," Harry cut in. "What's it to be? You have only a few minutes to make a decision before they get here."

"What decision is that?" Elaine came on before Dorothy could reply. "To spare her? What does that do to me?"

"It tells you what a damn fool you are for believing him," Dorothy said. "And it tells me that I was also a damn fool for eight years of living with him."

Harry laughed. "Divide and conquer, huh? It won't work, darling. Your lover is going to get it and you'll see him die."

"You shoot us and it will give you a way to our friends," said Jim.

"We'll take care of your friends," chortled Judith, holding up a grenade.

Jim's hopes sank. They could shoot both of them and then lob a grenade into John's group. John was still several minutes away, unknowingly walking into a trap. Jim's and Dorothy's rifles were still on their horses, but both had their sidearms. So far they had not been ordered to drop them.

He had only seconds to make a decision. The three were lying down to conceal themselves from the approaching group. Their rifles were pointed upward to cover the two. The angle of the pieces was the key, but it would only give him a couple of seconds at most before they could adjust.

He leaped sideways, away from their line of fire and knocking Dorothy to the ground. At the same time he was clawing for his gun. Judith screamed and hastily fired. Jim swung his gun in her direction and snapped off two shots. All three shots missed.

Harry shot and he didn't miss Jim.

Dorothy scrambling to seek shelter saw Jim go down and screamed. She pulled her own gun and started firing.

Judith, face contorted with hate, plucked the pin from a grenade and swung back her arm to throw it.

Harry saw it too and shouted. "No! No! They're too close!"

Then the grenade exploded.

CHAPTER TWENTY

July 1, 2020

"Gentlemen, the President of the United States."

The four men in the room scraped back their chairs and stood up. They had been seated at a long table reserved for cabinet meetings.

The President came in, nodded at the four men. "Please be seated." He sat in the presidential chair, two men on his left. The other two men sat across from him. The man who had opened the door and made the announcement sat down on the President's right. "For the record," the President spoke, "present are the Secretary of Defense and the Attorney-General on my left. Mr. MacNamara, my chief of staff, on my right. Our two guests are Mr. Shoster and Mr. Wells, respectively from the FBI and the CIA."

"You have some news to report?" he looked at the two men across from him.

"Yes sir," the tall thin man answered. "The area is clearing up, I've just been told."

"And?"

"We propose to cordon off the area until we can determine the effects of the weapon. Our people are already on station. No one must be allowed in or out unless properly authorized by the Agency."

"What about survivors?"

"We don't believe there are any survivors, sir, but on the off chance there are, they shall be quietly picked up and confined at an undisclosed location, for their safety and debriefing, of course."

The chief of staff nudged the President with his knee. Then he got up and sauntered around the room until he was behind the two men and facing the President.

The smaller man now spoke up. "Mr. President, if we're not careful, we'll have the media swarming over the place. And don't forget the shysters, looking for some reason to sue the government."

"You need my consent on this?"

"Yes sir, the area is so large that our people can't possibly cover all of it. Defense is the logical one to give us support."

The President glanced over their heads at MacNamara. Mac shook his head and raised his hand, palm outward, stop, or was it wait?

"How many people do you have out there?"

"3000 of our own. The Army has 15,000."

"We realize it shall put a strain on the budget," the other one said, "but the catastrophe has already knocked it out of kilter."

"A catastrophe that never should have happened," Mac said loudly.

"What have you done about Fischer?" he continued.

"Nothing. We need him and his group to analyze the effects of the weapon once we get in there."

"You mean that you still trust this man that disobeyed orders? A man that didn't have the brains to point the weapon at the wide expanse of the Pacific Ocean, but instead, points it east where it could hit any one of hundreds of population centers?"

"Mr. MacNamara, once it was determined the weapon was out of control, it was exploded over a desolate area."

"Desolate!" Mac stared at the man. "Don't you men read the papers? Watch TV? Over and over until the senses reel. Over two hundred thousand dead or missing. Half the state of Arizona gone, not to mention parts of Utah and New Mexico. Over fifty thousand square miles! Is that your definition of desolate?"

"Mr. President," the tall one whined to the president..

"That's quite a large piece of real estate you have to cover," he replied, ignoring his plea. "Just how do you expect to do this?"

"I've suggested we go in with platoon-size search parties..."

"Platoons?" the President exclaimed. "You're sending in armed men into a devastated area? Don't you need medics or medical teams if there are any survivors?"

"Sir, this is a classified weapon. We have to protect..."

The President cut him off with a wave of the hand. He turned to the Secretary. "Do you have someone down there we can talk to?"

"Yes sir."

The President pushed the telephone towards him. "Get him. I want to talk to him. As for you, Mr. Shoster, and Mr. Wells, effective immediately, both of you are off the case. I'm surprised Mr. Wells, domestic affairs are not your field."

"Ah, Mr. Shoster felt I should be aware of the situation. It could cause ripples overseas. In fact, it has, as you well know."

"Very well, you have been made aware of it. The State Department will now take over, which in fact, it already has. As for Mr. Shoster," he turned to the Attorney-General sitting next to the Secretary, "I believe he has other projects to occupy his time?"

"Yes sir."

"Before you and your people leave the limelight, Mr. Shoster, I want Mr. Fischer and his cohorts brought here to answer for this mess. I suspect quite a few people on the Hill shall be battling for his presence in front of their committees."

"Mr. President," the Secretary pushed the telephone towards him, "General Delfor is on the line."

"General," the President took over, "this is the President. As of right now, you are in complete charge of the operation there. Your primary mission, repeat, your primary mission is the search and rescue of any survivors.

"Get the armed commandos out of there and send in medical teams. Also some engineers might help clear out obstacles that might hamper the rescue efforts. In addition, seal off the area. Keep the media out for the time being. If they holler, refer them to the White House. That's my job. Keep out the looters and sightseers, and the spooks," he glanced at the two men, squirming in their seats. "If they give you trouble, restrain them in any manner that will get their attention. You shouldn't have trouble with them. They will shortly be given orders to withdraw.

"Any change of orders shall come from the Chairman, the Secretary or myself. If you need extra people, just yell. We have big ears. And General, if you find any survivors, you call the White House direct, you hear?

"Now I'm turning you back to the Secretary. You tell him what you need. Then you get back there and get the hotshots out and send in the mercy types. After what they've gone through, no survivor deserves to be greeted by looking into the barrel of a cannon," he turned the phone back to the Secretary.

"Mr. Attorney-General, I believe you and these two gentlemen have your orders and duties spelled out. Get on them."

They withdrew and the President slumped back on his chair and sighed. "Mac, why does anyone spend half a lifetime seeking this job?"

Mac shrugged. "You've heard the old joke, 'someone has to do the dirty work.'"

He laughed. "That didn't come out right, did it?"

"I know what you were trying to say. It's too late now. I'm getting it from all sides."

"Mr. President, you did the right thing. When this blew up in your face early in your term, you told the country there would be an immediate investigation, no holds barred. You're in the clear."

"That's right," the Secretary joined the conversation. "I have everything on record. I told Fischer to chop it off. He didn't. It's cut and dried. The only thing we might be faulted is that we didn't monitor him, but that's minor. The only way out is for someone to give him a loaded pistol and tell him to do the honorable thing."

"Not that! For God's sake, we need him alive until everyone gets sick and tired of seeing him on TV, over and over," Mac put fingers to his temple, rocking his head from side to side.

"What about Shoster and Wells?" the Secretary asked.

"Yes, they were all too eager to cooperate with Fischer," the President mused. "Somehow I got the impression that if they found any survivors, they wouldn't have survived too long once those two got their hands on them.

"I'll have to replace them, which the media will love. Well, I'd rather the media have their field day with survivors, if any."

"Still we don't want to overlook these scapegoats," Mac persisted.

"No, not scapegoats. That implies passing the blame to someone else and covering your ass. We don't need that when we have the real culprits."

"There's still a lot of fallout to answer," Mac continued. "The catastrophe wiped out Flagstaff, Prescott, Gallup and dozens of other towns. The Grand Canyon is blocked. Everyone from Colorado to Southern California, even Mexico, is howling about the cutoff of water. All the Indian tribes are screaming genocide."

"That's why I want to handle it out in the open, Mac. Without secrecy or intrigue. We don't need a Nixon cover up or a Kennedy assassination mystery that runs on for decades. Nor do we need any more 'gate' investigations at great expense to the government and that end up slapping the criminals with a slap on the wrist."

He looked at the Secretary. "Just what was this weapon supposed to do?"

The Secretary grimaced, shaking his head. "According to Fischer, and I don't know how straight he was with me after all that has happened, it is supposed to affect the weather. Exploded in an already existent low pressure area, it quickly drops the air pressure to incredible lows. The combination causes damage with sudden drops in pressure and accelerates wind velocities to tornado-like force, something like 300 miles an hour. But unlike regular tornados that drop down, cut an uneven and narrow path, this weapon made this force remain over an area for longer periods of time, thereby causing more damage, isolation and, of course, killing people."

"How can that be?"

"I don't know the particulars, and I don't think I want to know. I believe what got them interested was the history of bad weather over battlefields supposedly caused by the excessive exploding of gunpowder. There were chemicals in the gunpowder that aggravated bad weather over the area. I suppose it can be compared to seeding clouds to induce rain. Anyway, the whole project got started back in the eighties along with the Star Wars weaponry of the Reagan era."

"What possible help would that be in a battlefield?"

"Absolutely none," replied the Secretary. "Used on a battlefield, it would affect both sides equally because of the area it covered."

"So it could serve only one purpose," said the President. "A terror weapon. To be used against your foe's country and civilians as the target."

The Secretary nodded. "Exactly, sir."

"That's all the world needs, another terror weapon," said the President.

"And that is going to present problems in prosecuting Fischer and his cohorts," said Mac. "His attorney will want to bring out the details, figuring we won't do it. Then there's our publicity-hungry congressmen who might grant immunity in order to get their names and images in the media."

"Well, it might be possible to keep out the specifics on how to make it," said the Secretary, "but the results are there for the world to see. Every spy in the world will make it their top priority to steal the secret. And don't forget we have our own nut cases in this country who will feel it their duty to pass on our secrets because we shouldn't have exclusive rights to blowing up the world. So it will out. Look what happened to the A bomb. Every tin-can nation now owns one and has it pointed at their favorite enemy."

The president sighed. "There's no way of stopping it then?"

"Well, we're back to handing him and his buddies a loaded pistol," the Secretary looked at him. "Or else using it ourselves to make sure the deed is done. Then burning all the plans. Then five years from now the Germans or the Japanese will come up with the same thing, only better."

"This is a democracy with constitutional rights," said the President.

"There are times when humanity would be better served by suspending them for a few minutes," said Mac.

The President looked at the Secretary. "Keep me informed wherever I am or whatever the time of day or night. And Mac, let's look at my schedule. Unless it is important, cancel it and make arrangements for us to fly over the area. Maybe by that time we'll know if there are any survivors."

July 2, 2020

The line of skirmishers stopped. The people behind the barricade waited, firearms thrust over the barrier. Finally, Oscar stood up, left arm upraised, his right holding his rifle at port.

"Who are you? What do you want?"

One man detached himself from the skirmishers and advanced a few paces from the barricade.

"I can ask the same question. Who are you and what are you doing here?"

"What are you? A comedian?" Oscar replied. "You think we're out here for a picnic? This is our town, what's left of it. Then you come here with your assault weapons and chemical equipment and question our right to be here. That makes us mad as hell, and we're ready to defend ourselves."

"You people survived this?" he sounded less truculent.

"For almost two months now," said Oscar. "You want to identify yourself?"

"Uh, sorry. I'm Lieutenant Crowther, United States Army. We're supposed to contain this area. You're trespassing. The area has been declared off limits except for authorized personnel. Furthermore, you're compounding your problem by the bearing of arms. I must ask you to lay them aside and step away, otherwise we shall be forced to take action."

"I can't believe this!" said Oscar. The others had now risen from behind the barrier. "We've spent two months scraping for food, shelter and clothing. We've been shot at and have sustained casualties. We don't know what's happened out there, but we're damn sure not going to stand here and have you kick us out of our own land,"

"You'd better get someone out here with more rank before you screw up and end your military career here," Aaron spoke up. "I know a few people in Washington that can book a reservation for you in Leavenworth, Lieutenant."

The young man was a mixture of belligerence and astonishment. Before anything more was said, one of his men came running towards him. He had a radio strapped to his back.

"Lieutenant, captain's calling."

The officer took over the radio while keeping an eye on the people in front of him. "Yes, sir. This is Fox Two."

He listened for a few minutes. "But, sir, I have encountered a group of armed intruders who are threatening resistance. They claim to be survivors."

There was another long silence on his part, then: "Yes, sir. Of course, sir."

He hung up. Meanwhile the radioman had been looking at the group and now he spoke.

"Sir, I recognize that man. He's Tom Wadley, the quarterback of the Wolves."

"Great!" cracked Sylvia. "Save him. The public needs him. Let the rest of us rot."

"You're all saved," said Crowther." The general is excited at finding you. The President told him to call the White House collect if we found anyone. So we're supposed to move you out."

"Your change of attitude is encouraging, Lieutenant." said Oscar, "but we're waiting. We have ten other people out there. We're not leaving until they come back."

"You can't keep the general waiting."

"Watch us. The general and the president can wait. We've been waiting for two months for you. So here we stay until the others return."

July 2, 2020 (the same day)

247

The grenade exploded, shattering and dismembering everything in close proximity of the blast. As the sound faded away, only the splatter of debris was heard and then that too faded away and replaced by the silence of the doomed forest.

It was minutes later that it was broken as two riders came galloping up, the hooves of their horses crackling the underbrush. It was John and Frank, weapons at the ready.

"Look! My God!" yelled Frank. "Bodies, what's left of them?"

John had already seen the carnage and his stomach was ready to revolt. Then he saw the remains of the clothing. He knew of only one group that wore such clothing. He heaved a sigh of relief.

"There's some more over here," Frank shouted. "Oh my God! It's Dorothy and Jim!"

John hurriedly dismounted and ran to see Frank's discovery, steeling himself to see a grisly repeat of their earlier find.

He joined Frank who was tearing away brush and dirt that partially covered the two bodies.

"I think they're alive," said Frank.

It was Dorothy who recovered first. She had taken shelter immediately after Jim knocked her down and she suffered only cuts and bruises. Jim was breathing, but unconscious. He had a long gash across his back and a smaller one on the back of his head.

Meanwhile, the rest of John's party arrived. Martha put hand to mouth as she saw the shattered remains. Josh led her away. The others gathered with John and Frank as they tended to Jim and Dorothy.

"Jim!" Dorothy screamed and then threw herself on him attempting to turn him over, but was restrained by John.

"Here, let me help," said Jean. "We'll have to cut that shirt to treat his back, but it's the head wound that looks serious."

Dorothy was crying and Thelma and Anna did their best to comfort her while Jean and John attempted to clean out the cuts and bandage them.

Frank came back after rounding up Jim's and Dorothy's horses. "We can start back if they're ready."

"Jim's still under. I don't see how we can move him short of tying him to a horse," said Jean. "Let's give it a few more minutes. If he doesn't come out of it. We may have to send for Walter."

"Can you tell us what happened?" John asked Dorothy.

She explained Oscar's suspicions that some had survived the blast of the mountain top. How they had set out to warn him fearing an ambush of his party. Then being ambushed instead by the survivalists and their threats to kill everyone including John's people. Finally Jim's desperate gamble to save their lives.

She kept looking at Jim. Then unable to wait any longer, she ran to him, cradling his head and whispering in his ear, urging him to respond.

John shook his head as the others gathered about him.

"From what I've seen and from what Dorothy says, it looks like they blew themselves up. Either Jim or Dorothy's shots caused them to drop the grenade as they pulled the pin or got shot before they could throw it and it exploded among them."

"I guess we should try to bury them," said Frank.

"Yes, let's do that. It looks like one of us shall have to ride to camp to fetch Walter."

"If it's not too late," Frank whispered.

He did regain consciousness, however. Opening his eyes, everything was spinning, so he promptly shut them.

"Stop the merry-go-round, everything is spinning, I want to get off," he groaned.

Dorothy quickly gathered him to her arms. "Oh, darling, you had me worried."

"I had ME worried," he grimaced, his eyes still shut. Is it my head or my brains inside that are spinning?"

John came up. "Think you can ride a horse? We'll get you to Walter."

"Maybe blindfolded. It could be temporary."

Dorothy on one side and John on the other, walked him to one of the horses. But before he was mounted, everyone froze as they heard the sound

"Thuck! Thuck! Thuck! Thuck!"

"My God! I can't believe it," cried Jim. "I can't see, but I'd swear that's a helicopter. Am I hallucinating?"

249

Everyone was looking at all corners of the compass. Then it came into view, from the west.

"Well, I'll be damned!" exclaimed John. "The world didn't end after all."

CHAPTER TWENTY ONE

J uly 14, 2020, Washington, D.C.
That evening after dinner, they gathered at one of the meeting rooms of the hotel. The past two weeks had gone swiftly for the forty three surviving members of the class. Jim and Dorothy had been picked up by the helicopter and flown to Stonecliff where Jim had insisted on going and where Walter treated his wounds. John and the rest of his party had arrived two days later, united at last, the whole group had been transported to the nearest airfield where they met the President briefly. The entire group was then flown to Washington where they underwent a complete medical checkup. They spent four days at the hospital and were given a clean bill of health and allowed to contact any relatives, friends or associates.

A service which Aaron, Tom and the Longleys took advantage to straighten their affairs. They were then transferred to a major hotel chain to await further word from the government, namely the President. Of course, it also brought on the media and their Congressmen and Senators made the obligatory and politically correct visit.

"This is an informal meeting requested by this gentleman," Jim informed them. "You saw him the other day when the President met us at the airport. For those who don't remember, he is Mr. MacNamara, the President's chief of staff. Sir?" Jim stepped aside as MacNamara stood up to polite applause.

"Good evening, folks. I hope you are doing better now after two harrowing months of the holocaust. The President has asked me to be available to you. I shall try to explain what happened to you and yours and your town. It's not a very pleasant story, but I assure you, the President wants to correct the wrongs and make amends for your losses. Not all losses, unfortunately. He cannot bring back to life those of your loved ones. Those responsible have been detained and we intend to prosecute to the full extent of the law. It was done without the President's knowledge. However, he is ultimately responsible for the actions of his subordinates.

"I'll make the bad news short. Indeed, I'm limited in what I can tell you because it is a classified weapon that should not have seen the light of day. The President and the Secretary of Defense ordered its development stopped at the beginning of his administration. Certain individuals chose to ignore those orders and you experienced the results.

"What I'm allowed to tell you is that this weapon could alter the weather over a specific area. It could be applied where a low pressure area already existed and enhance bad weather into, well, you already know what happened. Tremendous explosions followed by cyclonic winds of horrendous speed that drops air pressure within seconds and brings down everything standing."

"Initially it felt like an earthquake," said Jim. "It might have caused that too."

"Yes, and the air pressure readings at the entrance to the basement were out of this world," contributed Carl.

"Your observations are very interesting, gentlemen. If possible, I hope you will consider passing on these observations to Defense officials. The weapon is being shelved, but we need all the input on its performance for future reference. We hope it shall not proliferate as others have, but once it's out of...I think you understand.

"The people who ran the program did not cease operations as they were ordered by the Secretary. It is all on paper. These people were so immersed and confident of their research that they decided to make one last effort to bring in the project to a successful completion and thereby avoid cancellation.

"Well, the weapon worked, but the guidance system didn't. Instead of heading over the Pacific Ocean, it went inland. The experts decided to explode the weapon 'over a desolate area.' their exact words. You know the rest.

"All the facts have been turned over to the Attorney-General. The Congress, as usual, is vying over which committee shall handle the investigation. Which means the culprits stand a good chance of going free after some congressional committee grants them immunity in exchange for the free publicity. The media is going ape trying to decide the appellation to describe the whole mess. 'Weathergate', perhaps? "Fortunately for you, The Congress is also falling backward in their efforts to compensate the survivors, all of whom are present in this hall. The President concurs with this. The President believes in being open and aboveboard on this incident, so nothing shall be held back or covered up. It was outright insubordination by individuals in an agency that was supposed to be dissolved. Nevertheless, it happened on his watch and he takes full responsibility. Not only in prosecuting the offenders, but in making amends to the victims.

"The President heard your story of survival from Mr. Fenzer and several others. He believes your ordeal and survival is in the great American tradition of resourcefulness that has carved this nation out of a wilderness for the past two hundred years. This country is in need of heroes. For too long we have worshipped flawed men and women whose only accomplishment was that they could act, sing or hit a ball."

"I wonder what offices he's running for?" Oscar whispered in Esther's ear.

"The President is aware that due to lack of communication with the outside world, you believed yourselves to be alone. You set about forming your own community, electing a leader, appointing a judge and starting families. Today, the President personally called the Chairman of the Judiciary Committee and submitted the name of your appointed judge to be the new United States District Judge over the devastated area. The Chairman and the Majority and Minority Leaders promised the President full senate approval bypassing inquiry by the committee."

MacNamara was interrupted by applause and Susan stood up to acknowledge it. Smiling, Mac continued. "The President had an ulterior motive for pushing this nomination. He understands that several relationships have flowered and the couples wish to legalize those relationships. As I understand from Mr. Fenzer, that was one of the reasons for her appointment. What better way than to have one of your own to do the honors as you had originally planned. As I said, your representatives in The Congress are eager to sponsor legislation to compensate you for your losses and provide for your future. Although I suspect the entertainment industry shall be vying for your stories and dangling handsome profits for them.

"To continue, the area of your home town shall be cleared and temporary housing and provisions shall be provided if you wish to return there. Your meals and lodging at this hotel are assured for a week. After that we can transport you to your destination of choice. Perhaps a honeymoon for several of you. One of the local department stores has offered to provide a complete outfit for each of you. And you're going to need them tomorrow night. The President has invited you for dinner at the White House. But don't splurge on fancy gowns or tuxes, business suits and cocktail dresses will be fine. I believe that covers everything I can think of, unless there are some questions you want answered."

"In what form is this compensation?" Sylvia asked.

"That's up to The Congress to decide. It could be in the form of cash, housing, low interest loans. You might talk to your representatives and make your wishes known. They are in an expansive mood."

"Some of us no longer reside in Stonecliff," said Susan Longley. "Now I'm a district judge there. As of right now, my husband and I are thinking of resettling there. However, we still have a business in the East which may cause us to change plans later. What then?"

He shrugged. "You can resign, of course. On the other hand, you're getting a judgeship at an early age and with this notoriety, the possibilities are endless. You could end up back here in an elective or appointive office."

Susan beamed.

"That did it," said Sylvia, tactlessly.

"If that's all, I have to be going. I won't say good-bye. You'll be seeing me tomorrow, and don't forget, you have a news conference in the morning. You're free to say anything, except about the weapon. A press officer shall be here to assist you. Thank you and good evening ladies and gentlemen."

"Do we have to attend this press conference?" Esther asked after MacNamara left.

"No, but it's limited to one hour," said Jim, "and maybe we ought to get it over with, otherwise they'll be hounding us all the way back to Stonecliff. Don't worry, the next big story that breaks will have them swarming after it like ants headed for a picnic."

"How much bigger would a story have to be to top this?" groused Oscar.

Jim ignored him and addressed the others. "What are your plans? Dorothy and I plan to get married day after tomorrow, Susan officiating. Do any of you care to join us?

"A multi-wedding ceremony? You can't leave us out of it," said David, holding Nancy's hand. She nodded in agreement.

"You can include us," added Jean, holding up her hand. She looked at John who bent down and kissed her.

"Esther and I are still married according to the Church," said Oscar, "but I guess we can make it legal all the way."

"We have a couple of days. Whoever decides to join us," said Jim. "Mr. MacNamara has promised to expedite any legalities required."

Aaron reached over for Linda's hand. "During my illness, I kinda got the idea you cared. Now we've been rescued, you seem a little distant."

"You saved me from Larry and he shot you. Of course I cared."

"And that's all?"

When she didn't answer, he withdrew his hand.

"Well, that's it then. I'll stay for the weddings and congratulate the happy couples. I owe them that much."

"Where are you going?"

"I still have my business in California, New York and Texas. Luckily they didn't blow up like Stonecliff. If you ever need help, I'm in the book."

She stood looking after him as he left. Sylvia came up behind her.

"Boy, that husband of yours must have been a paragon. How dreadful to spend the rest of your life without him, knowing no one else can equal him."

She turned around and threw her arms around Sylvia. "Oh God! Why do I do that? Maybe I am cold and incapable of feeling. I don't think I ever cared for Ed. Perhaps I married him on the rebound. Perhaps I carried a torch for Jim. Jim didn't care, or at least he didn't show it. He got on Dorothy right away even though she was married."

"Dorothy told me," Sylvia looked at her. "She met Jim at Stonecliff back in June, almost a year before the reunion. They met several times after that, though always in regard to that Indian legend and those artifacts Jim was working on. I believe that's when they fell in love. Dorothy was having problems in her marriage, with divorce a possibility, but even so they couldn't do much at the time. So, the reunion and your actions there didn't have anything to do with alienating Jim, And, of course, you were married as you so often told us. Happily, we assumed. I'd give Aaron a chance. He changed out there. Can you honestly say you don't love him?"

"I think I do, but every time he asks, I can't say yes. Why is that?"

"Don't ask me. At least you get offers."

"Oh, Sylvia. If you dressed up, fixed your hair, get the whole beauty treatment, who knows."

"Well then, join me and we'll both get the treatment. Maybe you'll change your mind or I'll get an offer. Anyway, the treatment is on the house."

July 15, 2020

"Thank you, ladies and gentlemen of the press. You understand we have a date with the President this evening and we all have some shopping to do to be presentable. Thank you." Jim ended the conference and the news types were ushered out while the rest of the class milled about. Linda came up behind Aaron and tugged at his sleeve. He turned to face her.

"I looked for you in the book," she said. "I'm in trouble. I need help."

He arched an eyebrow, just the faintest sign of a grin on his face. "What kind of, not THAT kind of trouble, is it?"

She arched an eyebrow in return. "What if it was? What could you do?"

"I'd deny it, of course. Not mine. But for an old friend like you, I'd find the culprit and beat him up until he did the decent thing."

"Happily it's not that kind of trouble. Actually, the culprit is, well, not a he."

He frowned. "You mean a woman? Is that, My God! Are you in a relation, Are you..." He stopped. He couldn't say it.

She looked at him in wonderment, then she let out a peal of laughter. "You think I have a thing going with another woman?"

"What am I to think? You say the culprit is a woman. You've shied away from any commitment with me or Tom.

"Yes, I guess it's possible to think that."

"I guess it's my fault. I thought I was going about this in a cute and humorous way. No, it's not about another woman. Just one woman, me. I'm the culprit."

She stopped him, fingers to his lips as he started to reply. "Let me finish. You see, there's this man that comes on to me, but I can't respond. Then he goes away, we part and I'm despondent."

"I'm a direct man, Linda. Is it me?"

"Yes."

"Then be honest with me," he grasped her arms, looking into her eyes. "Do you love me?"

"Yes, I think so. It must be so, otherwise why would I feel like I'm losing something precious when you leave."

"But you say you think so. What does it take to be sure?"

"I guess what I'm saying is that we need more time to explore our feelings."

"I know what my feelings are," he said. "I told you, and I've had two months to explore them."

"What it comes down to is that, I don't want to be cut off from you. We'll be leaving in a few days and you're going off to look after your business interests."

"True, I've neglected them, but a few weeks, maybe a month should be time enough to bring me up-to-date. I've got a construction company. I could set up an office in Stonecliff. They'll be needing homes there. Come with me while I make the rounds. We can get to know each other better and under different conditions. All aboveboard, naturally, separate rooms. If your feelings solidify, we could make it permanent when we return to Stonecliff."

She closed her eyes, then let out a sigh. "All right, I'll go with you. I don't know what my friends will think."

"I think your friends are way ahead of you. Besides, if they are really your friends, they won't think the less of you. We don't know what's ahead of us. We've just come through an experience that vividly illustrates how unknown the future can be. Let's not lose time with indecision."

He embraced her and she presented her lips.

IT WAS EVENING AND they were gathering in the meeting room awaiting transportation to the White House. All were dressed in their new clothes and admiring each other.

"I didn't think I would ever put on another pair of high heels," said Nancy.

"You think this is conservative enough for a new judge?" Susan was asking.

"Do you have a partner for the evening?" Tom asked Jane.

"I don't have an 'escort' if that's what you mean, but you're asking for a date, I'm available."

Tom colored. "I'm out of the escort business. And yes, I'm looking for a date."

"Look no further," she took his arm.

"When do the limos arrive?" asked Esther.

"There are no limos. We're getting government transportation, buses," said Jim. "Actually, one bus."

The door banged open, causing everyone to look in that direction.

It was Sylvia, but a transformed Sylvia. Her hair beautifully done, makeup, high heels and a short, black flared dress that did its job as she twirled around. She ended with hands on hips regarding her awed classmates.

"Take a look then feel sorry for yourselves," she declared.

"Sylvia!" Carl gasped. "Is that you?"

"It ain't Twiggy," she sniffed.

Carl fell to his knees in front of her, staring at her knees which he addressed. "I love you...Will you marry me? I know you come with excess baggage, but I can learn to love the rest of you."

Sylvia let out a scream of laughter, then she knelt also and threw her arms around him. "Gotcha! If you were joking, it's too bad. I've got forty witnesses."

"What does that mean?"

"It means I accept, dopehead."

"Aw, sweetcakes, you love me too."

Sylvia, still embracing him, head on his shoulder, made a face at the endearment. Then she saw Oscar, hand to his throat, making a gagging motion.

"Aw shucks," Oscar moaned. "Does that mean we break up that great team?"

She stuck her tongue at him, then brought her hand up with a "thumbs up" signal.

"Now we can make it a foursome," cried Esther.

The laughter subsided into a normal buzz after Sylvia's entrance and subsequent proposal. John took this moment to sidle up to Jim and Dorothy, making sure the three were undisturbed.

"Jim, there's something you should know. I haven't had a chance to tell you with everything that's happened in the last two weeks, dating back to you getting hurt at the pass."

"Is it serious?" Jim asked.

"It's been nothing but happy days since that day, but this concerns the three of us. We've been in it from the start."

"Is this about Martin?" Dorothy asked.

He nodded. "Yes."

"Did you find his body?"

"No sign of him, but, Jim, the tablets are gone."

"What? How could that be? There were hundreds of them. How could anyone move them in so short a time?"

John shrugged. "I can't explain it. They disappeared between my last two visits. That means about a week's time when no one was at the cave, at least none of our group."

"They're gone, not destroyed?" Dorothy asked.

"Yes, if someone had vandalized them, they wouldn't have gone to the trouble of picking up every piece. The place is clean, as if they never existed."

"Could it have been Harry and his bunch?" Jim regarded him.

"That's really stretching. You said they were waiting to ambush us at the pass. If they had been at the cave, they could have done a better job of getting rid of us. Besides, there's a time limitation here. How could they find the cave, remove all the tablets and hide them all in one week? No. Given Judith's hate and impatience, she would have smashed them on the spot and called it part of her revenge. Further, none of the supplies in the cave were broken into. Any stranger entering the cavern would have opened some of the containers, out of curiosity at least."

Dorothy nodded. "I agree with your reasoning."

"I had to ask because there was no one else," said Jim.

"Except for Larry. But he would have broken into the food at least, so that lets him out."

"There's one more we haven't considered," said Dorothy. "Martin."

John stared at her. "You can't be serious. He's dead. If he isn't, where is he? Why would he hide from us?"

"The mystery of their disappearance is as mysterious as their appearance," said Jim.

"They've been there for ages, as far as I know," John replied.

"But you knew about them only a few months earlier than I did," said Jim.

"What are you implying?"

"That as far as we know, only four people knew about them and saw them. Three of them are here now. Martin was the other. That anyone else knew about them is hearsay. That, going back to when we first saw them until they disappeared, is a time period of a year and a half. We're left with no proof they ever existed."

"Except for the three of us. We took pictures," John's face fell.

"Yes, they're gone too," Jim smiled.

"The tablets that never were," said Dorothy. "Perhaps it was an illusion."

"You can't photograph an illusion," said John.

"Their appearance was a mystery to start with," Jim continued. "They were out of place there, in the cave, in this part of the globe. Who or what would place the tablets there? Were they supposed to serve a purpose or was it just a storage place? If it was for a purpose, did they disappear when that purpose was served? Martin is the tie-in. Everything centers on him. The tablets were there. I saw them. I handled them. We photographed them. I'm convinced they existed as much as anything exists in this world."

"So what is the answer?" John asked.

"There is no logical answer that's acceptable to a scientific world, or even common folk like us. Which leaves us only the science fiction mumbo jumbo. That some unknown or supernatural force or entity put them there and later reclaimed them."

"Yes, but for what reason?" insisted John. "And was Martin in on it?"

"It's inescapable. Martin had to know something. He wouldn't let me bring in qualified help while pushing me to finish translating the tablets."

"And you never did," said Dorothy. "Yet Martin stocked his cave and we were all saved at my basement. Whether or not the tablets prophesied the future or were supposed to warn us, they never did."

Jim shook his head. "There are just too many inexplicable events that cannot ever be explained. If you try to discuss them openly and frankly, you invite ridicule and get labeled as a nut. So, the best thing is to keep quiet."

"And speaking of mysteries, what ever happened to Larry?" John asked.

"No one knows," replied Jim. "The authorities have been told what he did, but have found no trace of him. He may be dead somewhere in that mess out there, or maybe he walked out. Remember that the area was beginning to clear up at the time he ran off. So his whereabouts shall remain a mystery."

"Martin went to South American once," said John. "It was his pilgrimage, he said. He wanted to see the city in the sky at the top of the mountains. I can't pronounce the name."

"Machu Picchu? Tiahuanco?"

"Yes, something like that."

"I'm bringing this up because he said this was the land of our ancestors. The cities were in the clouds and there were numerous caverns underneath. The way he said it, well, he intimated there are caverns all over the world where the Ancients dwell with their secrets of the ages. Could it be this cave is in that network? There are passageways in that cave that we never explored. We don't know how far it extends. Could that be how they got there and how they disappeared?"

Jim nodded. "I've heard those stories and I've seen some of those caves, though I didn't go too deep into them. The natives are afraid to enter them. Many of these caverns have been covered up. The stories are that the treasures of the Incas are sealed in caves or at the bottom of lakes, put there to keep them out of Spanish hands. There is a large cavern in the Yucatan with many corridors, most unexplored. No one knows how far or how deep they may extend.

"Back in the 1950s, some miners in Utah uncovered some old tunnels that were very ancient. They couldn't be dated. Yet there is no evidence that mining was ever done by your ancestors in this area. On the other hand, considering the large amount of earthquake activity from South America to Alaska, how many of these caves could have survived after these many centuries?"

"Ours did."

"Yes," Jim sighed. "And that puts us back where we started. I'd like to explore that cave when we get back."

"If it's still there," said Dorothy.

"And we still don't have a clue on Martin's disappearance," added John.

Jim shook his head. "From time to time in the history of this planet, personalities have emerged and brought about great changes in our lives. Some like Jesus and Mohammed, caused changes that have endured for millenniums. Others like Napoleon and Hitler, Roosevelt and Churchill affected us for a shorter period of time. But there were many more who did not make the history books or who were barely mentioned. Fathers, mothers, teachers, friends, they changed our lives, although we were not immediately aware of it until later. And some never got any credit at all. Sometimes all that is needed is to inspire or to make us think. Martin was such a man. We denied him, but as we saw our plight and our problems mount, we acted on his premise and I think that saved us all. I am not nominating him for sainthood, but the three of us know what he did and he will always be remembered."

Dorothy nodded. "Amen."

"The bus is here!" someone shouted.

Dorothy got between the two men and linked her arms with theirs. "Come on. Tonight it's the President. Then tomorrow we start our date with the future. The rebuilding of our lives and our new homes. That's Martin's new world. Let's do him proud."

ABOUT THE AUTHOR

Peter J. Flores is a veteran who served his country during WWII. After the war, he went into Civil Service, developing work standards and computer software that would test jet aircraft engines. After retiring in 1981 he began to write stories and novels. Now, after 30 years of trying to get published, he is a first time author at age 93. When asked about his age, he merely says, "But, why stop at 93? This is just the first novel. The response to it from the public will be an indication if I should continue writing books, or whether I should confine myself to writing unprintable letters to the Editor.

Don't miss out!

Visit the website below and you can sign up to receive emails whenever Peter J Flores publishes a new book. There's no charge and no obligation.

https://books2read.com/r/B-A-WIYG-IUBV

BOOKS 2 READ

Connecting independent readers to independent writers.